SHAUNTA GRIMES

Albert Whitman & Company
Chicago, Illinois

Library of Congress Cataloging-in-Publication data is on file with the publisher.

First published in the United States of America in 2024
by Albert Whitman & Company
ISBN 978-0-8075-0412-3 (hardcover)
ISBN 978-0-8075-0413-0 (ebook)

Printed in the United States of America
10 9 8 7 6 5 4 3 2 1 SMI 28 27 26 25 24 23

Jacket art by Jess Vosseteig
Design by Erin McMahon

For more information about Albert Whitman & Company,
visit our website at www.albertwhitman.com

For the girl at the pool who inspired this story. Thank you.

CHAPTER 1

Lou Duncan pulled away from me, and I forced myself to stay on my side of the sofa.

If I moved toward him, even an inch, I'd lose a silent war. A secret war. One where my only mission was to keep myself from begging for his attention. So, instead of chasing Lou, I rebraided my hair.

When I was done, I said, "You're kind of a jerk, you know?"

"Come on, Celly."

"It's not fair to Vivi." As if he didn't know that already. As if he hadn't said the exact same words to me a dozen times. At least. "She thinks you love her."

Knowing that I wasn't being fair to Vivi either didn't stop me from wanting him to say she's wrong.

What he did say was, "She loves herself enough for the both of us."

Lou handed me the hair tie he'd pulled from my braid as soon as he was inside my house, when he kissed me. Just like always, he had the elastic wrapped around his wrist.

I won't lie. Sometimes I braided my hair just so he could do that.

He stood up and walked to the sliding glass door that led to my back patio. Nice, high walls. The better to keep out prying eyes.

Lou was about to start spring training and had a baseball scholarship for the fall, but that didn't stop him from taking a pack of cigarettes out of his back pocket and lighting one. I followed him outside and sat at the picnic table where my family sometimes ate dinner in the summer. Lou didn't look at me.

I inhaled when he did, breathing in through my nose, and wondered if the smell of tobacco smoke would always make me think of him. "It's not fair to me, then."

"Don't give me a hard time, Celly." Inhale. Exhale slowly, his face turned just enough so that the plume of smoke bloomed away from my face. "Let's just keep this fun, OK?"

Fun. I was good at fun. I smiled and made an attempt at shoving a stick into the spokes of my spiraling mood.

"You're such a jerk." I reached for him, and he came closer so that I could rest my forehead against his stomach. "All I want is to go to Morp with you."

Morp was a reverse prom. A seriously outdated and homophobic concept. Girls ask the boys, publicly, with a rose delivered during school lunch. Tomorrow.

"I'm your jerk, you know?" He wrapped my braid around his

hand, his thumb rubbing the elastic. "For real."

My teasing tone had worked, even if my heart wasn't in it. Problem was, I couldn't hold it in today. It happens. The stick broke. I sat back again and looked up at him. "As long as no one else knows."

His smile fell. "Don't do this."

If it wasn't fun, he didn't have any reason to be with me. I knew that. We had a kind of contract between us, and I never had any delusions about what we were.

It wasn't like I went into this thing with him with my eyes closed.

I stood up and went back inside to sit on the couch. He finished his cigarette, leaning against the doorjamb. I'd have to light a candle after he was gone.

Whenever Lou texted me something like Noon? I knew he meant at my house.

Both of my parents spent all day at the gym they owned. He had a stay-at-home mom. That's what she called herself, even though Lou was the youngest of her four children and he was a senior in high school.

His mom wasn't the only reason, though. He could get away with saying that he was at my house to see my sister, Jenna. She was a freshman, but she was also on the school dance squad, and she offered him plausible deniability.

He could say he was hanging out with her, if someone at school asked. The idea triggered my gag reflex, but it was true. He'd rather people thought he was hitting on my fourteen-year-old sister than me.

If one of his friends saw me knocking on his door, there'd be no good explanation. None they'd accept, anyway.

I shoved all of that out of my mind. It was too ugly to keep around for more than a few seconds.

Lou flicked his cigarette onto our lawn, then came in and sat next to me. He smelled like smoke now, but I didn't mind. He pulled me closer to him and kissed me. Finally, he leaned back just enough to whisper, "I'm sorry."

What he didn't say was *I'm sorry, so let's stop this bullshit.* He didn't promise to break up with Vivi. He didn't say that he wasn't really ashamed of wanting to be with me. He didn't tell me that he wanted to go to Morp with me.

Any of that would have been a lie. All of that would have been a lie.

I told myself it meant something that he didn't lie to me the way he lied to Vivi.

I made another attempt to drag myself away from my bad mood. Lou and I were both going to school in Las Vegas in the fall. We hadn't planned it. That's just the way it'd turned out.

Vivi was headed to Brigham Young.

"To me, you're beautiful," he said.

Right. But his friends wouldn't understand the switch from Vivi Hughes, a pom-pom girl they all wished they could be with, to Marcella Boucher, the fatass they'd called Moocella since the first grade.

CHAPTER 2

Mom sat at the kitchen table with her back ballerina-straight and tracked me as I moved around the kitchen.

"What?" I finally asked when she'd literally turned around in her seat to look at me.

"Are you buying a rose today?"

I gave a box of cereal a shake and looked at her, trying to decide if she was serious. Oh my God, the sincerity in her face was going to kill me. "No, Mom."

"You're not going to Spring Fling?"

"No. I'm not going to Morp. No one calls it Spring Fling anymore."

She stood up, took the Lucky Charms from me, and replaced the box with Special K. "I remember buying my first rose. I was a freshman. Tom Norton was a junior. I wonder whatever happened to him."

“They don’t let freshmen go anymore,” I said.

She looked up at me. “Oh. Right.”

Oh, right. They didn’t then either.

Replace two meals a day with a bowl of Special K, the back of the box promised, and wear a bikini by summer. “I don’t have anyone to give a rose to.”

My mother stuck the smiling leprechaun back in the pantry, deep behind my father’s protein powder. Right. I only had ten inches on her and had surpassed her ability to put things out of my reach before I hit puberty.

She also seriously overestimated my desire to eat stale marshmallows for breakfast.

Back at the table, Mom had a cup of unsweetened herbal tea and a single slice of sprouted wheat toast with half an avocado smashed over it. Sprinkled with black pepper. No salt. “I’m sure there’s a boy.”

“Of course, there’s a boy.” He smoked a Marlboro Light on our back patio yesterday afternoon. “I’m fat, not dead.”

“Celly.”

“Mom.”

“There’s no need for that.”

I wondered what she would think if she knew the boy was Lou or how often he came to our house to do things with me that she wouldn’t approve of.

In her senior year, Mom had a huge, ratted pouf of platinum-blond hair and icy blue eyes. She weighed maybe a hundred pounds and was a cheerleader with a scholarship and big dreams that were squashed when she learned that she was already pregnant with me by the time they handed her a diploma.

She was not the kind of girl that boys dated only in private. My mother was the Vivi Hughes of her generation, and she wouldn't understand why Lou had a strict no-one-can-know rule.

Or why I've gone along with it all year.

I looked down at the Special K again. The box had a picture of a measuring tape wrapped around its middle.

OK, maybe she would understand.

Mom was fond of saying that she was glad she didn't have to worry about me repeating her mistakes. Not the way she worried about Jenna.

Because I was such a good girl.

What she really meant was that I was too fat for some boy to accidentally impregnate in a motel room after prom or in the back seat of his car after the big game.

Or wherever she had given it up to our dad and wound up with me.

"Your hair's like spun gold, you know that?" She leaned in closer to me and pulled a strand through her fingers. Thick, straight, white-blond hair was the only thing I'd inherited from her. Mine fell to my waist and was the one part of me that I knew, for sure, was pretty.

Everything else—height, definitely weight, green eyes—came from Dad. I was what happened when the prom queen procreated with the linebacker captain of the football team.

I put the cereal away. "I'm late."

"Wait." She took a half-bite of her toast, chewed it, and swallowed. “I haven’t seen you at the gym lately.”

My parents had opened a strip-mall gym with a loan from my dad’s father when I was two years old. And because being the fattest kid in school wasn’t torture enough, the gym was called Belly Busters.

They named it after me.

Marcella became Celly, which became Belly when I was a fat baby. Mom called me Celly Belly one day at school, when I was in the second grade.

That was a gift that kept on giving.

“Really, there’s no reason for you not to be there every day,” Mom said.

“Yeah, I know.”

“Come by after school and work out with me. It’ll be fun. And get a dollar out of my purse for that rose, OK?”

I found her knockoff Coach bag by the front door and dug out her wallet. She had several dollar bills, but I took a ten and wondered if she thought when I left the house every day I went through a time portal to Twain High School circa 2002, when she was prom queen and a rose still cost a buck.

○ ○ ○

As I approached the school bus stop a few minutes later, I tried to take its temperature.

I wasn’t above walking the two miles to school if the bus stop had a fever. The only thing worse than being surrounded by assholes is being trapped in a giant metal Twinkie with them.

A group of girls huddled together at the curb, looking at something around the corner out of my line of sight. They all wore the same uniform: skinny jeans, fake-vintage T-shirts, and Uggs. Even though it was seventy-five degrees.

Two guys with patchy facial hair and trucker caps stood behind them.

None of them paid any attention to me.

Four more kids stood half-hidden by a pine tree, sharing a cigarette pinched between forefingers and thumbs, looking over their shoulders like their mothers might come up and smack it out of their hands. Ninth graders.

A couple of them looked at me, but none seemed inclined to leave the herd. When I came around the corner, I finally saw two boys, one of them a strawberry blond with a face full of cystic acne and the other a short, muscular fifth-year senior with a mustache and a tribal tattoo around one bicep, standing in front of a small crowd, taking turns karate kicking at the backpack of a very tall boy I had never seen before.

The new kid made me think of a woodland creature—pointed chin, wide dark eyes, big ears—topped by a mop of curly brown hair. He would have looked like he belonged at the middle school, if it weren't for his impressive height.

He was easily six or seven inches taller than me. I was six feet tall, so that was saying something.

Nathan Bernstein and Jossue Cruz laughed too hard to get any of their regular wisecracks out. Their half-uttered jokes only made them laugh harder.

"I wonder if he's gigantic everywhere," one of the pretty girls said as I passed by.

Classy.

The kid kept turning to get away from one jerk, only to find himself assaulted by the other.

Then the boy lifted his face and looked around. He used the back of his hand to wipe at his nose, and his cheeks were flushed a blotchy red. Anger pulsed from him, but it made him look like he was about to cry.

I knew from hard experience that tears were an aphrodisiac to Nathan and Jossue. I adjusted my bag over my shoulder and whispered under my breath, "Come on, kid. Suck it up."

"Ah, shit, he's crying."

One of the groupies started it, and within seconds, the sheep had picked up on the taunting. It was weird, to be surrounded by it, but not the focus of it. A little like being in the eye of a storm.

The new kid was caught in the crosswind.

Nathan reached up and pinched the boy's cheeks, making his lips pooch out like he was pouting as well as crying. That should have undone the new kid. So, I actually gasped when he reared back, wrenching his face from Nathan's fingers, and then stepped forward.

I don't know what I expected. A fight, maybe. Nathan and Jossue and boys like them win fights before they even start just by being aggressive assholes. People assume they're going to fight dirty. But there was something about the way the new kid held himself that made me think this was going to be different.

I was still trying to figure it out when Nathan fired his knee up like a piston and caught the boy square in the balls. A low blow that was too low, even for Nathan. Where had that come from?

I don't even have balls, but the wind went out of me anyway as I watched the kid bend forward and let loose a gagging, choking retch.

"Oh, no," I whispered.

Oh, yes. He vomited all over the sidewalk. And Nathan's black low tops.

Jossue busted a gut laughing at the poor kid, who stood up as well as he could and wiped his mouth on the edge of his T-shirt, exposing a wiry torso.

Nathan's face was bright red behind his zits. "You puked on me!"

"Why don't I knee you in the nuts and see what comes out of you." The sound of my own voice shocked me. Panic reared up when they all turned to stare at me. Where in the hell had that come from?

"What did you say, Belly?" Nathan looked back at his friends for approval. Maybe someday I'd forgive my parents for that particular nickname. I hadn't gotten there yet.

Oh, God. Walk away. But something about Nathan, with that shit-eating grin on his face, and the sound of the new kid wheezing gave me a little boost of adrenaline. "When are you ever going to grow up?"

Jossue laughed, which triggered the ninth graders to join in, and Nathan shot him a glare before leaning closer to me. "You're such a fat bitch."

Clever. "Yeah, and?"

It wasn't bravado or a tidal wave of self-esteem causing me to speak up. I'd made my decision about Lou. Either he would say yes and my life would change, or the backlash would be so epic that nothing these kids could do would compare.

I'd reached a weird kind of bottom, and at least in this moment, there was nothing anyone could do to hurt me.

Jossue tipped his head toward me. "I think fatass found herself a man."

It took me a minute to realize that he was talking about the new kid, who was now standing right next to me.

As one, the whole group erupted in laughter.

"Gross," one of the trucker hat boys said. "That's like a giraffe trying to hump an elephant."

One of the girls he was trying to impress groaned. "He puked all over the sidewalk. I think I need to go home."

"Go to hell," I said, but before I could leave, because there was not a chance of me getting on that bus today, Nathan grabbed onto the fat at both sides of my waist and twisted hard.

I tried to turn out of his grip, but he only twisted my flesh in the opposite direction and stepped forward, which forced me to step back.

He flapped his lips together, making a motor sound.

I smacked Nathan's hands, my face burning, but his fingers dug into me deep enough to bruise, and he walked me backward again.

Like we were some kind of grotesque Fred Astaire and Ginger Rogers.

"Let her go," the new kid said.

"I don't need your help." I meant it, but it was obviously not true. I couldn't get Nathan to let me go.

Nathan stopped twisting my fat but didn't take his hands off me. When I tried again to get away, he dug his fingers in deeper as he looked up into the new kid's face.

I was definitely going to have bruises.

"You really have something to say to me?" Nathan asked.

The blood had drained from the new kid's face, and he looked to me like he might faint. When I drove my elbows down, trying to dislodge my parasite, the tall boy lifted his chin and held his ground. "I said, 'Let her go.'"

Jossue made a move for the kid and squeaked in surprise when he caught a bony elbow jab in the forehead. His head would have gone rolling down the road if it weren't attached to his neck. Jossue went sprawling off the curb and onto the blacktop, flat on his back, gasping for air like a fish out of water.

The whole bus stop went deathly silent, except for Jossue, who sat up and blinked. "What the fuck?"

As Jossue stood up, I pushed Nathan with both hands on his chest until he dropped his hold on me and stumbled back. He glared and spit out a few obscenities but didn't get any closer to the kid and his flying elbows of doom.

Then the school bus was there, belching exhaust. I adjusted my backpack again and watched Nathan and Jossue both line up with the other kids.

"You are so dead," Nathan said before he filed into the gaping yellow mouth. To me, to the new kid, maybe to both of us.

"Yeah." Jossue rubbed the spot between his eyes.

Whoever this new kid was, he'd reduced the two baddest boys at Twain High School to caricatures of themselves and I took a mental snapshot.

If I'd had more time, I might have pulled out my phone and taken a real one. Or video. Video would have been awesome, even if it did show me being driven around the bus stop by my belly fat.

"You coming?" the bus driver asked me. I shook my head and he shrugged, shut the door, and drove off.

I stood there until the bus was gone and then turned to the tall boy who stood near the pine tree. "You OK?"

"I'm good. Thanks for all of that."

"For almost getting us both killed?"

"They wouldn't have killed us."

He was probably right. "Still."

I yanked on the strap of my book bag and started to walk toward school. No point in going home and expecting a ride from my mother. She would pat my arm and say that the walk would do me good. Probably tell me how many calories it would burn.

The boy caught up with me. "My name's Jason."

"Marcella." He'd catch on soon enough to the fact that most people called me Celly. We'd see if he fell into the "Belly" camp.

"Can I ask you something?"

I stopped walking and turned to face him. His eyes drifted from my feet slowly up to my face. Right. Belly it is. "Three twelve."

"What?"

"I weigh three hundred and twelve pounds. I eat lard for breakfast and cause earthquakes during PE. Just ask anyone, they'll tell you. Anything else?"

He opened his mouth and a strangled noise came out, like whatever he wanted to say was stuck in his throat. Good. Let him choke on it.

○ ○ ○

Buy a rose, Celly.

Easy for my mom to say.

I stood in front of the cafeteria during the break between second and third periods. Why couldn't my parents have moved away from their hometown when they grew up, like normal people do? Especially when their hometown is somewhere as boring as Sun Valley, Nevada.

The idea of skipping this whole thing was appealing. I was pretty sure that Former Prom Queen Robin didn't expect a boy to actually accept her fat daughter's rose anyway.

It would have actually screwed up her entire world view if I came home with Lou Duncan as my Morp date.

So, I could have skipped the whole thing. That's what everyone—literally, everyone—wanted.

Or I could have gone home that afternoon and told my mother that I'd tried and failed. She would look at me with pity and determination to somehow fix what was fundamentally wrong with me. She'd offer me a spot in her 5 p.m. Zumba class or serve me a dry salad for dinner. Or both.

I love my mom. But, I swear, she could be dense as hell. I have tried to tell her that high school is not such a magical place for me.

Kids will be kids, she'd said over and over. They'll like me if I give them a chance. And, besides, it wasn't all easy for her. Chloe James hated her guts.

I've never been able to convince her that Chloe James drooling all over my dad and campaigning against her for senior class secretary wasn't in the same world as my problems.

She thinks I need a thicker skin and to remember that boys always tease the girls they like the most.

Because Robin's real world is a romantic comedy. I wish I could say it wasn't even a good one, either. But it was. She thinks I need to be more like Jenna, who is as much like our tiny dancer mother as I am like our linebacker dad.

And the whole world agreed with her.

In the end, that was what gave me the nerve to push open the cafeteria door. My mom needed to see exactly what I was dealing with. And my dad had to see that being the girl version of him wasn't all that awesome.

I had a feeling that this would turn out very badly, but I just didn't care anymore.

I had a strange disconnection going on. Like I was floating above myself, watching what would inevitably be a train wreck, incapable of stopping it.

I walked up to the long table where members of the student body government stood with boxes of flowers. Another table sat perpendicular to it, crowded with girls bent over, writing on little white cards.

"Oh, good for you, Celly!" The junior class president held out a yellow rose to me. Abby Morales was so perky she made a Chihuahua look sedate.

"Thanks."

"Holly didn't think you'd come in, but I told her I bet you would. Who're you inviting?"

Holly Stephenson, senior class treasurer, lifted her perfectly manicured eyebrows, daring me to take the flower. Holly didn't try to drive me around by my spare tire or call me Belly. She rarely said anything at all to me, which, if I'm being honest, was the worst kind of pain.

Practically from birth until the summer between eighth and ninth grades, Holly was my best friend. We'd been inseparable. Then her parents had sent her to spend the summer before high school with her aunt in Florida while they got divorced.

She'd had a serious glow up.

She'd lost forty pounds, traded her glasses for contacts, had her braces off, and came home with a brand-new wardrobe. And sudden popularity.

For a while, she'd tried to include me with her new friends, but when it came down to choosing, there was no choice.

Walking away from the table would mean admitting that Holly was right. I handed my money to Abby, took the change and the rose, and walked to the end of the long white table. After I printed my own name on the card, Lou's name stuck on my fingertips.

Some of the boys at Twain were so far out of my league that they were barely on the same planet. They were too high in the social stratosphere even to bother with acknowledging me.

The second-tier boys would do anything to move up to the stratosphere. Boys like Nathan and Jossue. I dismissed them out of hand. They were the most dangerous.

Giving a flower to anyone might be a social death wish, but I wasn't completely stupid.

That left the boys like Hayden Clark.

He spent half of every day taking classes at the university and because he'd skipped sixth grade, he was a year younger than the rest of us. He was going to Stanford in the fall.

Hayden was a good choice. A safe choice. He'd say no, but he wouldn't make me pay for asking. I actually started to write his name, but then pulled the pen back up.

Lou was one of those stratosphere boys. He was beautiful, popular, and had been dating Vivi Hughes off and on since freshman year.

But he'd spent all last summer with me at Belly Busters. And at my house. I expected that to end when school started, but it didn't.

I'm not stupid. I knew that, at least in the beginning, I was just the fat girl who would go further than his socially acceptable girlfriend. But there was something else, too.

We were friends. I really believed that was true.

I wrote his name in block letters. Either the stunt would fail spectacularly, or I'd go to the dance with Lou. I tied my card to my rose, then pushed the flower deep into the box beside Abby that was full of them, before I could change my mind.

○ ○ ○

By the end of my fourth-period class, my stomach was in knots. I'd had bad ideas before, but this was truly on another level. Skipping the cafeteria and the Morp roses was a serious option. It was too late to take my flower back, but I didn't have to be there when my stupidity was exposed.

Except, I couldn't let go of the chance that Lou might say yes.

It would be spectacular if he did. He'd stand up in the crowded cafeteria and turn slowly, looking for me. I'd be in the back, with Vivi somewhere between us, literally overlooked. He'd part the crowd to get to me. He'd pull the tie from my hair, and there might be kissing involved.

In my daydream, he would definitely say yes in front of the whole school.

Every breath hurt, and my chest ached with the effort to keep my heart beating as I took my place at the back of the cafeteria, against the black-and-white tiled wall.

I fiddled with the end of my braid and wondered whether it was possible to actually die of anticipation.

After a few minutes, student council members came in carrying boxes full of roses. They took turns calling names into the microphone set up in the center of the room, and eager freshmen passed out the flowers.

"Harley Morris, from Emily Carver!"

"Chris Jones, from Cassidy Bates!"

Barbaric. What was the point of calling out the girls' names as well as the boys? Or having the invitations be so public in the first place? It was a miracle that any girl had the nerve to offer a flower to any boy.

Tradition, Mom would say. She'd done it. Plenty of other girls at Twain had mothers who'd done it, too. Some probably even had grandmothers who had. Morp flowers were a rite of passage.

"Oh, my god." Abby stood on her toes at the microphone and found me. She gave me an exaggerated are-you-sure look and mouthed, "Really?"

She was giving me an out, and my brain screamed, *No, not really*, but the words didn't make it out of my mouth. The edges of my vision went black, and my blood pounded like a breaking tide in my ears.

I lowered my eyes to the floor and took a couple of breaths, focusing on not passing out. When I looked up again, Abby had the microphone in one hand and my yellow rose in the other.

"Lou Duncan!" Lou raised one hand without bothering to look up from his jock friends. As if it were possible that Abby and every other girl in the room didn't know exactly where he was. He did not betray even an ounce of excitement that his name had been called.

Of course his name had been called. Lou was a high school god. Dark hair slightly messy, but in an expensive way. Six-two, with deep brown eyes that had just the right hint of sadness. And a letterman's jacket, for God's sake.

"Wait." The word slipped out, but my voice didn't travel beyond my own nose.

"From Celly Boucher!" *Bow-chur*, she said, not *Boo-shay*.

I'd gone to school with Abby since the third grade. How did she not know the right way to say my name?

I almost called out a correction. But every single person in the cafeteria, student and adult, turned and looked at Lou as he came to his feet and took the rose. Heat rose up my neck and over my face as awkward silence stretched on and on.

Lou might say yes.

It could happen.

He could choose me, in front of everyone.

He found me, and for a split second, I was sure he was going to. I stood up straighter. He tilted his head slightly, and his tongue darted over his bottom lip. He gave me a look that made me inhale, hard.

Apology. That look was apology.

And then the silence broke in a waterfall of laughter.

"Holy shit, Lou."

"Jesus, that's disgusting."

Lou blinked, like he was waking up. Then he turned around and the room went silent. He parted the crowd, just like I knew he could.

I held on, for a few more seconds, to the hope that he was about to say yes.

Held on like a drowning person holds on to a lifeline.

But life isn't a romantic comedy. Sometimes it's just a disaster movie. This was going to be bad. *Bad* bad. I opened my mouth, but nothing came out.

What could I say anyway?

I'm sorry for having the nerve to ask you out?

I'm sorry for reaching out of the fat-girl gutter?

Remember all those hours of making out on my couch?

Sorry for pretending, for the five seconds it took to write your name on that stupid card, that I'm a human being?

Vivi came through the opening Lou made. She was like a five-foot-tall, ninety-eight-pound honey badger out for blood. I glanced around, looking for an adult. None of them looked me in the eye.

Vivi had almost-black hair, the front bleached blond. She wore it in a ponytail that curled up at the end. Honey Badger Barbie. She came as close to me as she could get without actually touching me and pointed one finger at my nose.

I'd read somewhere that the human jaw is strong enough to bite through a finger like a carrot, but the brain won't let it happen. I had an urge to test that theory out.

Vivi didn't speak right away. That had the effect of the entire room, including me, leaning in to catch whatever it was she might say.

The quiet was almost total, and Vivi's voice was clearly audible even though she didn't raise it. "Moocella."

"Moocella," someone in the crowd yelled. And that was answered by a ground swell chorus of mooing.

I tried to just breathe and let the noise roll over me. If I shed a single tear, if anger or misery showed on my face in any way, it would be like trying to use aerosol hairspray to put out a fire. I willed my insides to go numb.

It took a full minute of *Moocella* and barnyard noises for the vice principal to start trying to make it stop. A full minute of standing there, blocked from leaving by the crush of students filling the cafeteria. And by my own stubborn refusal to let them make me run.

A minute might not seem like a long time. In fact, when something will be over fast, we say, "This will only take a minute." But when you're counting in half-seconds, it's a lifetime.

Especially if you count them while making eye contact with the boy who did not say yes, over the head of his girlfriend.

Once I finally made my escape, no one came after me. None of the kids and none of the teachers or administration. I spent the rest of lunch hour in the big handicap stall in the girls' bathroom, where I finally let myself cry.

I didn't cry out of shame or embarrassment. The tears were pure anger. It wouldn't have surprised me if they burned channels down my cheeks.

Before the bell for fifth period rang, I sat on the closed toilet lid and forced myself to calm down. I would not let them see me this way, and I would not let them chase me out of school for the rest of the day.

I wasn't always so stubborn. I often skipped the bus to avoid conflict. I was an expert at manipulating the system so I could miss classes without being caught.

For some reason, that day, I'd had enough of pretending like I didn't really exist. I walked to my PE class after the bell rang.

My fifth-period and sixth-period teachers kept order during their classes. The hallways were quiet, too. But it felt like days had passed between lunch and my final class.

By the time I walked into trigonometry, I was exhausted, physically and emotionally.

The tall boy from the bus stop, the one with the woodland face, sat in the empty desk next to mine. It was the first time I'd seen him since that morning.

He turned in his seat to face me and said, "Hey."

"Seriously?" I said under my breath. "Jason, right?"

He was as wedged behind his desk as I was behind mine, just for a different reason. He couldn't bend his legs under his; they were too long, so he had them opened with a knee protruding from each side and his back hunched in a way that looked incredibly uncomfortable.

"Yeah," he said. "Jason Daley."

"Could you sit somewhere else?"

He didn't move. Just sat there and lifted his eyebrows. His eyes were so dark they were nearly black, but they looked right into me in a way that screamed pity. I hadn't seen him in the cafeteria, but I was pretty sure he'd heard the story somewhere.

Everyone had heard the story by then.

Before I could tell Jason, again, to leave me alone, Daniel Holstrom turned around in the seat in front of him and gave a loud, realistic moo. I might have pointed out that someone who could replicate a bellowing bovine so perfectly probably had no place calling someone else a cow, but it would have been useless.

The teacher shushed Daniel, who rolled his eyes and flopped back into his seat, facing the right way. I got through the forty-five-minute class without learning a single thing, but also without crying, so I called it a draw as I waited until everyone else was out before standing up and leaving the classroom myself.

Jason stood just outside the door. When I looked at him, he asked, "Is everyone at this school an asshole?"

"Pretty much." At least that's how it felt right then.

He walked with me all the way to my locker. I finally turned to him and said, "What are you doing?"

"Just waiting for you."

I spun the dial on my locker and threw it open. I was still turned to Jason when I heard a thick, wet pop, and something smacked me in the chest. Like someone had hocked the world's biggest loogie at me. A nasty blob of something clung to my white top. The bottom of my locker was coated in the same sticky, whitish fluid that dripped from my sternum to my waist.

It was disgusting, covering my books and papers and PE uniform. The remains of some kind of balloon were attached to the far wall, with a string that had pulled and popped it when I opened the door.

I reached in and lifted one edge of it, then dropped it when I realized what it was.

A condom. From the smell, the oozy substance was hand soap from a school bathroom, but more condoms—they looked used, and I could only hope they'd been coated in the soap—were stuck to the things inside my locker.

Jason sputtered, working on getting something out that just wouldn't unstick. Finally, he just said, "Jesus."

I closed my locker again, carefully, and looked up at him.

My heart was in my throat, choking me, and I had to stand there for a moment before I trusted myself not to scream. The laughter behind me started before I had fully pulled myself together.

Vivi stood across the hall with a group of cheerleaders and girls from the dance team. I didn't see my sister with them, which was at least something. Vivi lifted her eyebrows and tilted her head, waiting to see what I might say or do.

I had a brief, intense fantasy of pulling my ruined T-shirt over my head and grinding it into her perfect, delicately-featured face. My fingers were actually gripped on the hem, when Jason put his hand on my upper arm and said, "Let's get out of here."

I yanked my arm back and stalked away from him and my locker, toward the door at the end of the hallway.

"Miss Boucher!" The librarian tried to stop me when I passed her. Jason on my heels. "Marcella, are you OK?"

I heard Jason say, "She's fine," before I pushed through the door.

CHAPTER 3

Somewhere along the two-mile walk home, I lost Jason. Probably when he asked me for the tenth time if I was OK and I unleashed a flood of curse words at him.

I walked fast, with my backpack hugged over the sticky mess covering my chest. I couldn't put any of my books in my locker, so my bag weighed roughly two tons, and my arms were like dead weights by the time I got home.

The muscles between my shoulder blades were on fire, and I was covered in sweat and tears and snot—as well as hand soap that was supposed to look like something a lot more disgusting. I'd cried myself out, though, so there was that.

Nothing could hurt me anymore, because the part of me that could get hurt had snapped in half. If I looked back, I'd see bits of myself left all along the way between school and home. I just didn't care. I dropped my soapy backpack at the front door and went upstairs to my bedroom.

At my desk, I woke up my computer.

The Google search bar stared back at me for a while. I wanted to ask it something, but I couldn't figure out what.

How do I make this not hurt?

How do I make it go away?

How do I...?

I couldn't ask the Internet something I couldn't even put into words myself. My fingers moved anyway. On their own.

I didn't think about what I was doing as a cohesive plan. Not *I'm trying to figure out how to die*. I was just doing research.

So, I typed in *how to tie a noose*.

A strange, almost alien calm settled over me. Like learning how to tie a noose had nothing at all to do with what I might actually want a noose for.

I found a YouTube video first and watched it twice. Then I clicked around until I found a website with a picture tutorial and printed out the instructions.

My father had two ropes hanging in loops from hooks on the garage wall. A place for everything and everything in its place. It must have been so hard for him to have a daughter who oozed so far outside the lines.

One length of rope was rough and white. The other was smooth, neon-orange nylon. I picked up the smooth rope, because it slipped between my fingers and reminded me of the snake I touched once when our parents took us to Bonnie Springs.

I took the rope and the printed instructions to the second floor, pulled down the attic entry stairs and went up them. The attic was stuffy and hot. Dust caked my pores and the ick on my shirt as I found an old dining-room chair and positioned it where I wanted it.

I sat and focused on learning how to tie a noose. I didn't think about why I was tying it or what I might do next. It took three tries to get it right. I held it in my lap for a while, thinking about undoing it and taking the rope back to the garage.

Maybe if I just got the chair in the right spot. Maybe then I'd feel better. I stood up and pulled it, looking up at the beam over my head, three feet in front of the support post behind me.

I knew I had the right spot when my heart pounded in my ears and throat.

The first time I threw the noose, trying to get it over the beam, it fell back onto my face. I kept waiting, with every step, for something inside me to say, *Don't do this, Marcella.*

It didn't happen.

Not when I got the rope over the beam on the second try.

Not when I tied the other end of the rope to the support post.

Not when I stood on the chair to test the length of the rope.

Not even when I slipped the noose around my neck.

The noose was not uncomfortable. It was snug against my skin but didn't hurt or make it hard to breathe. Still, my hands and feet tingled, like all my blood had rushed away from my extremities to protect my internal organs from the very idea I was flirting with.

I thought about my parents. They would be sad, but I was reasonably sure my mom would also believe that I was in a better place. A place where everyone was skinny in God's eyes.

I couldn't decide how my dad would feel.

My sister would be home soon. She'd go to her room, maybe with that last bowl of Lucky Charms, and see the attic stairs down. If she came up to investigate, she'd be the one to find me swinging heavily from the rope Dad used to tie down our gear during summer camping trips to Lake Tahoe.

Or she might just close the stairs, thinking someone else forgot to do it. Then no one would know where I was. They'd know I was gone, of course, but they'd probably call me a runaway.

It might take days or weeks to find me up here, rotting in the heat and dust.

And there was that voice I was looking for. That give-a-damn that said, *Hey, Celly, you don't want to do this.*

It was like waking up from sleepwalking and finding myself standing on a rickety chair with a noose around my neck. Only I had been awake the whole time. And suddenly I knew, for sure, that I didn't want to be here.

I leaned forward, trying to get a little more ease in the noose as I reached behind me to loosen the knot. It didn't work. At all. The crack of the chair's front legs breaking was earsplitting in the quiet attic. I clawed at the rope, trying to get my fingers between it and my neck. It wasn't comfortable anymore. The more I struggled, the tighter it pulled.

The next few seconds went by in slow motion. My toes balanced on the broken chair, chin lifted as high as possible, numb fingers trying to work the knot. Panic squeezed my throat even more than the rope did.

I couldn't get purchase on the knot. My slipping hold on the chair, balanced for the moment on its back legs, kept causing the noose to dig in deeper

I don't want to die. Please, I didn't mean it.

And then I lost the chair. I inhaled like I was going underwater and wrapped my hands around the rope over my head. It pulled tight and hurt me, like a giant hand lifting my head from my shoulders, trying to separate it from my body.

A jolt shot through my spine when the rope was brought up short by the knot on the post—but instead of hanging there, I kept falling. All the way to the floor with a thud that slammed my brain against my skull. The rope flew over the rafter above my head and piled on top of me.

"Shit." I tugged on the noose. It tightened at first, and for a panicked moment, I was sure I was going to suffocate to death anyway. But then it loosened and I could breath again.

I lay flat on my back, staring up at the ceiling. Totally inappropriate laughter burbled up and chased away the self-pity I'd been swimming in since Shannon had read Lou's name and mine that afternoon.

Since the ninth grade, when Holly had stopped eating lunch with me, if I was being honest.

Or, hell, since the first day of first grade when Nathan had poked me in the ass with his pencil and said my butt was bigger than his mom's.

For the first time in I didn't even know how long, I knew for sure I didn't want to die. It was like taking a deep breath after years of not even realizing I'd forgotten how.

I sat up and pulled the rope through my fingers. The noose had held, but I obviously didn't know how to tie a decent square knot.

Another uncontrollable burst of laughter hurt my raw throat. Finally, I took several hard breaths to try to get myself under control. The attic smelled like mildew and dust and the hand soap from the girls' bathroom at school.

I pulled my shirt over my head and sat cross-legged, wearing just my jeans and a white cotton bra. I felt light. I'd been walking around with my body filled with lead, weighing twice as much as it needed to, and suddenly it had drained out of me, and 312 pounds wasn't so bad anymore. At least not worth dying over.

I untied the noose and coiled the rope, then took it and my ruined shirt down the attic stairs to my bedroom, where I pulled a T-shirt over my head before I went downstairs.

No one but me would ever know what I'd almost done. It was my secret, and I doubted that even if someone found out, they'd understand why accidentally almost killing myself felt so good.

Some little voice in the back of my head said that this wasn't any more normal than how I'd felt a few minutes before. The word *mania* felt about right. But I didn't care.

I was flying high, right up until I came to the bottom of the stairs and found myself nose-to-nose with my father.

I'd gone from feeling nothing earlier to feeling everything now. I was caught, at the moment, between wanting to throw my arms around Dad and a sudden sharp anger that he was home early. I settled on "You scared me."

He put a hand on my shoulder and pulled me into a hug that surprised me. "Are you OK?"

My face burned, and I knew it had gone beet red. It always does when I'm caught off guard. "Yeah. Why?"

"Mrs. Fitzgibbons called me at work."

Oh. Right. Mrs. Fitzgibbons was my school counselor. She'd been his, too, when he was at Twain. "I'm fine."

He moved his hand to my head and smoothed it down one side of my hair, back to my shoulder. "Are you sure? She said something happened."

I couldn't believe the school had bothered to call him at all. Maybe it was because the prank Vivi had pulled was more public than usual. And someone would have to pay for my damaged books. Before I could tell him again that I was fine, his eyes followed his hand and rested on the coil of rope around my shoulder.

I stood up a little straighter, trying to look non-suicidal.

It was too late. Dad's eyes moved from my shoulder across to my neck.

"Daddy." I hadn't called him that since I was ten years old. The look on his face made me wish I could crawl into a hole and hide forever.

He put his fingers under my chin and lifted it. "Oh, God."

"I'm OK. I really am."

He took the rope from me and threw it to the floor, like it was dangerous in its own right. I inhaled as he lifted my chin again, gently, taking in the chafing that burned now that the adrenaline was wearing off.

"What did you do, Celly?"

I opened my mouth, but nothing came out except a sob that hurt my throat. Then tears started, and they streamed down my flushed cheeks. I wanted to make him see that I'd really figured out I didn't want to die. This wasn't helping. "I'm sorry."

"What did you do?"

I shook my head, trying to think of some way to make him understand. All I could manage was "I changed my mind."

He pulled me to him and hugged me again. Hard. I closed my eyes and for a minute, everything was all right. He smelled the way he always smelled—like Belly Busters and toothpaste and laundry detergent.

I didn't want to let go, but he pushed me away from him so he could look into my face. "You can't do this. Do you understand me? You don't get to do this."

"I didn't…"

He took a step back and sat down hard on the fourth step up on the staircase behind him. "Marcella."

"I know, Dad, but really I'm OK now."

He looked at me, but his eyes didn't lift higher than my neck.

"I'm taking you to see Doctor Harrison."

Oh, no. "I don't—"

"Go put something around your neck," he said. "A scarf or something."

○ ○ ○

We had to sit for ninety minutes in Doctor Harrison's waiting room before his receptionist fit me into his schedule as a drop-in patient.

Three toddlers and a croupy seven- or eight-year-old played on the floor in the middle of the room with a kid-sized kitchen and a collection of fake food. One of the younger children handed me a pink plate with a piece of plastic bacon and a sprinkled doughnut on it. I'd missed breakfast and lunch, and my stomach growled.

"Don't you think I'm too old for a pediatrician?" I asked my dad.

He turned in his chair, facing me completely. I realized, suddenly, that my dad was a thirty-six-year-old version of Lou. Tall, athletic, broad-shouldered, expensive-messy hair. He still carried himself like an athlete, like Lou would long after he'd settled into his adult life. My stomach did a queasy belly flop.

"I'm really sorry I worried you," I said. "We can go home. I swear, I'm fine."

"Celly, I need you to tell me why we're here."

"You're the one—"

He shook his head. "Don't put this on me."

"I don't want to be here. Let's just go home."

"You tried to—" My father looked around to see that no one was paying any attention, then lowered his voice. "You might have hurt yourself in some way that isn't obvious yet."

That was as close as he could get to acknowledging that he thought I'd tried to do more than hurt myself. A wave of guilt over the worry I'd caused him washed over me.

The door to the back office opened, and a nurse in purple scrubs with yellow puppies all over them came out with a clipboard. "Marcella Boucher?" *Boo-cher*. Almost right.

"Dad." I tried for the pleading tone that always worked for Jenna. He stood up and waited until I sighed and stood as well.

"In here." The nurse opened the door to a bathroom. She was maybe thirty, with a brown chin-length bob and bangs. She was clearly used to working with small children and didn't quite know what to do with me. "I'll get your weight and height and then you can pee in that cup for me."

The nurse pointed to the sealed plastic cup on the sink.

Dad nudged me into the bathroom before I could ask what my pee had to do with anything. Because the day hadn't been awful enough, he stood right on top of me as I stepped up on the scale. The nurse slid the balance to two hundred pounds, and the arm stayed firmly down.

She inched the weight up a single pound at a time.

The silence in the bathroom, except for the metallic scraping, was hideously awkward. The nurse moved the big weight up to two hundred fifty pounds and went through the same process. I couldn't decide if she was trying to be polite or if she really thought I might weigh fifty or even a hundred pounds less than I did.

At two sixty-two, I moved the heavier weight over to three hundred myself, and the arm finally lifted. The nurse focused intently on the scale for a moment, adjusting it slightly until it was perfectly balanced.

"Three hundred and twelve." She whispered my weight, as if my father might not hear. His breath brushed my cheek.

"I know," I said.

The nurse fiddled with the scale for another second, then wrote down the number and looked up at me. "Well, my goodness, you're a tall girl, aren't you?"

Yeah. "How about if I just tell you how tall."

"That should be all right."

She was maybe five foot two. I wasn't convinced she'd be able to reach high enough to measure me anyway. "I'm six feet tall."

"Well, I guess you are. My goodness." She twisted her wedding ring, and I thought I was probably going to be the topic of conversation around her dinner table that night.

You wouldn't believe the size of the girl who came in today. My goodness.

I looked at my dad. He had his hands in his pockets and was looking at the print that hung over the toilet—elk frolicking through pine trees. I hoped he was getting what a useless waste of time this all was.

He and the nurse left me alone in the bathroom. When I came

out, the nurse took the pee cup from me and we all marched down to an exam room.

"You don't have to wait with me," I said to my dad. "I'll be fine on my own."

He sat in a chair and picked up a two-year-old special Oscar edition of *People* magazine. We sat in silence until Doctor Harrison came in, looking at my chart.

"Marcella. I haven't seen you in quite a while."

He looked up, did a double take, and looked back at the file, turning the page. I'd gained more than a hundred pounds since he'd treated me for strep throat in the summer when I was fourteen. I'd grown a good six inches since then as well, but I was pretty sure that wasn't what caught him up.

"What brings you here today?" he asked my father, not me.

"Take off your scarf, Celly."

What I wanted to do was run. Get the hell out of there as fast as my long, chubby legs could take me. I pulled off the silk scarf my grandmother had given me out of her magic, never-ending drawer of them when I was a little girl. At the time, I'd loved the bright orange poppies all over it, but now it just made me feel like I'd taken a highlighter to what my dad wanted me to hide.

Doctor Harrison sat the file down on the counter and came closer. "What happened here?"

I cut my eyes to Dad, wondering how much he'd let me get away with. And how much he really thought he knew. "It was an accident."

Doctor Harrison probed my neck with his fingers, which were

long and narrow and almost too soft. Then he took a tongue depressor out of the front pocket of his long, white lab coat. "Open wide."

I looked at my father again as I did as I was told. His mouth was pinched closed.

"I don't see any real damage." Doctor Harrison lifted my chin and touched my neck again with that feathery light pressure that made me want to yank away. "I'm afraid this bruising is only going to get worse, and you already have some swelling. You should have had ice on it right away. How did you manage to do this to yourself?"

"It was just a stupid mistake," I said as much to my father as I did to the doctor.

He sat back and looked at me long enough to make me squirm. "You've gained a lot of weight, Marcella."

I bit back a sarcastic response and just said, "Yeah."

The wheels on the doctor's steel stool squeaked as he scooted closer. He spoke low, just like the nurse had when she'd announced my weight. As if my father wasn't right there in the room listening to everything he said. "I think you'd be happier if you slimmed down some."

Was he serious?

"It's a matter of simple math," he went on, which at least saved me from having to come up with an answer to that little bit of completely shocking wisdom. "Move some more, eat less, and you'll be leaner before you know it."

Right. Why hadn't I thought of that? "I lost some weight over the summer, but—"

“That’s great! Just keep at it.” The doctor slid back on his stool and stood up. “Why don’t you just relax here for a minute while I talk to your dad in my office.”

○ ○ ○

“I should have told him what you did,” Dad said when we were in the car driving out of the medical center parking lot. “Why didn’t I tell him?”

I wasn’t sure how to answer that. “What did he say?”

“He wants you to go to the ER if the swelling gets bad and makes it hard to breathe.” He pulled a card from his shirt pocket and handed it to me. “And he wants you to see this woman.”

Betsy Hamilton, board certified therapist specializing in eating disorders and childhood obesity. The back of the card looked like the cover of a book.

“*Healing Childhood Obesity from the Inside Out*,” I read out loud. “Dad, I’m not doing this.”

“You’re going to see her, just as soon as I can get you in.”

“Dad!”

“Tomorrow, if at all possible. Doctor Harrison isn’t stupid.”

“I never said he was.”

“I didn’t tell him what you did, but that didn’t stop him from suggesting a three-day stay in the hospital to make sure you won’t try it again.”

I didn’t try to kill myself. Not really. But there wasn’t any way for me to get him to see that. "I don't need—"

"I'm sorry, baby, but you can go see Betsy Hamilton or I can turn this car around."

○ ○ ○

We pulled into the driveway before Mom made it home from Belly Busters.

My father put a hand on my arm to stop me when we were on the front porch. "Let's just have a peaceful dinner."

It took some real effort not to roll my eyes. "Maybe I should just hang out in my room. That way I won't bother anyone."

He didn't pick up on my sarcasm. "No. You'll worry your mother if you do that. Put that scarf back on before we go inside."

"Seriously."

"I don't want you to upset your sister. We'll talk to Mom tonight."

Not better. I took the scarf from my bag and tied it around my neck. I knew I looked ridiculous. The gaudy thing didn't hide the bruises. If anything, it drew attention to my neck.

Jenna was home, sitting on the living room floor in a full split, her chin in her hands and her elbows on the floor in front of her, watching television. She had to have heard about that stupid rose and my locker.

"Hey," she said, without looking at us.

"Homework done?" Dad asked.

She mumbled something that sounded like *yes*, but probably wasn't.

"OK then." He left us alone and she finally looked up.

Normally, he would have asked about her day. Spent some time talking to her about her dance competition that weekend or something. She looked at me, and I just shrugged.

"What are you wearing?" she asked.

I put my hand to the silk around my neck. "Nana's scarf."

"Why do you go out of your way to look ridiculous?"

She wore a pair of running shorts that slid up to her hips in her current position and a tank top that left two inches of her midriff exposed. "Why do you go out of your way to look like a prostitute?"

She grunted but didn't move out of her split or look particularly put out by my insult. "I'm stretching."

"Yeah? I'm sure your friend Vivi would appreciate your technique."

Jenna did sit up then. "Vivi isn't my friend."

"That's good."

She got to her feet. "She isn't. And I didn't know about your locker before it happened."

I nodded and went to my bedroom before I could start to really wonder what my sister would have done if she had known.

o o o

Dinner was awful.

When I went for the bread basket, Mom moved temptation to the other side of the table, in front of Jenna who reached in with a nasty little grin and took a roll.

"You look lovely," Mom said. "It's nice to see you with some color around your face."

"Thanks." I guess.

"It's a myth, you know, that black makes you look slimmer."

"I actually did know that." She'd only told me about a thousand times. A stench of stale Chanel No. 5 wafted up from the scarf, and I wanted, badly, to take it off.

Breakfast and lunch had both been a complete wash, and I was hungry. Not just regular hungry. Cookie Monster hungry.

Jenna reached for a second roll, tore off a piece, and dipped it into her spaghetti sauce before taking a bite.

"I had a call from the high school counselor today," my father said.

I froze with a bite of pasta halfway to my mouth. My appetite was almost killed. Almost. My stomach rumbled in protest when the bite didn't come, like the empty sides of it were flapping together.

"Oh?" My mother stopped her fork, too, only it was filled with dry romaine lettuce and a cherry tomato. She didn't eat carbs past noon. I doubted she'd eaten ranch dressing since middle school. "And?"

"Marcella has an appointment tomorrow. She'll have to miss her first classes."

"What kind of appointment?"

I took my bite and twirled my fork in the rest of the half-cup of pasta my mother had used a Pyrex measuring cup to dole out onto my plate. I chewed slowly while my parents talked about me like I wasn't there.

"It's with a specialist," Dad said.

I stared down into my plate and wished my spaghetti would swallow me up instead of the other way around.

Mom turned to look at me. "Are your grades down? Why am I just hearing about this now?"

I forked up another bite. "My grades are fine."

She pushed her mostly full plate away from her. "Grades are important. Especially for you."

I tried to remember that a few hours ago I didn't want to die. I still didn't want to die, but I wanted to be anywhere but inside my own skin at the moment. "My grades are fine."

"This woman's job is to help Celly figure out how to lose weight," Dad said.

Jenna, who wasn't even five feet tall and weighed something like eighty-five pounds, looked from our dad to our mom to me. This must have been like seeing some sort of weird cross between a zoo exhibit and a freak show. Watch the fat girl try to eat while her keepers talk about her blubber like she isn't there.

"Well, good, then. That's good." My mother retrieved her plate now that she wasn't concerned about my grades anymore. "Was it the nurse that called?"

"May I be excused?" I asked.

"Marcella." My father lowered his voice. "You'll see her tomorrow."

As if I had a choice. If I didn't agree to go on my own, one or both of my parents would visit Betsy Hamilton, childhood obesity expert, with me. That was just about the only thing worse than having to go at all.

I picked up my plate and left the table without waiting to be told I could. In the kitchen, I shoveled the rest of my spaghetti into my mouth without even tasting it. My insides were too hollow to ever be filled. But I tried.

I ate more, right out of the pot. But I was a fucking bottomless pit. That empty feeling wouldn't go away. It was a black hole that threatened to eat me up from the inside. That scared the shit out of me. It had been too much like that afternoon, and I had to do something to make it stop.

I opened the pantry, took out the box of Lucky Charms, and pushed a handful of the sweet, crunchy marshmallow mess into my mouth. I heard my parents and my sister in the dining room, talking about Jenna's dance competition. Like it was just a regular night. I didn't even register that I'd eaten the rest of the cereal until I reached my hand into the box and came up empty.

I wanted to hate someone other than myself. My sister, for being so goddamned perfect. My parents. Lou. Vivi. The idiots at the bus stop. Anyone but myself.

I opened the bag of rolls on the counter, ripped pieces off, and dipped them in the leftover spaghetti sauce before shoving them into my mouth and swallowing almost without chewing.

I picked up the pan of organic, gluten-free brownies that were supposed to be dessert for everyone but me. I didn't bother with a plate—just dug a fork into the center. I didn't care that even if no one came into the kitchen and saw me inhaling the whole thing, it would still be obvious that I'd eaten them.

They tasted awful, but I didn't care about that either.

The funny thing was, this was the best way to make sure I didn't get another invitation to work out with my mom in the morning. She'd act like it hadn't happened at all. They all would. Dirty 312-pound secrets were best kept quiet.

Dad wouldn't push me to talk to her about what had happened yet, either. He'd wait until I was more settled.

The empty feeling was finally replaced by the pain of being overly full, and I went upstairs to bed.

CHAPTER 4

My appointment with Betsy Hamilton meant I could stretch two parent-sanctioned missed classes into the first half of the day. I'd have to take a city bus the six miles north to Reno, after all. I didn't have a car. And since my appointment wasn't until nine thirty, I could eat breakfast alone after Jenna and our parents had gone for the day.

I made myself scrambled eggs and sourdough toast with real butter, not the spray-on low-calorie shit my mother bought for me. I added strawberry jam and tried not to think about my binge the night before.

I didn't want to think about school, either, but the fact was I'd have to face it that afternoon, like it or not. By the time I got there, it was a sure bet that everyone at Twain, including the janitor and the lunch ladies, would know that Vivi had filled my locker with hand soap and condoms.

They'd all seen the Morp rose disaster firsthand.

Everyone at school had witnessed Lou rejecting me. I was the only one who had any expectation that he might call me to make sure that I was OK.

He hadn't.

My PE uniform and half of my textbooks were covered in hand soap. That meant no PE fifth period either. This day was shaping up not to be as bad as I'd thought it might.

I was dead sure I'd be the one to pay for the mess in my locker. Hell, even if I had video of Vivi loading that condom and rigging it to break when my locker opened, somehow she would avoid responsibility, and it would land squarely on my shoulders. Some people just have that get-away-with-anything magic.

I was not one of those people.

I doubted that I'd ever even know how Vivi got into my locker in the first place.

The more I thought about it, the less I hated the idea of visiting Betsy Hamilton. Putting off school until fourth period was fine by me. In fact, make it after lunch just to be on the safe side. And no need to get back in time for PE, so it could be a long lunch.

I still had the change from buying the rose. I could pick up some tacos or something.

The directions my father gave me took most of an hour and two bus transfers. The address was a three-story, very narrow brick building sandwiched between a tattoo parlor and a restaurant called Stew, which specialized in stew.

How meta.

The door was locked, so I pressed my thumb into the doorbell that read "Betsy Hamilton." I'd wrapped my grandmother's scarf back around my neck that morning, and now its stupid ends literally waved in the breeze. I pulled it off and stuffed it into my school bag.

The front door was opened by a woman with a perfectly round face that was only accentuated by her closely-cropped jet black hair. She was much younger than I expected a woman named Betsy Hamilton to be. "Marcella?"

I thought about telling her I was there selling Girl Scout cookies or something. And then I thought about my dad bringing me here himself next time and just said, "Yes."

The woman smiled and exposed straight white teeth and a dimple in each apple cheek. When she spoke, her voice was soft and pleasant. "I'm Betsy. You found me. Come on in."

Betsy was six inches shorter than me and reed thin. She moved with grace, like maybe she had been a dancer in another life. I followed her, with pretty much no grace at all, through a foyer and up a narrow wooden staircase.

Everything about her was the opposite of me. As dark as I was fair on the outside; as light and breezy as I was stormy on the inside.

"We have an elevator, but taking the stairs is an easy way to get some exercise." She looked back as I turned slightly sidewise to get through the cramped stairway. She radiated pride. Like she'd invented the idea of taking the stairs instead of the elevator. "You don't mind, do you?"

I didn't bother to answer. I was too busy trying to keep my breathing even so I wouldn't puff like the Little Engine That Could by the time I got to her office.

On the third floor, Betsy led me into a room that spanned the width of the building and had large windows along the back wall. Potted plants sat on every available surface that wasn't already occupied by books. More greenery hung from hooks around the perimeter. A couple of large plants sat on the floor. She'd trained some sort of ivy to cling to a network of string running across the ceiling.

Betsy swept one long-fingered hand toward an overstuffed chair.

"Sit there, Marcella. I was just watering my babies." She picked up a watering can as I sat. "It's hard to keep them healthy here, you know? It's so dry all the time."

I sat in the middle of this jungle, watching Betsy move from plant to plant, watering and picking out dead leaves. Sometimes she murmured something, but I couldn't make it out. She wasn't talking to me anyway. She was talking to her "babies."

"So," I finally said when I couldn't take it anymore. "My dad said Doctor Harrison recommended you."

Betsy put her watering can on the floor, pushed her handful of dead leaves into a wastebasket, and turned her full attention to me. "Do you know what one of the greatest parts of growing up is?"

I shifted in my chair. "You only have to do it once?"

She gave me a look that said *good one.* "Figuring out who you want to be and making a plan to get there."

I suppressed a groan. Barely.

"When you're seventeen, everything is fluid. Every possibility is still open." Betsy sat in the chair next to mine. She crossed her legs under her long white sundress. Excitement thrummed from her. "I know it doesn't feel that way when you're in the middle of it and everything hurts, but it's true."

"I'll let you know when I'm on the other side of it."

"High school sucks, doesn't it?"

This was going great so far. "You have no idea."

I was pretty sure she really didn't. Girls who looked like her weren't mooed at in the hallways.

"You might be surprised," she said. "But you know what? I wish someone had told me when I was seventeen that I didn't have to let high school define me."

Barf. "How can high school not define me? It's my whole life."

"It won't be your whole life forever. And you get to decide, right now, whether you want to emerge from high school the same way you entered it."

"You mean fat."

Betsy leaned in closer, her angular body nearly touching my rounder one. "Believe it or not, I was a fat kid, too."

I didn't believe it. "Really."

"Really. I lost twenty-eight pounds in college, and it changed my whole life."

Twenty-eight pounds. Seriously? Twenty-eight pounds more than what she weighed now did not make a fat girl.

"If you'll make the commitment, Marcella, I'll help you make sure your weight problem doesn't follow you to college."

I leaned back in my chair and stared up at the ceiling. I went on my first diet when I was in third grade. I went on my latest last summer. I'd never lost a pound that didn't find its way back, with friends.

I hated that something inside me wondered if Betsy had some kind of magic shrink-the-fat-girl bean. I didn't want to care.

"Are you OK?" Betsy asked. "You look a little pale."

Betsy reached for me, and I pushed myself deeper into the chair, away from her long, brown fingers. "I'm fine."

"You don't look well at all." Betsy stood up. "Stay right there."

"Seriously. I don't need anything."

She came back with a bottle of water and spun the top off before handing it to me. "Drink this."

I took the bottle and felt a little like Alice. Did her bottle make her shrink or grow?

The cold water soothed my throat, but also highlighted that it was sore and swollen. I waited for her to say something about the bruises around my neck. I was pretty sure my father had talked to her about them.

But she didn't, so I finally asked, "What exactly does a childhood obesity specialist do?"

"We'll work on figuring out what's causing your weight problem and make a plan to help you realize your best self."

I drank again. This was so stupid. "So, basically you're Oprah? Only without the money."

"How does your weight make you feel, Marcella?"

"I'm not happy having my locker filled with fake semen and a bunch of condoms and then having the whole school call me Moo-cella while no one does anything to stop them."

Betsy hesitated. "That happened to you?"

"That happened to me yesterday."

"I'm so sorry."

"Yeah, well. I'm pretty sure that your plan for helping me realize my 'best self'"—I shot her some air quotes—"isn't going to be much help."

Betsy's face relaxed again into a mask of concerned care. "I can help you. But you have to be willing to help yourself, too."

Smooth, Betsy. So, if I swallow the magic bean and don't shrink, it's all on me. "I lost weight last summer. Did my dad tell you that? It only made things worse at school, and I gained it all back plus thirteen pounds."

"Your dad told me you were on a diet. I don't do diets here."

Right. A childhood obesity therapist who didn't do diets felt about as real as a whale that didn't do the ocean. "Then what do you do?"

"I help you recover."

"Recover from what?"

Betsy looked at me hard enough to make me squirm. "I specialize in eating disorders."

"I don't have an eating disorder." Except you ate a whole pan of disgusting gluten-free brownies last night, Celly Belly. I was mortified to feel a hot flush move from my chest over my face.

"Maybe you don't. How about if we just talk for now and see what we find out together?"

"I've been to therapy before." It was true. My mother took me to see a therapist in ninth grade, after Holly stopped talking to me and I stopped talking to everyone.

I'd decided the day before that I didn't want to die, but I'd been close enough to hanging myself that I was still a little shaky just thinking about it. A therapist might not be the worst thing ever, even if I'd never tell her that.

For the first time since I walked into her office, Betsy took a long look at my neck. Then she shifted her gaze to my face and said, "I have something for you."

I stayed in my seat while Betsy went to a shelf and took a book from it. "I'd like you to read this."

She held it close to her chest, then thrust it toward me. *Healing Childhood Obesity from the Inside Out*. "Wow."

Betsy pushed the book into my hands. "You don't have to read the whole thing. Just look at the chapter that describes eating disorders before we meet again. I think you might be surprised."

"When am I supposed to come back?"

"We'll find a time that doesn't interfere with school. But we still have half an hour today. Why don't you tell me about what you eat every day? No judgment here, Marcella. I just want to find our starting point."

The idea of refusing to talk about food flirted around my brain, but in the end, I decided it wasn't worth it. "My mother gives me half as much to eat as my sister, who weighs a third of what I do."

"How old is your sister?"

"She's fourteen. You won't be meeting her, though. She's perfect."

"Is that what you think?"

I shrugged one shoulder. "It's what my parents think. It's definitely what she thinks."

"No one is perfect."

"My mother thinks giving me less to eat will make me lose weight, but all it does is make me hungry all the time. I eat more later." I hesitated, then added, "Sometimes a lot more."

"We can talk about that."

"I should get to school."

"OK." Betsy stood up. "Will you come again? I know your father can probably make you, but this won't work unless you want it to."

It didn't matter what I wanted. If I said no, my father would have me back to Doctor Harrison in a heartbeat. And like he said, Doctor Harrison wasn't stupid. "Fine."

"Good. What time are you done with school?"

"Three."

"So next Thursday, then. Four o'clock."

"Fine."

Betsy tilted her head and looked at me for a long moment. "Promise me something, Marcella."

"I already said I'd come back."

"I want your word that you won't hurt yourself between now and then."

She didn't get it. "I'm not going to hurt myself."

"Good. Read the chapter and keep a food log for me. I'll see you next week."

CHAPTER 5

I took the stairs back down from the third floor of Betsy's building, even though the elevator was right there, because she stood in her doorway and watched me.

Rule number one of being a fat girl. You have to avoid even the appearance of laziness.

She was crazy if she thought I was going to write down everything I ate this week, though. I didn't care if she did think I was lazy.

After I was outside, I checked my cell phone and found a text message: Where are you?

Lou always spelled out every word in a text. That quirk was one of the things I loved about him. But today I wasn't in the mood to love Lou Duncan.

Like you care? I still hadn't decided to hit send when a second message came in.

He never sent a second message.

Your house, lunch?

My house would be empty. He knew that. He probably assumed I was ditching to avoid dealing with what happened yesterday, and because I was so heartbroken over him.

In fact, everyone probably thought I was ditching to avoid him. I hated that.

I knew why he wanted to see me in my empty house, and what I really wanted was to be the girl who could say no to Lou Duncan.

I actually backspaced my original message and keyed in Fuck you.

But then I remembered: Lou never, ever sent more than Where are you? He'd wait for me to respond, then tell me what time he'd be over.

What if he actually wanted to apologize? Maybe he'd broken up with Vivi over the prank she pulled.

Maybe Vivi had finally gone too far.

I erased my f-bomb and typed something a little less salty. Fine. And sent it.

Tacos could wait. I went to wait for the bus that would take me home.

○ ○ ○

An hour later, I was intensely aware of how far Lou sat from me on the couch. He was pressed into one corner with his long legs stretched out in front of him. No part of his body touched me.

I wanted not to care. I wanted to be glad, in fact, but my hand twitched next to me, wishing he'd take it.

He had apologized as soon as I opened the front door and let him in. Sort of. As he looked over his shoulder to make sure no one had seen him come in, he said, "I'm sorry, Celly, but you shouldn't have done that rose thing."

If I could step back out of my body and see what the pair of us really looked like, the image would probably scar me. Him, beautiful, sitting on his half of the couch, laid back and comfortable in his own skin. Me, doing what I could to condense myself by folding my arms over my chest and pressing my legs tight together, ankles crossed.

Like trying to fold a Mack truck into a Mini Cooper.

Since he'd shown up, there hadn't been a nanosecond when I was not aware of how much space my body needed. That was a familiar feeling, but I didn't usually have it with Lou. Today it was on hyperdrive.

"Did you see what she did to my locker?" I asked.

"Vivi was pissed off. What did you expect?"

"Not that."

Usually Lou touched me. He liked to hold my hand. Or he'd touch my leg or put his fingers in my hair—which was still braided, because he hadn't tugged the elastic out of it.

Whenever Lou kissed me, he didn't hold back. At least, I didn't think he did. He hadn't kissed me today, at all.

"Did you know what she was doing?" I held my breath and wished I could take that question back as soon as it blurted out of me.

He shook his head. "Why did you give me a rose, Celly?"

I exhaled. "I told you I wanted to go to the dance with you, and you said you wanted to go with me, too."

Reach for me. I wanted him to show me some sort of affection. I was alarmed by how badly I needed it. He didn't move.

"I can't do this anymore." My voice was barely more than a whisper.

"You broke the rule, Marcella. You can't blame me for this."

It wasn't that I didn't know better. I did. Of course I did. I knew Lou didn't love me. He didn't love Vivi, either. But this was the first time I really believed that maybe he didn't even like me. I was sitting beside him with bruises around my neck, and he hadn't even asked me about them.

I struggled out of the couch, trying not to touch him as I did. "I'm not doing this."

Lou's face darkened. His eyes narrowed and, for a split second, I was scared of what he might say. But then he shrugged and stood up, too.

"You'll be my project," he'd said at the beginning of last summer.

Somehow, I'd convinced myself that not only was being a popular boy's project OK—it was kind of cool.

By that time, Lou had been picking up dirty towels and cleaning toilets at Belly Busters for two years. He'd wanted the experience of working as a trainer before he left for college and had figured that if I lost weight and he could take credit, my parents would notice and promote him.

It had worked, too. Between junior and senior year, I'd lost nearly fifty pounds. I'd bought new clothes, two sizes smaller. I already had good hair. I didn't have braces or glasses to get rid of, but I bought some new makeup and spent hours practicing putting it on.

I'd thought about asking Jenna for help but couldn't bring myself to do it.

A makeover had worked for Holly the summer before ninth grade. But the new me had not been not absorbed into Holly's new clique. Or any clique at all. So far, senior year had been a nightmare that taught me a lesson about whether there was really a difference between 299 pounds and 253 pounds. Or 312 pounds, for that matter.

There wasn't.

Lou finally touched me. He brushed a hand over my cheek and then down my braid to the pink elastic at the end of it. When he spoke, his voice was nearly irresistible. Nearly. "This doesn't have to be such a big deal. We graduate in May. I'll break it off with Vivi then. She's going to Utah, anyway."

He pulled the elastic from my braid and shook my hair loose. His hand brushed my arm, and I let myself feel his fingers on my skin, just for a moment, before I opened my eyes. "It does have to be such a big deal."

He pulled his hand back.

It was on the tip of my tongue to apologize. *I'm sorry your project failed.* Instead I just kept my mouth closed. Something I probably should have figured out how to do around him a long time ago.

He reached forward and tangled his fingers in my hair again, trying to pull me into him. "I really like you. But you have to follow the rules."

Follow the goddamned rules. "I can't do this anymore."

Lou tilted his head and looked at me the way I might look at someone who was so crazy it was cute. "You're just mad."

Hell yes, I was mad. "Just leave, Lou."

"Celly."

I didn't trust myself to hold my ground if I kept talking, so I just looked at him. Lou stood there for another few seconds.

I'd spent the last nine months confused about him. He spent so much time with me all summer. We talked about old movies that I loved and old music that he loved and about our plans for after graduation.

We talked about being in Las Vegas together for school next year.

We were friends.

And then one day he wanted to do more than talk. He wanted to do more than work out with me. And he was perfect. I was sure most girls at Twain would trade places with me in a second.

Lou had three rules.

Rule number one: No one needed to know Lou's personal business. I was his personal business. Vivi was his very public business. He was a point guard on the basketball team and captain of the baseball team. He was supposed to be with someone like her. It was expected.

Rule number two: No kissing. I spent all summer expecting Lou to break this one, like Julia Roberts did in *Pretty Woman*. And around the time school started again, he did.

I guess that meant he really only had two rules.

Rule number three: Lou texted me when he wanted to see me. Never the other way around. This one was unspoken, but still ironclad.

By the time I started having second thoughts, it was too late to change the rules. I'd already agreed to them by following them. I'd even agreed to let him be the one to change them by letting him kiss me.

That made giving him a Morp flower in front of the entire school an even bigger crime. Which annoyed the hell out of me. Why was it such a crime to make my own rules anyway?

So far, I hadn't had the nerve to test what would happen if I just didn't answer one of his texts. I figured there were two possible outcomes.

In the first, I stood him up and he had a come-to-Jesus moment where he realized how much he truly loved me and how stupid he'd been. He'd hold my hand in the school hallways and kiss me when his team won, and we'd get married after college graduation. We'd have a couple of kids, maybe a golden retriever. Live happily ever after.

In the second, I stood him up and he didn't care. It took accidentally almost killing myself for me to realize that I shouldn't care either. I had no idea what it would take for me to get to actually not caring.

I admit it. I had harbored some major Cinderella fantasies about our future.

In every one of them, I lost weight. That was the center of my dream world. Then Lou would be so impressed that he would kiss me on the mouth in front of all of his friends, or...

“Fuck it,” Lou said. He left me standing in front of the couch and went out the front door without looking back.

I was tempted to skip the rest of the school day. But if I didn’t show up for fifth period roll call, the school would call my dad. That was worse than going, so I went. Even though all I really wanted to do was crawl into bed and cry myself dry.

My life often felt like a series of choices between bad and worse.

○ ○ ○

Five minutes after the bell for fifth period rang, I sat in my street clothes halfway up the bleachers while the rest of the PE class played dodgeball on the basketball court. The first ball that flew at me might have been a mistake. The fifth definitely wasn’t. It hit me square in the face while I was busy deflecting the fourth.

“Christ, Marcella.” Mrs. Prichard had a habit of reminding me, as often as possible over the past four years, how I was nothing like my mother had been when she was in her class.

I saw her picture in Mom’s senior yearbook once. In the early aughties, Helen Prichard had been young and rather pretty. She had some wear on her now. Like she’d aged forty years instead of less than twenty.

“Really?” I pinched the bridge of my nose. I was surprised it wasn’t bleeding. “I was just sitting here.”

“If you choose not to dress out, you have to stay out of the way.”

The dodgeball game had come to an end, and everyone stared at me. "I didn't choose not to dress out."

"Go to the office." She turned her back on me, leaving no room for argument, and yelled, "Throw the balls, ladies, or you'll be giving me the push-up position!"

I somehow made it down out of the bleachers, lugging my backpack and still pinching the bridge of my nose. I stopped long enough in the gym bathroom to assess the damage and clean myself up some.

I was a hot mess. My neck was every shade from black to blue to purple in a weird necklace-like ring around the top of my neck and under my jaw. As long as I kept my head down, it wasn't really noticeable, but when I tipped my chin up, it was awful.

My nose was red and starting to swell, but not bleeding at least. I had dark circles under my eyes, and I'd left for school without putting my hair back up, so it was a tangled disaster.

All I had to work with were my fingers and water, but I did my best before I walked to the office.

Mr. Ellis had been the vice principal of Mark Twain High School practically since Samuel Clemens himself wrote his first article for the Virginia City *Territorial Enterprise*.

I could have gone to the nurse's office instead, which is where Mrs. Prichard probably meant me to go, but there was a better chance that she'd call my parents.

"Miss Boucher," Mr. Ellis said when I stood in his doorway. He leaned back in his chair, hands clasped in the center of his narrow chest, bald head shining in the fluorescent light. "I was going to call for you anyway. Come on in."

I sat in a chair across his desk from him. "Mrs. Prichard sent me."

We stared at each other for an awkward moment, then Mr. Ellis said, "Are you going to tell me why Mrs. Prichard sent you here?"

"Apparently, halfway up the bleachers isn't far enough out of the way during a dodgeball game."

He drew his hand along his graying goatee. His gaze slipped to my neck, and then he jerked his attention to the top half of my face, like he'd never seen eyes so green. "And why weren't you participating?"

Really? "Well, Mr. Ellis, yesterday someone filled my locker with soap and rubbers and ruined my PE uniform. I'll have to take it home tonight and wash it. You know. If my locker isn't vandalized again."

His eyes narrowed, and he lowered both arms to his desk. "What are we going to do with you?"

Was I supposed to answer that? I opened my mouth, but couldn't think of anything to say, so I shut it again. When he really seemed to be looking for an answer, I finally said, "I didn't put that stuff in my locker."

"I know that, and it will be dealt with. It doesn't excuse you from your schoolwork."

I almost laughed but managed to hold it back. "OK."

"It's what precipitated the prank that I want to talk to you about."

He seemed to be weighing his words. I waited a minute, but when he didn't go on, I said, "OK?"

"Sometimes a person needs to take preventative steps to avoid unwanted attention."

"Preventative steps?"

He hesitated again, clearly trying to make sure he said the right thing. "There are two sides to every story."

"Are you seriously putting this on me?"

"I was in the lunchroom yesterday."

I dragged a hand through my hair and grunted in frustration when my fingers tangled in it. "You were there when people were mooing at me, you mean."

The tops of his cheeks went pink. "Before that, when you had a rose delivered to Lou Duncan."

"Everyone was having roses delivered."

Mr. Ellis at least had the grace to look uncomfortable, like he was picking his way through a mine field. "It might have been best to ask him to the dance more privately, is all."

"I didn't want to ask anyone at all. My mom—"

Mr. Ellis leaned forward in his chair, waving his hands to cut me off. "I'm not saying you shouldn't have asked someone. I want that to be perfectly clear."

"Well, I—"

"All I'm saying, is sometimes we have to make choices that are best for us. And perhaps giving Mr. Duncan a rose wasn't the best choice for you."

"I can't believe this."

"The janitor cleaned out your locker. Your books were a lost cause, but I sent someone around to collect new ones for you." He tilted his head toward a stack of books on the edge of his desk, then brought up a plastic grocery bag. "Here is your PE uniform. My wife washed it for you."

For some reason, the idea of that grossed me out. I took the bag. "Will my parents have to pay for the books?"

"No, no, of course not. No charge at all. If we can just work together to make sure nothing like this happens again, Miss Boucher, I think we'll get you graduated in June just fine."

"Don't you think that if you want to avoid more acts of bullying, you should be talking to the bully?"

Mr. Ellis took on a look of long-suffering patience. His eyes did not travel farther south than my nose. "I can't talk to you about how the other parties involved are being dealt with."

"You consider me a party to what happened yesterday?"

"Marcella."

The bell rang just then. I stood up, stuffed the gym clothes into my backpack, and reached for my new books.

"Please sit down."

"I need to get to my history class."

Mr. Ellis jotted something on a pad of paper and tore the top sheet off.

"Until things"—his eyes finally drifted to my neck again—"have calmed down some, I'm having your work sent to the ISS room."

ISS was in-school suspension. "What?"

"It's for the best, Marcella. For your own protection, really."

"Right. Because my bullies won't be in there with me."

"No," he said, quickly, as if to reassure me. "Of course they won't.

You'll be fine."

In his pea brain, he was protecting me by punishing me instead of Vivi and her minions. "This is unbelievable."

"We have to work within the system we have. Try to understand. You aren't under suspension. It's just the best place for you to work in peace right now."

I took the suspension slip and my books and walked out of his office.

CHAPTER 6

I'd never been sent to ISS before, but knew enough to know that it was basically a room where kids went to do classwork while the basketball coach sat at a desk and either ate, napped, or worked on his playbook. All. Day. Long.

Coach Phillips was stocky and on the short side for a man who specialized in basketball. He had heavy sideburns and a barrel chest, and he looked like he belonged in an old sitcom.

The ten or so other kids in the room all looked up at me, probably happy for something to focus on other than their endless supply of Xeroxed worksheets.

I handed Phillips the slip from Ellis.

"What're you in for?" he asked.

So much for privacy. Every student had ears tuned to this conversation. "My own good."

"Smart mouth." He tapped the eraser of his pencil on the desk before writing something down. When I just stayed standing there, he gave me an exasperated look and flung one wrist toward a shelf full of big red books. "There's no work for you yet, so get yourself one of those dictionaries and start copying."

"Seriously?"

He raised both bushy eyebrows. "For your own good."

God. I grabbed a dusty dictionary and wedged myself behind a desk in the back of the room. The effort of turning around in their seats proved too much for everyone else, and they went back to pretending I didn't exist.

Zero moos were given.

I flipped the book open to the *D*s and found what I was looking for, then dug out a notebook and wrote:

douche: **Noun**. a jet or current of liquid (such as a cleansing solution) directed against or into a bodily part or cavity (such as the vagina) **Verb**. the act of cleansing with a douche

I was about to look for Webster's definition of the word *anus* when something at the door caught my eye.

Jason peered in through the small window at me.

I waved him away as inconspicuously as I could. If being bullied landed me in ISS, I couldn't imagine what might happen to me if I actually did something wrong. Expulsion? Decapitation?

He waved back at me, then shook his head when I pretended not to know what the come-here motion meant. He held up a finger and disappeared.

And then he pressed a piece of notebook paper to the window. He'd written on it with a ballpoint pen, going over it and over it until the letters were thick and furry looking.

The note said: *Ditch?*

What in the actual hell. Who was this kid?

I looked at Coach Phillips, who wasn't paying attention to anything but his open playbook. I was so tired of trying to be good and getting punished just for being alive. I wanted out of this smelly, stuffy room. I put my notebook back in my backpack and side-walked through the aisles of desks to the front of the room.

"What is it, Boucher?" he asked when he finally looked up. At least he pronounced my name right.

"I need a bathroom pass."

"You've been here five minutes."

"Still. I need one."

He looked at me for a long moment then shook his head. "You can wait."

I hefted my bag higher on my shoulder and leaned toward him to whisper. "Girl emergency, Coach Phillips. I really need to change my—"

"Oh, for God's sake!" He tossed a laminated picture of a toilet at me. "Hurry back."

Jason was standing down the hall, near an exit door, waving at me to come to him.

"What are you doing?" I asked him. "Trying to get in there with me?"

"No." He held up his own ISS slip.

"On your second day of school?"

"Not my fault everyone in this school is an asshole." He shrugged and shoved it into his pocket. "Almost. What did you do?"

"I gave a Morp rose to Lou Duncan."

His eyebrows shot up. "Seriously?"

"Sadly. What are you doing out here?"

"If this school is anything like my last school, sixth and seventh period are practically optional, as long as you're there for fifth period roll."

I nodded slowly. "So?"

"So, let's get the hell out of here."

"How did you even know I was in here?"

He lifted on shoulder. "Everyone knows."

Great. Even the new kid.

"Coach Phillips is going to notice if I don't come back. And if you never show up." I held up the laminated toilet. "He'll miss this."

I didn't do things like this. I was a good girl. Not because I didn't know how to manipulate the rules, because I did. I knew how to stretch two missed class periods into four today, plus lunch. But in general, I try to follow the rules.

Lou's. My parents'. The school's. Everyone's.

Jason pushed open the door and a wave of cool air blew over me. I followed him outside, still holding that stupid laminated toilet.

He started toward the student parking lot. I shoved the pass into my pocket and followed him.

"Wait a minute," I said. "You have a car? What were you doing at the bus stop yesterday?"

"My foster mom made me promise to take the bus the first day. To meet people." He looked back over his shoulder at me. "Her plan met with mixed results."

"Hmm."

Turns out he didn't have a car. He had a cherry-red Vespa. "Marcella, meet Francine."

I ran my hand over the front fender.

"She's French." He reached over and inserted a key, then turned it without kicking the engine over. The kickstand came up with a nudge from his toe, and he started to walk the scooter out of the parking lot.

I walked with him. Jason was so tall that he had to bend over at an awkward angle to keep his hands on the handlebars. "Where exactly are we going?"

"To drop Francine off at home, first," he said. "After that, you'll just have to wait and see."

I stopped walking. "Go ahead and ride home. I'm going back to school."

"Don't be stupid."

"I'm not stupid."

Jason turned Francine in a wide U-turn and came back to me. "I know you aren't. I didn't mean—"

I looked over my shoulder, back at the school. The idea of going back there made me nauseous. "If you didn't mean it, you shouldn't have said it."

"You're right. I'm sorry. Let's just get out of here. I really want to show you something."

○ ○ ○

With Jason pushing the scooter, it took almost an hour to walk to our neighborhood. He lived two streets over from me in a small house with a front porch and an overgrown yard that still had a "for sale" sign stuck in it.

They'd just moved in, but the yard was already cluttered with two bicycles, a skateboard, and an impressive arsenal of water guns.

"Wait here," he said.

Jason parked his scooter in the driveway and used his keys to get into the house. I stood where I was, on the sidewalk, and slowly became more and more self-conscious. I tugged the edge of my blue-and-white striped top over the waist of my jeans. Then I took a hair tie from my backpack and pulled my hair into a messy bun.

Finally, the garage door opened, and Jason stood on the other side of it.

"Here." He ducked under the garage door and started to wheel his scooter in. "Leave your backpack. We can pick it up later."

I hesitated for a moment but then went into the garage. Maybe I should have just gone home. But the truth was, I didn't want to be there anymore than I wanted to be at school. The garage was filled with skis, inflated inner tubes, more bicycles, and a mountain of grocery store cardboard boxes.

"How many people live here?" I asked.

"My foster parents have three boys. And me." Jason took my bag and set it inside a wheelbarrow against the wall of the garage. "Ready?"

As I ever was going to be. "Where are we going?"

"It's a surprise."

"I hate surprises."

"You'll like this one." He stopped and looked at me as I got a few steps ahead of him. "I think."

We walked to the bus stop on the corner, halfway between his house and mine, and sat next to each other on the bench until the number sixteen showed up. Before I could dig a dollar in change from my pocket, Jason pushed two dollars through the feed.

We sat on the far back bench seat, facing the front of the bus.

"You didn't have to do that," I said.

"You can get it next time." His words flowed out easy, like there was zero doubt we'd be on the bus together again.

I crossed my arms over my chest and pressed as close to the window as I could get. "Are you going to tell me where we're going?"

He shook his head.

"When will we be there?"

"Soon."

It took twenty minutes for the sixteen to make it to the main bus depot in Reno, where we got off with transfers. We didn't talk much during that ride, although the silence was not exactly uncomfortable. Not totally lacking awkwardness, but OK.

When we got onto a bus that took us through downtown Reno, toward Betsy's office, the silent portion of our little ditching adventure was apparently over.

"So," Jason said as soon as we were seated, and the bus had started moving. The sixteen had been nearly empty, but this bus was packed. "We should probably get it over with."

"Get what over with?"

He lifted his chin toward my neck.

Something in the vicinity of my chest cavity closed like a clam and made it hard for me to breathe.

I almost lied and said it was an accident, but at the last second was sure he wouldn't even pretend to believe me. Then, I almost got defensive and told him to mind his own damned business. But something stopped me.

Something like not minding that finally someone other than my dad looked at my neck and didn't turn away.

So, instead of anger, I went with honesty. "I don't want to talk about it."

"OK," Jason said. "Well, since I'm not blind or stupid, and I was there yesterday, you don't really have to talk about it."

"I'm OK."

"Are you really? Because you don't look OK."

I inhaled hard, trying to catch a breath that slipped just out of my reach. "I am. Really."

He leaned back in the bench seat and stretched his long legs so they seemed to go on for half the length of the bus. "Good."

I waited to see if he was going to say more. Maybe lecture me about my worth as a person or guilt me about upsetting my family.

None of that happened. The semi-awkward silence, although strangely less awkward now than before, was back until we got off at a stop near the university.

I didn't bother to ask again where we were going. After we'd walked about half a mile, we came to a huge, gray cinder block building like a hangar, with a massive double door that stood wide open. It was a little weird to be led by a boy I didn't know to a place that looked like a warehouse. In the next town over. When my parents didn't know where I was.

But we were close to the university, and there were people around. And he walked in like he belonged there. So, I followed.

When I was a kid, I loved to watch *The Wizard of Oz* with Jenna. We had it on DVD, and we watched it a thousand times, even in fast forward and reverse. I loved that moment when Dorothy opens her front door and finds her dull Kansas world suddenly in Technicolor, full of singing flowers and glittering shoes.

That's what walking into that warehouse was like.

Music pounded through it. I didn't know what I was listening to, but it hit like a train. The walls were covered in posters and graffiti. The warehouse floor was lined with rubber mats and stacked with weights and other apparatuses that I recognized from Belly Busters. Arnold Schwarzenegger would have been right at home here.

Except he'd be the only guy, other than Jason.

There were maybe twenty women, all dressed in stripes and bright colors and booty shorts. Some of them were lifting weights. Others were cheering them on. A few were running around the perimeter of the warehouse.

"What is this?" I asked Jason under my breath. I was a little afraid that raising my voice might break the spell.

"This is the Hive."

"What?"

A woman came toward us. She was maybe thirty, with dark hair in short curls around her face. Tattoos covered both arms from shoulder to elbow and peeked out from the neckline of her tank top. She was no taller than my mom, but sturdier. Stronger.

"Shouldn't you be in school?" She had to crane her neck back to see either of our faces.

"It was one of those days," Jason said.

"Already? Like, day two? Shit." The woman turned to me. Her almost-black eyes opened wide.

"Marcella," Jason said, "this is Suzy. My foster mom."

"Oh my god." Suzy reached up and pushed one of my shoulders. "Oh my god! You're a Beast. Jason, tell me this girl is a Beast."

"What?" I looked at Jason, who sighed and shook his head.

Suzy pushed my shoulder again, harder this time. I moved with the pressure but didn't step back. I was too stunned to do anything else.

"You are a Beast," she said again. "With awesome balance. Where did you find her?"

"The girl section of the grocery store," Jason said without skipping a beat.

The music, which had been exciting a few minutes ago, was too loud now. I walked away. I didn't skip school to get more of the same bullshit here. Jason reached for me, but I was faster.

Asshole. I'd trusted him. *What an idiot.*

I was halfway to the double doors before Suzy ran around in front of me. She was the fastest.

"Hey," she said. "Don't go. You just got here."

Jason caught up then and said, "She didn't mean anything bad, Celly."

"Right." I lifted my eyebrows. "She called me a beast."

Suzy put a hand on Jason's chest when he started to say something else. "You are a Beast. Oh my God. You're the Queen Beast."

"Thanks for pointing that out. I'm going home."

Suzy pushed my shoulder again, even harder than before. Tears pricked my eyes, and I was mortified. I had one rule for myself: I didn't cry in front of them. Ever. I inhaled hard and fought to control my breathing.

"Look at you," Suzy said. "I bet you're as strong as an ox."

Jason looked about as horrified as I felt. "Calm down, Suzy."

I am so out of here. I turned and walked back toward the door. I made it three steps before the next thing she said stopped me.

"Can she move?"

I turned around.

Jason's whole face changed. He smiled and shrugged one shoulder. "Like she was born for it."

Panic started in the pit of my stomach and contracted my lungs. But I didn't leave. "Born for what?"

"How old are you?" Suzy asked.

"Seventeen, but I really don't—"

"Your parents will have to sign a waiver. You can talk them into it."

"I have no idea what's going on."

Jason waved an arm back into the warehouse. "This is the Hive. Suzy and everyone else—they lift weights, go to competitions. Kick ass. Celly, they're all Beasts."

Suzy grinned, causing deep crinkles around her eyes. "We all have names. It's part of the fun. I'm Banshee. You know, like Siouxsie and the...?"

"Who?"

"Google it. You can thank me later. Come watch the rest of practice. See what you're getting yourself into."

As if there was no doubt that I was getting myself into anything. And then she walked away and left me standing there with Jason.

"Are you OK?" he asked me.

"What just happened?"

"I think you were just invited to join the Hive. I knew she'd love you."

"That was love?"

"I'm sorry she's not more subtle. I guess making it a surprise wasn't the best idea."

I inhaled through my nose again as two women jogged past us, but I was surprised to find that I wasn't that upset anymore. It was too hard to be when I was so freaking curious.

Another pair of women across the room from me walked up a

set of bleacher steps. Sideways, like crabs, facing each other. The one whose face I could see was pretty old. Maybe as old as my grandma. She had short graying braids and huge dark eyes. And a smile.

A real one. I'd spent God only knew how many hours at Belly Busters, and I'd never seen anyone look that happy on a Stairmaster.

"Have you ever lifted weights before?" Jason asked as we sat on the bottom row of the bleachers.

"Some, at Belly Busters, but—" I'd never done anything like this. Ever.

"What's Belly Busters?"

"A gym in Sun Valley." I looked slowly around the Hive again. "My parents own it."

Jason lifted his eyebrows. "Your parents own a gym?"

"Yeah. But it's nothing like this."

He bumped me with his shoulder. "Kismet."

"What?"

"Obviously, we were meant to be friends."

There were eighteen women in the gym, including Suzy. And one man whom I'd missed on my first glance around the room.

"That's Dirk," Jason said. "Suzy's husband."

He pointed out each woman and gave me their names. There was a Chaos, a Devilette, and a Lusty. The women were in every shape and size between Suzy and me.

When he was done, Jason leaned closer to me. "Want to try?"

"I don't think I can do this."

"Sure you can."

I watched Suzy lift a long bar with what looked like an impossible amount of weight on each side. She drew it from the floor to her chest and then hoisted it over her head before letting it drop to the mat.

"How can she be so sure I'll be good?"

"You're strong, Celly. It's obvious just looking at you."

I couldn't stop the sharp sting in the center of my chest. Was *strong* a euphemism for *fat*? No one would look at Vivi Hughes and say she was strong. She was delicate.

But in this place, she'd be in the minority. These women wanted to be strong. They were working hard at it. And having fun.

Suzy waved at us before bending to pick up the bar again.

"You'll need some gloves," Jason went on like I'd agreed to something. "Some fishnets if you're going to do it right."

"Fishnets?" I half-expected some kind of crack about whale nets.

Instead he just laughed and said, "I'll help you get it all together."

"You come here every day after school?"

"Most days. Sun Valley is farther than our old house was, so I might not be able to as much now that we've moved."

"Do you work out?"

"This is a women's gym, but Dirk and I help out some, so they let me lift with them."

I leaned back against the row of seats behind me. "Do you wear fishnets, too?"

He looked over at me, deadpan, and said, "I've never found any that were long enough."

CHAPTER 7

Suzy drove me home after she was done with her workout and we'd stopped to get my bag from her garage. It was dark, and she insisted on coming to the door with me.

"I should have made you call," she said.

"Really, it's OK. You don't have—"

My mother opened the door, mid-lecture. "—worried sick. The school called and said you ditched ISS. You were suspended? Why were you—"

"You ditched ISS?" Suzy asked. She looked over her shoulder at Jason.

Mom's momentum ground to a stop.

"I'm so sorry." Suzy stuck her hand toward my mom. "I'm Suzy Oliver. I should have had Celly call you when we ran so late."

My mother looked from Suzy, whose hand was still hanging out, waiting to be shook, then back to me. "Late doing what?"

"She was watching us work out and time got away from us."

My mother finally noticed the hand that Suzy still hadn't taken back. She shook it while Jason and I stood back on the porch, watching. "What kind of workout?"

"My husband and I own a gym over off Washington in Reno. Marcella has a waiver she'll need signed."

My mother took her hand back, not quite snatching it, and looked up at me. "What's going on?"

"Your daughter blew my mind tonight," Suzy said before I could answer. "She's our Queen Beast."

Mom grabbed my sleeve and pulled me toward her, into the house. "My daughter is not a beast. What's wrong with you?"

Suzy opened her mouth to say something, but the door slammed in her face before she could.

I wanted to open the door again, but Mom stayed between me and it.

"Jesus, Mom. That was embarrassing."

"Calling you a name like that, right in front of me."

"It's not what you think. You embarrassed me."

"Don't be ridiculous."

"I'm not—"

She waved a hand toward me. "Anyway, do you know what time it is? I was about to call the police."

"The police? Seriously?" I reached into my back pocket. "Why didn't you just call my cell phone?"

"I did. A dozen times at least. You missed dinner. And we have to talk about this suspension thing."

"I wasn't—"

She held up a hand to stop me. "Whatever you did, I don't want you to do it again."

"I gave Lou Duncan a Morp rose."

That stopped her in her tracks. A look of shock spread over her face and then she shook herself and said, "What did you say?"

"Don't worry. That will definitely not happen again."

"Celly."

"You said it was tradition, remember?"

"But Lou Duncan? Really?"

"Yes, really. We—" I swallowed. "We worked together all summer."

"You gained back every pound he helped you lose. What did you think was going to happen?"

Maybe my head was still full of the music and the people at the Hive. Or maybe it was the heady feeling of being instantly accepted like I'd always belonged there. Or how well that crazy world fit with my newfound determination that I did not want to die.

For whatever reason, I couldn't get mad at my mom. "I don't know what I thought. I didn't expect to get suspended from school for it."

"Well, there had to be more to it than that."

I pulled the paper Suzy had given me from my pocket and smoothed out the creases against my thigh. "Will you sign this?"

"Don't change the subject." She took the paper and asked, "What is it?"

"A permission slip."

"For what?"

"Suzy's gym. The Hive."

"You don't need to join another gym. You can go to Belly Busters anytime—"

"I'll use my own money. I really want to do this."

My mother inhaled through her nose, then pushed the breath back out again the same way. "Go do your homework."

"I don't have any."

"You always have homework."

"I wasn't in school today."

"Go to bed, Marcella."

I was hungry, and any other day I might have complained about not getting dinner. But today I just turned and went for the stairs. Once I was far enough up to be out of sight of my mom, I turned sideways and crab-walked the rest of the way, like I'd seen the women at the Hive do.

"What are you doing?"

I looked up and saw Jenna standing at the top of the staircase looking down at me with an expression somewhere between bewilderment and disgust.

"Conditioning."

She stared at me for another second, then went into her bedroom.

I threw my backpack on my bed and sat on the floor at the foot of it. On second thought, I got up again and locked the door. After throwing the edge of my comforter over the top of my bed, I pushed my hand and lower arm between my mattress and box spring and came out with an envelope.

I had $248 saved from birthdays and babysitting. I didn't even really know what I was saving it for. A car, maybe, although at that rate it would take me the rest of my life to earn enough for even an old beater.

But maybe $248 enough to pay for at least a couple of months at the Hive. And some fishnets. I counted the money again, then pushed it back under my mattress.

I pulled my backpack toward me and dug into it for my phone. My mom had called five times, not a dozen. I hadn't heard my phone in the warehouse over all the noise, and it had never occurred to me to check until now.

Lou had texted me. Twice. The first time, he wrote: Where are you? The second time: Fuck it then.

I'd never missed a text from him before, and it gave me a rebellious feeling that I kind of loved.

I leaned forward, resting my cheek on the cool comforter. Before I could even decide how to feel, my doorknob turned. When it didn't open, there was a knock. "Celly?"

My mother. I stood up and unlocked the door. "I'm sorry I didn't answer the phone. I didn't hear it."

"I need to know where you are. I get worried."

"I know, Mom. I'm sorry."

She reached forward and touched my neck. I pulled back. "Did you get those bruises lifting weights today?"

I shook my head a little.

"You aren't the most graceful girl, you know? You get it from your dad."

Yes. I knew. I'd been told often enough. "Suzy says I have great balance."

"She looks so trashy with all those tattoos, don't you think?"

Was $248 was enough to join the Hive and get a tattoo? "No, I don't think so."

"Well, I do." My mother smoothed a hand over my hair. "You have to go to school tomorrow. I want your word."

"Who called you today?" I asked.

"The vice principal. He was very upset with you."

I was very upset with him, too, but I didn't mention that. "Did he say how long I have to stay in ISS?"

"No. He didn't say."

"I don't deserve to be there at all. It isn't fair."

"You skipped school, Marcella. You can't expect to do that and not be punished."

"Did he tell you about my locker?"

She nodded. "Kids can be jerks, Celly. That's still not an excuse for ditching."

I couldn't tell if she was being obtuse on purpose or if she really didn't get it. "Is Dad home?"

"He's in the living room."

I stood up and left her in my room.

○ ○ ○

"I need you to sign a permission slip for me," I said to my dad when I found him watching Fox News in his easy chair. He wore his Belly Busters T-shirt and sweatpants and tipped his face up to me without really taking his eyes off the screen.

"Permission for what?"

My mother stood in the doorway between the living room and the kitchen. "I really don't appreciate that. I already said no."

"No to what?" Dad asked.

"Joining a weightlifting gym," I said. "I really want to do it, Dad."

"Weightlifting? I can help you with that."

"This is a special gym, just for girls. For women. And they invited me to join."

"Who is they?"

"A woman named Suzy, who is absolutely covered in tattoos," my mother said.

My parents did that thing. The one where they looked at each other and somehow discussed me telepathically. Finally, my mother said, "We'll talk about it again after you're done with your suspension."

○ ○ ○

Early the next morning, a knock on the front door caused a little flurry of concern in the kitchen where I was eating my Special K and Jenna was drinking the colored milk left over from her bowl of Lucky Charms. Mom must have bought a new box.

"I'll get it!" she said.

"Finish your breakfast." Mom put her teacup down. "I'll get it."

"Marcella." I looked up a few seconds later when she called from the front of the house. "Marcella!"

I left the rest of my bowl of soggy flakes and went to the front door. Jason stood there, his riot of brown hair slicked back and a short-sleeved button-down shirt tucked into dark-blue jeans. He wore a pair of Doc Martens that gave him an extra couple of inches so that he towered even higher above my mother.

"Hi," he said to me.

"Hi."

There was an awkward three-way silence as my mom looked up at Jason, then to me, and then back again. Her look of shock that a boy would come to see me was offensive, and she finally caught on and her face flushed.

She recovered by asking, "Are you going to introduce me?"

"You met him last night." I slid my feet into low-top Converses sitting near the door and picked up my backpack. "Oh, never mind. Jason, this is my mom. Mom, Jason."

Jason cleared his throat and said, "It's nice to meet you, Mrs. Boucher."

He said my name right.

My mom raised her eyebrows, then nodded slightly. "Have a good day at school."

I pushed Jason's arm to get him to move back and let me out of the house. My dad joined my mom and now both of my parents stood at the door watching us as we walked down to the sidewalk. It was a sweet family moment that made me want to vomit.

"What are you doing here?" I asked Jason once we were out of sight.

"I came to see if you were taking the bus this morning."

"Probably." I automatically slowed as we came near the stop. The same pretty girls and their groupies, the same wannabe-stoner freshmen. Nathan and Jossue weren't around, though. "Might not be too bad today."

"OK," Jason said and kept walking toward the corner.

"Wait a minute. Why are you taking the bus? What about Francine?"

Jason just shrugged one shoulder. We stood together, far enough away from the rest of the kids that they'd have to seek us out to get their fix. For a while, I didn't think they would. Then someone mooed.

"Jesus Christ," I said under my breath.

Jason looked at the kid who'd made the noise. He nodded slowly and said to me, "Let's walk."

"Go ahead and take your scooter. I'll be fine."

"Come on." He walked away, toward school, and I was left with a choice between being mooed at or walking with him. I walked.

"Why didn't you fight back?" I asked after we'd gone a few blocks.

"Fight back when?"

"When Nathan and Jossue were kicking you? You just let them. Why?"

"I don't fight."

"You practically knocked Jossue out with your elbow," I said. "Your elbow."

He shrugged. "I promised not to fight, so I don't. Or at least I try not to."

"Who did you promise?"

"My sister."

"Does she live with Suzy, too?"

"Suzy was her best friend."

Was. I didn't push anymore, because Jason wasn't looking at me, and he'd picked up his pace so that I was practically jogging to keep up with his long legs.

○ ○ ○

Jason walked to school with me every day for the rest of the week. I didn't bring up his scooter again, or his sister, and neither did he. Except to tell me that she'd been part of the Hive and her name was Danielle. We also didn't even bother with the bus stop.

"I'm glad to see you walking so much," my mother said on Friday morning. "And with a new friend."

A new friend. What a weighted statement. She meant that she was glad I was over the whole crush-on-Lou thing. That's how she saw

Jason: someone acceptable for her fat daughter. Her tone put far more into Jason walking with me to school than was really there.

"My ISS is done today," I said.

"And I hope it never happens again."

I was surprised to find that I didn't feel as strongly about that. My teachers had sent work by the second day, so no more dictionary copying. Best of all, most of the people who spent their time in ISS had their own problems and didn't bother me. It might not be so bad to spend the rest of the school year there and at the Hive.

"I still need that permission slip signed, Mom."

"Which?" She flipped through a fitness magazine while she sipped her herb tea and ate her avocado toast.

"Mom." I waited until she finally looked up at me, then watched her remember what I was talking about. I had the form in my hand.

"You have a perfectly good gym you can go to, for free. And I still don't know about that Suzy person."

"Don't call her 'that Suzy person.'" I put the form on top of the magazine she'd set down and held out a pen. "I have my own money. I really want to do this."

"I'd prefer it if you would just start going to Belly Busters again. Dad can set you up with a weights program if that's what you want. You really need some cardio though, honey."

I took the form back. "Forget it."

"You're always so angry these days, Celly. I don't like it."

Neither did I. "Please sign it, Mom."

She looked at me another long moment, then reached one hand

up. I handed her the paper and the pen I held in my other hand. She signed it and handed it back. "I hope I don't regret this."

I bent down and hugged her. She made a little surprised noise, which made me realize that I didn't hug her often enough.

"So, no more getting yourself into trouble, OK?" she said.

Right. I folded the paper into a square and stuck it into my pocket just as Jason knocked on the front door.

CHAPTER 8

When Saturday finally came, I stood in my bedroom looking at my closet with my heart in my stomach. I was as worried about what to wear as I would have been if Lou had taken my stupid rose and I was getting ready for Morp.

Jenna sat on my bed, watching me like it was an everyday thing for her to help me get dressed for something that was important to me.

It was *not* an everyday thing, and having her there was starting to freak me out. I grabbed a pair of gray sweatpants from the top shelf of my closet and tugged a purple T-shirt off a hanger.

"Wherever you're going, you aren't wearing that." Jenna sounded sure, like there was no chance that the reason I'd just pulled clothes out of my closet was to put them on my body.

"Just go away, Jenna."

She stood up. "No, I'm serious. You're not wearing that."

"What's going on with you? I'm just going to work out."

She didn't answer. Instead, she stood on her toes and tugged a pair of leggings with flowers all over them from the top shelf of my closet. My mother had bought them for me. I'd never worn them. Jenna stood back and looked at my wardrobe, then reached in and pulled out a pink tank top and an orange T-shirt. "Stay right there."

She left the room, carrying my size 3X clothes with her. Two of her would fit in each of the legs of those pants, I thought. With room to spare, probably, since they were stretchy.

I was halfway into the purple T-shirt when I felt my sister yank it away from me.

"I said no." She handed me the pink tank top, and I pulled it over my head, since the alternative was to stand there in my bra arguing with her. She gave me the T-shirt next. She'd cut away the neckline so that it slipped off one shoulder and the hem so that it hit a few inches higher than the top under it.

Like a crop top, only the tank top under it covered my stomach.

OK, so that was cute.

"Now put on the pants," Jenna said. "Trust me, OK."

I didn't have to ask her to leave. She closed the door behind her and left me there staring after her. Where in the hell had that come from? My sister A) had never cared what I wore, beyond telling me that I looked like a dork and B) had never tried to help me put together an outfit before.

That left pity because she knew about the condoms-in-my-locker thing. I didn't think she'd been part of it. But she had to have known it was going to happen. And now she felt sorry for me. Or guilty, maybe.

I looked at my closed door and then shook my head. If my little sister had known that Vivi Hughes was going to fill my locker with fake used condoms, she would have told me.

I looked at the leggings. They still had their tags attached. My mother had spent $24.99 trying to motivate her fat daughter to hit the gym. I pulled the tags off. I wasn't going to wear this outfit outside my bedroom, but I figured I might as well try it on.

The pants hit me mid-calf and were much tighter than anything I'd ever worn in public, except a bathing suit. When was the last time I'd actually worn a bathing suit in public anyway? I tried to remember as I stood in front of the full-length mirror.

OK. So, fashion is Jenna's thing. The outfit was cute. The DIY T-shirt made it look less like something my mother would have coordinated out of a catalog of fat-girl clothes. Still, my first instinct was to get out of it as fast as I could and put on the baggier, plainer, darker clothes that (as my mother constantly pointed out) wouldn't make me look thinner.

They would, however, give me a place to hide in plain sight.

Then I remembered what I'd seen at the Hive. Women wearing bright colors, fishnet stockings, even tutus. I wouldn't blend in there in my oversize sweats and a T-shirt that covered my butt.

I remembered Vivi pointing at my nose and calling me Moocella.

And I remembered what it had felt like, lying on the attic floor, a rope tight around my neck, staring at the underside of the roof.

I was done hiding.

○ ○ ○

The upside of wearing the outfit that Jenna put together for me was that it made my mom happy.

She insisted on driving me to the Hive. I agreed, with the stipulation that she would not get out of the car. I practically made her pinkie swear.

"I'm not going to embarrass you," she said.

"Good."

"I'm just curious. I want to know what's so great about this place."

"Mom."

"Maybe I can pick up some ideas for Belly Busters."

"No." I didn't leave any room for argument. "No, you can't pick up ideas for Belly Busters. Promise me."

She rolled her eyes. "Fine."

"OK."

"Not today, anyway."

She kept reaching over and patting my flower-covered knee as we drove. Telling me how pretty I looked. How much she liked my hair in braids, how nice it was to see my eyes for a change.

"Please," I finally said when she pulled into a parking spot and cut the engine. "Just drop me off. I'll be home before dinner."

"OK." She had hope in her eyes. Hope, I was pretty sure, that somehow this strange warehouse of a gym with eighties glam rock pouring through the open rolling door would somehow be the magic that would make her oversize daughter shrink to a socially acceptable size. "I'll make something with lots of protein tonight."

God, that hope. It made me want to scream. No amount of weightlifting, or Zumba, or protein was going to make me what she thought a girl should be: small and perfect. At least she had Jenna. "Bye, Mom."

Jason waited for me in the wide-open doorway. I turned around and looked at my mother until she finally pulled through the spot in front of her. I watched until her silver SUV had turned onto the street.

Truth: I was nervous.

I'd put on my yellow high-top Converses with the pink-and-orange outfit Jenna had put together for me, and I felt a little bit silly and a lot like everyone in the Hive was going to stop what they were doing to turn and stare at the fat girl in the bright colors when I walked in.

Jason wore gray sweatpants cut off at his knees and what looked like his PE shirt from his last school. It was purple. I wasn't sure whether to laugh or cry.

"I almost wore that exact outfit," I said when I reached him.

He lifted his eyebrows. "Funny. I almost wore that one."

I laughed, and some of the tension that had built up in my chest broke.

"Suzy said to start you off with some stretches," he said.

"She's not here?"

"She'll be here soon. She had a meeting at her son's school."

It's not like feeling awkward was something foreign to me, so I'm not sure why the feeling struck me so hard at the Hive. My eyes could see that no one was staring at me, or even noticing me, outside of a little curiosity about the new girl. My brain was on some kind of hypersensitive overdrive though. I felt like I was coming out of my skin.

"Relax," Jason said as he walked toward a section of the warehouse with a mirrored wall and blue mats covering the floor.

"This was a bad idea."

He stopped and came back to me. After a long pause, he said, "OK. Let's get out of here."

My mouth opened and closed and opened again. Great. Now I didn't just look like a clown. I looked like a clown fish. I clamped my mouth closed and shook my head.

"Then let's stretch."

We sat on the blue mats. I didn't recognize the music, but I was grateful for it. It seemed to cocoon us, wrapping us in a cloak of slightly-too-loud guitar riffs and screaming lyrics.

I just did what Jason did. Legs open in a wide V, body turned, leaning toward one foot. I felt the muscles in my lower back and my hamstrings tighten, then let go as I pushed deeper into the stretch. I shifted my weight so that I was reaching toward my other foot.

"You have good flexibility, honey."

I looked up at the mirror in front of me and saw a woman standing behind me in the reflection. I did what I always did anytime I ever came in direct contact with another person: I compared my size to hers.

She was probably fifty pounds lighter than me, but also six inches shorter, so our sizes were comparable.

How exactly do you respond to a random statement on your flexibility? I finally said, "Thanks."

"Your body's in the way, though."

I dropped my eyes and wondered why I'd had to inherit my dad's skin—the kind that showed every emotion in red splotches across my cheeks.

"Celly," Jason said. "This is Midge. She has about as much filter as Suzy does."

"Look," Midge said as she got down on the floor across from me, kneeling with surprising grace between my opened legs. "Do you mind?"

"Um." I gasped as she put a hand between my belly and my thigh and swept it toward my middle, adjusting my flesh.

I was speechless. Jason looked as surprised as I felt. "Jesus, Midge. Boundaries."

"What? I asked first. Someone had to show me, too." Midge looked at me. "Come on, try again now."

I bent toward my foot again. This time, I was able to wrap my fingers around the instep of my Converse and pull it toward me. The stretch was deeper.

"See." Midge stood up and wiped her palms on her hips like her job here was done. "You gotta learn to work with your body, that's all."

"Thanks." At least I wasn't completely speechless anymore.

"Maybe just tell her next time?" Jason suggested. Midge walked toward a group of women working with dumbbells.

I only realized that I was expecting her to say something to them about me, and for all of them to turn and stare at me, when it didn't happen. Nothing happened. They absorbed her into their group, and none of them paid any attention at all to me.

Suzy showed up a few minutes later.

"How'd it go?" Jason asked. It was pretty obvious by looking at her that whatever "it" was, it hadn't gone well. She practically had steam coming out of her ears.

"I really want to know how a bunch of educated people who should know better can't get it through their thick skulls that just because the kid's legs don't work doesn't mean his brain doesn't." Suzy shook her head a couple of times, hard, like she was trying to get rid of a bee that was buzzing around her. "Screw them, right? Let's see what our Queenie can do."

Queenie. That was me. The Queen Beast. I took a deep breath, as if having the full weight of her attention on me was a physical force.

"I stretched," I said, and then immediately felt like an idiot.

"Good. So, let's just start with deadlifts. Something nice and easy. Have you ever done them before?"

I'd seen Lou do them—deadlifts involved lifting a heavy bar from the ground to hip level and lowering it again. I'd never tried them myself, so I just shook my head.

As I came to my feet, Suzy turned around, slowly, standing on her toes and looking over the warehouse. She must have spotted what she wanted, because she put a hand on my arm and started walking toward a mat that had a barbell already set up with a forty-five-pound plate on each side. I knew that the bar itself weighed another forty-five pounds, so the whole deal was one-thirty-five.

A woman who looked as old as my grandmother was about to lift it, even though it might have been heavier than her, but she stood up when she saw us coming.

The old woman introduced herself as Hattie.

"I joined the Hive as a gift to myself for my seventieth birthday," she said. "That was four years ago. Never lifted a weight before that day. Best thing I've ever done, though. You can call me Nana. Everyone does."

She lifted the barbell when Suzy asked her to, showing me how to do it.

When Nana was done, Suzy stood me in her place. "You want your feet hip-width apart, not as wide as your shoulders. That's right. And the bar should go over your shoelaces."

I looked down at my shoelaces and hoped I was doing this right.

"Now, get your gorilla on, Queenie," Nana said.

I blinked at her a minute, processing what she'd said.

She demonstrated, bending her knees, keeping her back ramrod straight, sticking her butt out. "Like a gorilla about to sit in a chair."

Jason laughed and shook his head. I felt myself tighten up. I couldn't do this. I was making a fool of myself.

"It's OK," Suzy said. "Give it a try."

I was too embarrassed to say that I was afraid that I wouldn't be able to budge it off the ground.

I was too embarrassed to just leave.

So, I did the only thing I could think of. I bent my knees and stuck my ass out, trying to imitate Nana's posture.

"That's it," she said. "Now grip the bar—no, that's too wide—here and here."

My palms were sweaty. The barbell might as well have been welded to the ground. There was no way I was going to be able to lift it. The three of them watched me, and my brain compounded that to the dozens of eyeballs in the room.

This was going to be the cafeteria on Morp rose day all over again.

"Keep your head up and sit back. Lift with your glutes and your hamstrings—the backs of your legs," Suzy said, lightly slapping the back of one of my thighs.

I did what she said, mentally prepared to live through the mortification of failure in front of Jason and all of these strangers. Sitting back drove my heels into the ground. I thought about Lou and about Vivi, and I heard those stupid moos.

The bar came off the ground, slid along my shins, over my knees. My surprise must have shown on my face, because Jason laughed out loud. I stood all the way up, held the bar at the tops of my thighs for a moment, then lowered it back to the floor.

I looked up at Suzy, my fingers still wrapped around the barbell. "Again?"

"Yeah," she said. "Let's just get a little more weight on there first."

CHAPTER 9

By Monday, the bruises on my neck were fading, and I wasn't spending much time thinking about them. I'd spent two afternoons at the Hive, learning to deadlift and the proper form for squats. I was much more concerned with the callouses starting to form across the base of my fingers. I needed a pair of weightlifting gloves. I wondered if my dad had some I could use.

I walked through Twain High School with a smile on my face at school for what felt like the first time in forever.

"Celly." Lou stood in front of me, in the middle of the hallway. Kids parted around us like we were a couple of boulders in a stream.

"Hi." People weren't really looking yet. Lou hadn't exactly screamed my name, and he wasn't looking directly at me. No one who passed us would think we were on the verge of a conversation or anything. He was turned sort of diagonal to me, looking at the door to the social studies room across the hall. “Lou?”

I’d never seen him so uncomfortable. He’d texted me several times over the weekend. For the first time, I’d ignored him. I’d expected to have fallen off his radar by now. That didn’t feel great, but it helped that I’d been on an adrenaline high for the last two days.

When he still didn’t say anything, I said, “I was busy this weekend.”

A couple of heads swiveled toward us.

“Jesus.” Lou ran hand through his hair. “Just answer at lunch, OK?”

He was gone before I had the chance to respond.

Jason came toward me, turning to watch Lou as he passed by. “Everything OK?”

The longer I stood there, still forcing people to walk around me, the harder my heart beat.

Lou cared that I had ignored him.

“Celly?” Jason asked.

I smiled and finally focused on him. “Oh yeah, I’m fine. Let’s go.”

“What did he want?”

I stopped at my locker to pick up the books I’d need for the first half of the day. The janitor had done a good job of cleaning it out the week before. Vivi’s stupid little trick had left my locker smelling clean and scrubbed of the grime that went back to my parents’ days at Twain.

What did Lou want? I looked up at Jason. “I’m not sure.”

○ ○ ○

I really hoped that there wasn't anything vital in the work I did for my first period class, because it all just flowed through me.

Fifteen minutes after the second-period bell rang, I asked for a bathroom pass. After I had myself locked in a stall, I pulled out my phone and brought up Lou's texts from the weekend.

Where are you?

We need to talk.

Are your parents working this weekend?

Noon?

Fuck you, then.

Grow up, Celly.

Please just answer.

He was pissed off. Or maybe just confused. I'd never ignored even a single text from him before. I wouldn't have this weekend, either, if I wasn't so swallowed up by the Hive.

Hell, I was confused.

New rules. That's what we needed. No more hiding. No more Vivi. It was either me and him, or it was nothing. I lifted my chin, trying to hold on to the brave feeling that coursed through me.

Someone had drawn a picture of a penis on the door, right at my eye level. I wrinkled my nose and left the stall.

Lou wanted to talk to me, enough that he broke his own stupid rule and approached me in the hallway. I knew better, but I couldn't stop my brain from kicking up daydreams about him finding me at lunch and sitting with me.

He'd hold my hand and share my peanut-butter-and-jelly sandwich, and neither of us would care who was watching or what they said.

I should have known better, of course. But the only person who sat near me was Jason. He sat across from me at one of the picnic tables the janitor moved outside on nice days.

When I bit into my sandwich without looking up from my phone, which was infuriatingly silent, he asked, "Everything OK?"

"Why do you keep asking me that?"

"Because you seem like maybe everything's not OK, I guess."

Everything was not OK. I had no idea what Lou wanted. And it was driving me crazy. I hated to admit that, even to myself, and there was no way I was saying it out loud to Jason. I made myself remember how good I'd felt all weekend. My muscles were still sore, so that was easy.

I looked at Jason's lunch. Two ham sandwiches, a bag of chips, a banana. He had it all spread out like he didn't care who saw him. He probably didn't.

Jason pushed his books over and leaned closer to me, across the table. "He's not worth—"

I grabbed the first thing that caught my attention—the corner of a flyer of some kind that was sticking out from between Jason's geometry and chemistry books. "What's this?"

Jason grabbed it back. "Nothing."

I tilted my head, reading upside down. I recognized the logo for a local band I loved. I'd seen them play a couple of times.

"Soiled Dove is auditioning lead singers?" I looked up at him. "I wonder what happened."

He shoved the paper into his geometry book. "He quit."

"Are you going to audition? Can you sing?"

"Probably not."

"Probably you're not going to audition, or probably you can't sing?"

He shrugged.

"So, you're just carrying around an audition flyer for the hell of it." I wanted to snag the flyer and pull it back out, look at it more closely, but he looked so uncomfortable. "Can you sing, for real? Do you play an instrument?"

"The guitar. But it doesn't matter, because I can't do it in public. I really can't sing in public."

"Why not?"

"I choke."

I leaned back, taking in Jason's obvious discomfort, trying to figure out what to say to him. I was a little embarrassed that I hadn't known he could sing or play the guitar. I'd been so focused on myself ever since we started hanging out. Just as I opened my mouth to suggest that maybe I could come over after school to listen to him do his thing, my phone buzzed.

After school, your house.

And then: Please, Celly.

The last two words made my next breath catch in my throat.

Jason stood up. "I'll see you after school?"

I hadn't taken the bus since the day of the Morp disaster, and Jason walked with me every day, even though he could ride his Vespa.

I looked at my phone again.

Lou drove his mom's Honda to school every day. Maybe he'd start picking me up.

Right. And on Thursdays, he can drop me off at fat-girl counseling.

"Celly?"

I looked up again and put my phone in my pocket. My face was burning. Jason was taking in my distraction and analyzing it—I saw it in his face. "I'm sorry. Yes. After school."

Jason looked at where I'd stuck my phone, and then back at my face. I thought he was going to say something more, but he just walked away.

○ ○ ○

Jason's house was before mine, so usually we said goodbye at the end of his street, and I walked the last block on my own. Today, of course, when I was desperate to get home, Jason said, "So, you want to come over?"

"Hmm?"

"I think Suzy wanted to talk to you about training this week."

I did, actually, want to go to Jason's house. To talk to Suzy. To hear him sing. A genuine pull in a direction away from Lou made me feel good. Like maybe I wasn't as much of a loser as I was afraid rushing home to wait for him made me.

That didn't stop me from saying, "I do, but I need to get home."

"Oh." When Jason smiled, it elevated that woodland creature

thing he had going on. He had a gap between his two front teeth that was lethally cute. Unfortunately, he wasn't smiling right now. "OK, well—"

I hated how obviously his feelings were hurt. Somehow, he knew why I needed to get home. It shouldn't have bothered him, and I shouldn't have felt like I needed to keep the fact that Lou was coming over this afternoon a secret. But I did. "I'll come by later? After I check in with my parents and do some homework?"

"Yeah, sounds good."

Jason turned down his street and I watched him until he got to his front yard. He didn't look back. I shook myself and started walking toward my house again.

Lou's mom's blue Honda was parked two houses down from mine. My heart clenched—both in excitement that Lou was sitting in it, waiting for me, and in irritation that he didn't just pull into our driveway.

"Do you really think someone's going to recognize your car in front of my house?" I asked when I reached the passenger door.

"Your sister will be home soon, right?" Lou looked through the rearview mirror, like he was making sure Jenna didn't sneak up on him. "I just want a little privacy."

"I'm pretty sure she has dance practice."

"Let's go for a drive."

That was a new development. I opened the door. I was so preoccupied with wondering where he planned to take me that I didn't realize until it was too late that the last person who'd sat in this seat had pulled it all the way up. My knee banged against the glovebox and I couldn't get my ass into the car.

Vivi. I stood up again, my face burning for the second time in the last twenty minutes. I reached down for the lever to push the seat back.

"Sorry." Lou looked embarrassed for me.

"I'm a foot taller than her."

"I know."

I settled into the seat, now that my legs would fit under the dash. "Where are we going?"

Lou drummed his hands on the steering wheel. We never went anywhere but my house or Belly Busters. "Actually, we don't have to go anywhere."

Maybe he'd decided that me being pretty sure my sister wouldn't stumble on me sitting in his car made staying near my house the safest choice.

"OK. Want to go inside?"

More drumming and now his left leg bounced. "I just wanted to talk a minute."

"About what?" I was equal parts irritated and fascinated. I'd never seen him nervous before.

"You didn't answer my texts." He beat a little rhythm on the steering wheel. "I was worried, I guess."

Was he, really? I turned a little, leaning against the car door, so I could look at him. It was so easy for me to slip into elaborate daydreams that involved him. "Why do you even want to talk to me at all, Lou?"

He reached for me. I had enough time to imagine him cupping my cheek, looking deep into my eyes, before he pulled his hand back without touching me. "I wish you could understand—"

"Right. The rules. I have to understand the rules." Something had shifted. I'd lost the will to do whatever it took to spend a few minutes with him, and suddenly the rules made even less sense. "Screw your rules."

"Celly."

"Why do you want me at all, Lou?"

"Come on—"

"Why?"

He closed his eyes and I had another micro-daydream. Maybe he'd tell me he loved me, invite me to a party this weekend so that he could show his friends that we were together. When he opened them again, he didn't look at me. "I don't know what you want from me."

"Not being embarrassed to be seen with me would be a great start."

"I have a girlfriend—"

I opened the car door. "You should go find her, then."

Walk away, Marcella. Just walk away. Each step felt like wading through knee-deep mud. Don't look back.

I probably would have made it, too, except I heard his car drive away and couldn't stop myself from turning to watch it go.

○ ○ ○

Jason's room was clearly designed for someone much younger. The walls were covered in dinosaur wallpaper, left over from some unknown kid who'd lived here before he moved in.

"Suzy put her boys in two sets of bunk beds in one room so I could have my own space," he said. "I shared with Royce until we moved here."

Suzy had four sons. The youngest was a toddler. The oldest, who must have been Royce, was twelve and had cerebral palsy. "That was sweet of her."

He nodded, but his face tightened a little. Like the idea of it made him sad. "Yeah. It was."

Maybe he was thinking about whatever made him need to live with Suzy and her family in the first place. I was curious, but couldn't make myself ask.

"What's your favorite color?" I asked instead. He sat in the chair in front of a beat-up drafting table that served as his desk. I sat cross-legged on his bed.

"Blue, I guess."

"Do you think Suzy would let us paint over Jurassic Park?"

He laughed, which is what I was going for. Anything to break the tension that apparently followed him home after I went to meet Lou. "Yeah, maybe."

"You should ask her."

Another awkward moment of silence, and then he finally said what was on his mind. "So, did Lou come over?"

"Yeah." I didn't even know how to begin telling him what there was between me and Lou. I didn't really understand it myself. I wasn't proud of allowing myself to be Lou's big fat secret.

"Did he say anything about those bruises?"

That took my breath away. Truth was, no one but Jason had said anything about my bruises. Not even my dad, after we got home from the doctor's office. Not my sister. My mom thought I'd gotten them at the Hive.

Jason bent over and fiddled with some electronic equipment I hadn't noticed tucked under his desk. When he was done, he took off his shoes and socks. He wiggled his long toes as he lifted a guitar from where it leaned against the wall and plugged it into the electronics.

He picked out a tune I didn't recognize. "I don't want—I mean, if you've got a thing with Lou, whatever."

He stumbled over his words, but his fingers made the tune he played more intricate. He did something with his toes, flicking switches on the equipment on the floor, and the chords he'd just played came back through speakers that sat against the wall.

"It's complicated," I said.

He plucked another set of chords, using his foot to record that as well, then drummed a beat on the side of the guitar and added that to the mix. The result was the room filling with music that sounded like three musicians were playing instead of just one.

I closed my eyes.

"He has a girlfriend," Jason said.

"I know that."

"A girlfriend that isn't you, right? Vivi."

Stupid Vivi. "I said it's complicated."

"I know what he likes about you, but—"

I bristled and looked at Jason again. "What's that supposed to mean?"

He started to pick out the melody of his song over the chords and the drumbeat. The apples of his cheeks went dark pink. "I know you're awesome. I don't know what exactly you see in him. He's cheating on his girlfriend. That kind of makes him a scumbag, yeah?"

I rubbed a hand over my eyes. "Come on."

"What?"

I stood up. "Look at me, Jason."

He did, without skipping a note on his guitar. It was like his fingers weren't connected to the rest of his body. I didn't think I could ever multitask that well. "I look at you all the time."

He wasn't in the stratosphere, though. He didn't have anything to lose by being my friend. "I better go. I have homework."

Jason stopped playing and let the recorded part of the song continue on its own. "Can you stay another minute? I wanted to play you the song I was thinking about using to audition for Soiled Dove."

I sat back down on the edge of his bed. "You're really going to do that?"

He shrugged. "Probably not. But just in case."

He started playing the song I didn't recognize again, simple at first, then getting more and more complicated as the recorded chords and beats were added in.

Then he sang.

By the time he finished, my heart thumped in my throat. I wanted to say something, but I couldn't get the words to come out.

He used his foot to turn off the recorded tracks. He didn't look at me. "Did it suck?"

"Don't be an asshole." Heat rushed to my face. "You know it didn't suck."

He stood up and put the guitar away. "So, you think I should audition?"

I stood up as well. "I think you have to."

"Will you come with me?" he asked.

I nodded. "You're going to be a rock star, Jason."

He smiled, and something shifted in my chest. He was so close to me. One of his hands moved into my hair. Too much. Oh, God. I pulled away before he kissed me.

Jason had been about to kiss me.

CHAPTER 10

It surprised me how much I didn't mind heading downtown to Betsy Hamilton's greenhouse of an office for our second appointment. I hadn't cracked open her book, but I figured there wasn't much she could do or say about that.

I expected to feel, at best, ambivalent about meeting with her again. The truth was, though, I had a lot on my mind, and I was OK with having someone who was paid to listen.

She came down to open her door in a pair of blue jeans cuffed at the ankle, what looked like a man's white button-down shirt tied at the waist, and a pair of black ballet flats.

How very *Breakfast at Tiffany's* of her.

"Marcella!" She said my name like we were best friends who hadn't seen each other in ages. "Come on in."

We took the stairs up to the third floor again. Sneaking in

that exercise.

"You're looking much better this week," she said.

I'd probably looked like I'd been hit by a truck the previous week. "Thanks."

She kicked off her shoes and sat cross-legged in her chair. I sat with my feet on the floor. She just looked at me, and that feeling like it wasn't so bad to come to her office started to fade. Quickly.

"So, what's on your mind?" she finally asked.

It took everything I had not to squirm in my seat. "Aren't you supposed to ask me questions or something?"

"That was a question, wasn't it?"

I stood up and walked over to the windows where most of her plants lived. It was like a mini rain forest in her office. "You must spend a lot of time on these things."

"They're my babies."

"I remember."

"Celly." I turned back to look at her. My dad must have told her my nickname. "Come sit down and talk to me."

"Are you going to ask better questions?"

She smiled, and the affect was kind of startling—her face changed completely, brightening, making her look younger. "I'll try, I promise."

I sat down again.

"What's one good thing that happened this week?" she asked.

That was better. "I started working out at the Hive."

She leaned forward, like she was really interested. "What's the Hive?"

I told her about the warehouse and about Suzy and the other women. "I've been there almost every day this week."

"How did you meet these people?" she asked.

For no real reason, I didn't want to share Jason with her. So I just said, "Through a friend."

"Another girl who works out there?"

I was the one who asked her to ask me questions. Now I wished I hadn't. "No."

She tilted her head. "A boy, then?"

"Gender isn't binary, you know." Where did that come from?

"I do know."

Fine. Fine. "Jason brought me there. He's Suzy's foster son."

She just looked at me.

I was compelled to fill the silence. "It's no big deal. He just started at my school last week."

She nodded, and I knew that calling him no big deal gave away the fact that he kind of was. "So, he lifts weights, too?"

"Yeah, I guess, but he's really a musician."

She leaned back in her chair, getting more comfortable like maybe I was about to tell her a story. "Is he?"

"A good one." Why did I care if she believed me?

She smiled again. "I'm glad you have such a good friend, Celly."

"Me, too."

"Can we talk about what brought you to me in the first place?" Her tone didn't change, but suddenly we were done with the small talk.

I straightened my back. She absolutely wasn't going to make me talk about losing weight or her stupid book. "I don't mind coming to talk to you, but I'm not reading your book."

"That isn't exactly what I was talking about."

Oh. Shit. My throat tightened when I realized what she was talking about. "We don't have to talk about that, either."

She didn't say anything else, just watched me as I got more and more uncomfortable.

"Someone hurt my feelings, and I just—I snapped, OK? But I hurt myself. I guess. And now I know for sure I don't want to…" I couldn't say die.

"Who hurt your feelings? The kids who vandalized your locker?"

I shook my head. I didn't know how to describe Lou to her, so I just said "my boyfriend" even though Lou wasn't really that.

"Jason."

"No. Not Jason."

"Tell me about your boyfriend."

Why was I screwing this up so badly? "He's not really—I mean, we like each other, but there are rules, you know?"

"What kind of rules?"

All right. If she wanted to know, I'd tell her. "No one can know."

"About the rules?"

"What? No. About me and him."

"Why can't anyone know?"

Betsy was one of the most beautiful women I'd ever seen up close. How could she possibly understand? I just shrugged.

"What's his name?"

I took a breath and said, "I don't want to tell you."

"OK. You don't have to. But I want to make sure I understand." She inhaled and just looked at me a moment. "He's your boyfriend, and you aren't allowed to tell anyone about that."

Lou wasn't my boyfriend. I felt guilty for even saying out loud that he was. I also didn't particularly like hearing that rule stated so starkly by someone else. It gave me a bird's-eye view I didn't really like much. "We just like each other, OK?"

"Then why can't you tell your friends?"

"Because." She was some kind of big childhood obesity expert. How hard was it for her to look at me and catch the drift of my relationship with Lou? "Because he's beautiful and perfect, and I'm me."

"I don't understand."

The woman had written a freaking book about fat kids. Did I really have to spell it out to her? "His friends wouldn't understand why he's dating a fat girl, OK? Don't act like you don't know how the world works."

"But he likes you."

"Yes." I hated how my stomach sank when I said that.

"Does he treat you like you'd treat someone you like?"

I should have just clamped my mouth shut and sat there in silence until our hour was up. Instead, words just started pouring out of me. "He wants me, OK? He wants me more than her, anyway. I'm the one he calls when he wants—"

I couldn't make the words come out. My mouth was feeling more adventurous than my brain was allowing at the moment.

"Who is 'her'?"

Great. I tried to reel in the anger that was making me blurt out things I didn't mean to say. "She's his girlfriend."

Betsy still looked beautiful and serene, comfortably curled in her chair. "I guess I don't understand. I thought you were his girlfriend?"

Whatever. "You understand perfectly well. Don't pretend to be stupid."

"You're angry with me. We can change the subject if you like."

"That would be fabulous."

What I really wanted was to leave. I'd only been there for fifteen minutes though and leaving now would trigger a call to my dad, which would probably trigger Doctor Harrison's three-day psych hold.

"Tell me how Jason treats you that's different from how this other boy does."

"Jason's my friend. And that's the same subject."

"Isn't the other boy your friend, too?"

Heat rose up to my face and I knew my cheeks were flushed red. "I'm not doing this."

"Just one thing, Celly. Does Jason call you when he wants the same thing the other boy wants?" Neither of us was saying out loud exactly what that was.

"No."

"What do you think Jason would have done if you'd given him a flower last week?"

"We just met that day. I don't know what he would have done."

"Try to guess."

The day the Morp flowers were handed out, Jason had sat next to me in geometry class, even though it was obviously social suicide. He'd tried to walk me home. "He probably would have taken it."

"How does that make you feel?"

It made me wonder what was wrong with him. Why did he want to be my friend, if I wasn't doing the things for him that I did for Lou? Did he think I was easy, even though I hadn't let him kiss me?

I didn't realize I was crying until Betsy handed me a box of tissues. "I thought that therapy was supposed to make me feel better."

Betsy unfolded her legs and leaned toward me. "It will. Eventually."

I wiped my nose with a handful of tissues. "Yeah. Well this sucks."

"I know it does. Tell me about your friends. Who do you hang out with?"

I shook my head and blew my nose again.

She didn't say anything, just waited, which was infuriating. The silence was a living thing and the only way to get away from it was to fill it.

"I don't have friends," I finally said. "Not the way you're talking about anyway."

"No one you could hang out with tonight, if you wanted to?"

I started to shake my head but stopped. "Jason, I guess."

"Not the other boy?"

Only if he texts me. I wasn't about to say that out loud. "That's complicated."

"No girlfriends?"

Not since Holly went popular and never looked back. I just shook my head.

"Why do you think you don't have friends?"

"Because I don't." She didn't respond to that, and the silence got to me. Again. "I just don't, OK?"

Betsy nodded like I'd said something profound. "Will you do something for me?"

"Probably not."

She wasn't fazed by my negative response. "There's a Friday afternoon eating disorders group. I'd like you to come to it."

"I don't have an eating disorder."

Betsy sat back in her chair again, curling her legs under her. "I think it might be helpful anyway."

Suddenly I felt like a beached whale in the middle of Betsy's rain forest office. I took up too much space, and there was nothing I could do to pull my edges in. I was crying again, and that just pissed me off.

"You think I have an eating disorder."

"I think you use food as a coping mechanism," she said, softly. "And that you binge eat as a way to stop feeling the way you felt the day your locker was vandalized. It's human nature to turn to what makes you feel good. You self-medicate with food."

"You think I'm an addict," I said, my voice barely more than a whisper.

"That's not what I think. We can talk about it though. I do think you'll like the group. Will you come?"

"Will you call my dad if I say no?"

Betsy shook her head slowly. "I told you. None of this works if it's just me and your dad moving you from session to session. You don't have to come, but if you do, you need to make the decision yourself."

On Morp rose day, I'd known, for certain, that I wanted to live. That feeling had faded. Not completely, but it wasn't so Technicolor anymore, and that scared me. I didn't want it to go away completely, and I was afraid that I couldn't make that happen.

The Hive made me feel good, but who knew if that would last? And what in the hell was I going to do if it didn't?

"Fine," I finally said. "But I'm probably not going to talk."

CHAPTER 11

"How'd it go today?"

I looked up, startled away from my history homework by Dad standing in my bedroom doorway. It took me a minute to figure out what he was talking about. Betsy. "Fine, I guess."

My dad looked over his shoulder toward Jenna's room and then came in and sat on the edge of my bed. I couldn't remember the last time he'd been in my bedroom—two or three years ago at least. He looked as uncomfortable as I felt. The room wasn't big enough for the both of us. "How are you?"

"Fine, I guess," I said again.

"I'm worried about you, Celly." He looked down at his hands—big, with long, square-tipped fingers. I looked at my own. A more feminine version of his. "If you want to talk about—you know, last week—we can—"

"I'm talking to Betsy. Isn't that enough?"

"I'm trying to understand what happened."

It had to be hard for him to get it. He was bigger than most other men—but that was a good thing. He was like Lou. He'd married his Vivi. I could only imagine what a disappointment it was to realize that his genes and the prom queen's mixed into someone as wrong as me.

"I'm sorry," I said.

"Don't be sorry. Help me understand."

"I wish I was like Jenna." I'd never admitted that out loud before. Tears rolled down my cheeks and I just let them.

Dad reached forward and brushed my hair over my shoulder. "I'm pretty glad you're like you."

That surprised me.

"You're a great girl, Celly Belly."

I tried not to cringe. "Thanks."

"Things won't always be this hard. I promise."

"I'll always be too big."

Something crossed his face, but I couldn't decide what it was. Pity? Acknowledgment that what I'd said was true? "You take after me, that's all."

My dad had given me height, for sure. And for as long as I could remember, he'd fluctuated between having no extra body fat and having his gym-owner muscles covered in a layer of too many cookies after dinner. Still, I easily outweighed him, at his heaviest, by thirty pounds.

"I guess so," I said.

"When do you see her again?"

He was avoiding saying Betsy's name. I almost asked him why but decided I didn't really care. "She wants me to come to a group tomorrow after school."

"What kind of group?"

I thought about letting my dad decide for himself what kind of group he thought I needed. A near-suicide group, maybe? A trying-to-stay-out-of-the-mental-hospital group? Was there group therapy for fat girls whose fathers called them Belly?

In the end I told the truth. "An eating disorder group."

He seemed genuinely taken aback by that news. "An eating disorder? Did she diagnose you?"

Too much. "Can she diagnose people?"

"I don't know."

I shrugged. "Me either. She just thinks I should go, so I said I would."

My dad stood up and, mercifully, walked to my door. "OK, sweetheart. I'm glad you're getting something out of seeing her."

○ ○ ○

An hour later my history homework was done, and my sister called up the stairs for me to come to dinner. I heard our mom telling her she could have yelled for me herself as I started down.

I walked toward the kitchen instead of the dining room, meaning to wash my hands. I came around the corner just in time to hear Dad say, "Don't give Celly one of those. She doesn't need it."

"I don't need what?" I asked, but it was obvious. Mom was holding a Pyrex bowl filled with dinner rolls in one hand and the butter dish in the other.

Awesome. Now my dad was on bread patrol. And I had already been regretting telling Betsy that I'd come to her stupid group.

I inherited my tendency to achieve a hard blush from my dad, right along with his height and ability to put on pounds like a speeding bullet. Or something like that. His face looked sunburned as we both stood there staring at the stupid rolls.

I took them and the butter from my mother, who made a little noise but wasn't fast enough to keep them from me. "I'll take these to the table."

By the time my parents sat down, I had a roll split open and spread thick with butter. Real butter, because Mom wouldn't have margarine in her house. I took a bite and chewed slowly without looking at either of them.

Dinner was chicken with rice and spinach. When Mom tried to pass the rice to Jenna without it stopping at me, I reached out and took the bowl. She tried to serve me, but I grabbed the spoon before she could. She'd stopped serving Jenna when she was seven or eight years old. I did not want to have an eating disorder.

Besides, Midge had told me that carbs were energy food.

I spooned some rice onto my plate. "Looks good, Mom."

"Did you know that rice has one hundred and twenty calories per half cup? Just a half cup." She passed the rice bowl to Dad without serving herself any. "Spinach has practically none."

"Yeah," I said. "But it tastes like spinach."

○ ○ ○

The eating disorder group was held in a room behind a door in Betsy's office that I hadn't noticed before. She must've kept all her babies in the front, because there were no plants in the back room.

I'd imagined that we'd all sit in folding chairs, in a circle, and take turns moaning about our mothers or something. The chance to moan about mine might even have enticed me to change my mind about not talking.

For some reason, I'd thought the room would smell like coffee and that everyone in it would look like they'd rather be anywhere else on Earth.

Instead, Betsy's meeting room had a big rectangular table. Eight matching chairs stood around it, three on each side and one at either end. Their seats and backs were upholstered in peach-colored velvet. Instead of a conference room or a therapy room, it looked like she'd raided some 1950s sitcom for its dining room set.

It wasn't the furniture that really stood out, though. The walls were covered with a mesmerizing collection of needlework, what looked like old paint-by-number pictures, and framed bits of art-class projects.

"Holy crap," I said, under my breath, as I took a closer look at a painting of a big-eyed little girl in a tutu. It had to be two feet tall. "This looks like a deranged museum."

"I like other people's art," Betsy said. "It makes me happy."

"How am I supposed to concentrate with this thing looking at me?"

"Don't worry. Hildy won't tell any of your secrets."

"You named her?"

"Of course."

"You are so weird."

I was the first person to show up for the group meeting. I wasn't sure if that was good or bad. Maybe both. Good because I wouldn't have to make some kind of grand entrance into a room already filled with people who knew each other. Bad because my early arrival made my anxiety crystal clear.

"How big is this group?" I asked, in an effort to cover that anxiety.

"You'll make six."

"How does it work?"

Before she could answer, the doorbell rang. "Have a seat. I'm going to get that and wait downstairs for the others."

I sat in one of the chairs. They didn't have armrests, which was actually pretty thoughtful. I already didn't want to be here. Having my chair bite into my hips for the next hour would have made it even worse.

Even though I'd just had a conversation with myself about armrests, I was expecting to be the lone fat girl in a room full of anorexics. The first person up the stairs proved that theory wrong.

He was a fat man who looked to be in his mid-thirties. He had to be even more grateful for the fact that there were no armrests on the chairs than I was, since he must have weighed at least a hundred pounds more than me. He stopped just inside the room and said, "Hey."

I decided it was a greeting and not an accusation and returned the word. "Hey."

"I'm John." He came the rest of the way into the room and sat heavily, exhaling hard.

I wondered if Betsy had made him take the stairs, sneaking in that exercise. He was breathing hard and sweating, so I thought probably yes.

When I didn't speak right away, he said, "Not sharing your name?"

"Sorry. I'm Celly."

"First time, huh?"

Didn't he already know that? Maybe this was like AA and people came and went as the need arose. "Yeah."

He ran a hand through his dark hair, pushing it back from his forehead. "It's not so bad. I thought it was at first, though."

Before I could say anything else, two women came into the room. One was middle-aged, and the other looked old enough to be her mother. The more I looked at them, the more I thought they probably *were* mother and daughter. I was horrified at the idea of having to do this with my mother sitting next to me.

They were like a contained unit, both wearing acid-green T-shirts and black leggings, moving with matching posture. They didn't acknowledge me or John.

I was pulled out of trying to decide, for sure, if they were related by a familiar voice. "You have got to be fucking kidding me."

My heart did a sort of flip-flop. I would know that voice anywhere.

Vivi looked as much like a honey badger in Betsy's meeting room as she did in the halls of Twain High School. Her striped hair was pulled back into its familiar ponytail, and she wore her cheerleader uniform.

That kind of made sense. There was a baseball game that night. The cheerleaders came out for those, to practice. But it was also strange. Like something out of a movie or television show. Like she was playing a character who only ever looked ready for a pep rally.

At school, I was prepared for Vivi. Here, she was so out of context that for a minute I couldn't respond except to stare at her.

She turned back to the door and yelled, "Betsy!"

"Know each other?" John seemed pleased to have a little drama to catch his breath by.

I was trapped in the room. John blocked my way around the table one way and the maybe-mother-daughter team blocked the other. Even if I could get around either of them, Vivi stood in the doorway.

Betsy came into the room with the last member of the group—a girl maybe Jenna's age, but so tiny and fragile that I truly hoped she hadn't been made to walk up the stairs. "Everyone's here this week. I'm so glad."

"I'm not staying," Vivi said.

"What's wrong?"

Vivi pointed and everyone turned from her to me. The last time she'd pointed at me, she'd mooed, and I expected the same thing now.

But instead of mooing, she said, "She's what's wrong."

"You know Celly?" Betsy asked.

My face burned and I knew that it had turned lobster red. If I could have crawled under the table to get out of the room, I would have.

"I'm not staying here with her." Vivi started to turn away, but then stopped and interrupted whatever Betsy was going to say. "No. This is my group. Make her leave."

"It's not your group, Vivi," John said. "News flash. The world doesn't revolve around you."

"Mind your own business, fatass!"

John clucked his tongue against his teeth. "Language, language."

Betsy got the fragile girl into a chair. "That's enough of that. Sharon?"

The older woman looked up. "Yes?"

"Will you do me a favor and get group started? Celly, Vivi, you come with me."

Leaving the room meant Sharon and her maybe-daughter had to stand up and push their chairs in, then walk out of the way so I could squeeze past.

Betsy closed the meeting room door and walked to the middle of the jungle room. "You know each other."

"She's the one who asked my boyfriend to the dance," Vivi said.

I lifted my eyebrows. "She's the one who filled my locker with used condoms."

"Ew! They weren't used." Vivi scrunched up her face. "God."

How had Betsy not put this together? She clearly hadn't, because she sat in her chair with a sort of dazed look on her face. "OK. Let's think about this a minute."

"I won't leave," Vivi said. "You have to make her go."

I actually wouldn't have minded going home. It wasn't like I wanted to be here. I wasn't about to let Vivi push me out, though. "I'm not leaving. I didn't do anything wrong."

"One of you can transfer to the Saturday night group."

"I'm not spending Saturday nights here. She probably doesn't even do anything on the weekends," Vivi said.

She would have been right a couple of weeks ago. Now I had the Hive. And Saturdays were deadlift day at the Hive. Suzy wanted me there. That started a warm little glow burning in me. "Wrong."

Vivi's head snapped up.

"There are guidelines," Betsy said. "Vivi, you know them. Why don't you share them with Celly?"

Vivi rolled her eyes, then said, "No name calling, no weight loss talk, no interrupting, what happens in group stays in group."

"Can you live with those?" Betsy asked me.

"Of course I can." I was good at living with rules, after all.

"Vivi?"

"What? I've been coming to this group for six months. I know the rules."

"She called John a fatass," I pointed out.

"God, you're such a stupid—"

"Vivi," Betsy said. "If you can't follow the rules, then you'll have to go."

Vivi hummed with frustration, which was unusual and kind of fascinating to see. "Fine."

"Does either of you want to come back Saturday night?"

I wasn't going to miss the Hive for this. I hoped that Vivi would cave. She just shook her head though. She looked up at me and said, "I spend Saturday nights with Lou."

"OK," Betsy said. "Let's get inside then. We'll give it one meeting to see if you two can get something out of being in a room together."

I was worried that I'd get back to school on Monday and find everyone talking about how I was at an eating disorder group, but then I realized that would never happen. Vivi would have to out herself to out me.

When we went back to the meeting room, John was talking.

"I went to a movie this week," he said. "You know that theater that has loveseats? I sat in one of those. It was the first movie I've been to since I was a kid."

"Good for you," Sharon said.

Betsy took her seat. "How did it feel, John?"

John shrugged and waited until Vivi and I had both taken seats before he said, "It was good. I mean, people were looking at me, but then the lights went down, and I felt normal for a while. I'm getting used to not being in my house all the time anymore."

“I’m so glad to hear that,” Betsy said. “We have a new group member. This is Marcella.”

Everyone in the room, except for Vivi, replied at the same time. Like kindergarten. “Hello, Marcella.”

I blinked at them. “Hi.”

“Why don’t we introduce ourselves?”

John raised a hand in a little wave. “I’m John, but you already knew that. I’ve been homebound for the past five years, but this group is helping me get out more.”

He was obviously proud of himself. I smiled with what I found myself truly hoping was encouragement.

“I’m Sharon,” the older woman said. “This is my daughter Brenda.”

“Brenda can introduce herself, Sharon,” Betsy said, calmly.

“Oh, right. I’m Sharon. Nice to meet you.”

No information about herself at all, except at least now I knew that I’d been right about her being the other woman’s mother.

“I’m Brenda.” Nothing else. The poor lady looked like she wished she was anywhere on Earth but in this room.

Everyone turned to Vivi, who sat on Brenda’s other side. She just raised her eyebrows and kept quiet. The youngest member of the group finally said, “Hi, I’m Amber.”

“Hi,” I said back.

“OK.” Besty settled herself in her chair. “Is it still John’s turn?”

“I was just saying, I went to a movie this week.”

“Good. How did you get there? Did you go with someone else?”

“I went with my mom. Not exactly a hot date, but it felt good, you know?" John closed his eyes like he was remembering the awesomeness of the movie theater. I felt sorry for him, and then guilty for that because I was pretty sure he wouldn't want pity. Especially not my pity, since I didn't even know him.

"Was the movie good?" Amber leaned forward a little in her chair, her thin arms wrapped around her chest.

"Maybe you can go with him next time," Vivi said. The words were nice, but the tone dripped with venom. "Even you'd be a hotter date than his mom."

I looked at Betsy, expecting Vivi, for once, to be shut down. Her mouth tightened, but she didn't say anything.

Instead Sharon said, "Leave them alone, Vivi."

And, to my surprise, Vivi closed her mouth.

"The new girl should go next," Brenda said.

I had planned to refuse. I didn't know these people. I didn't know what to say. I actually turned to Betsy meaning to shake my head, but I was distracted by Vivi.

She looked so sure of herself. Like she knew I wouldn't speak.

"I'll go," I said.

Vivi frowned.

Betsy said, "OK, Celly. Just share something that happened to you this week. Remember, we don't talk about weight loss here."

I shifted my gaze to Vivi and said, "Someone filled my locker with condoms."

"Ew," Amber said.

I nodded without taking my eyes from Vivi. "It was pretty gross.

They looked, you know, used."

"Who would do something like that?"

Betsy said, "Amber, it's Celly's turn."

"And then I spent the rest of the day listening to people moo at me."

Vivi was so pissed, she actually seemed to vibrate. She couldn't say anything without giving herself away, and judging by the sympathetic sounds coming from the others in the group, she didn't want to do that.

I expected Betsy to stop me before I could tell the group that Vivi was the vandal. She seemed very calm though, like this was just another day in crazy town.

"How did that make you feel?" she asked me.

Worthless. Useless. I was blindsided by a rush of emotion and had to press my mouth shut to keep from saying more than I meant to.

Like: *I went home and accidentally almost hung myself in the attic. Mostly accidentally, anyway.*

That wasn't happening, though. Vivi wasn't getting that little sound bite.

"Like crap," I finally said.

Vivi put up a hand. "I'll go next."

"Celly isn't—"

"Remember last week, I told you someone invited my boyfriend to Morp, right in front of me? He's still distant this week, like something is really bothering him, only he won't talk to me about it."

I had a sharp pain in my stomach.

Not guilt. How could I possibly feel guilt? Vivi was a complete bitch, and she didn't deserve Lou.

It was hardly my fault if Lou finally started to see that.

"I'm really struggling to not start purging again," she said, keeping her eyes on her hands. "I know that it would make me feel so much better, but I try to remember that in the long run it will make me feel worse."

"Thank you for sharing," Betsy said softly. "Both of you. Amber?"

"I wish that eating wasn't so hard," Amber said. "I wish that restricting wasn't so easy for me. It's like having the world's worst superpower."

"Did something specific happen this week?" Betsy asked.

Amber shook her head but kept talking. "I had a fight with my grandma. She wants me to be able to just eat. It seems so easy to her, and I can't make her understand. I don't want to wind up in the hospital again, but asking me not to restrict sometimes feels like asking me not to breathe, you know?"

My mom would be great for someone like Amber. They could spend their time measuring out teaspoons full of food together. Except, of course, for the whole hospital thing.

OK. Not so great.

When Amber was done talking, Sharon went next. She had to be reminded twice by Betsy to talk about herself and not Brenda. Sharon, as far as I could tell, was actually afraid of food. She worried about everything from genetically modified corn to antibiotics in meat. She was gluten-, dairy-, and soy-free.

Apparently, she'd passed her fear to her daughter, who took it a step further and just wouldn't eat at all.

The rest of the group meeting went more easily than I expected. Vivi didn't speak to me. She didn't even look at me. Betsy encouraged everyone to talk but didn't single me out again. I didn't have anything else to say, so I just listened.

"Can you stay for a minute?" she asked me after the room had emptied.

My dad was probably downstairs waiting for me, but I sat in the jungle room and waited for Betsy to come sit with me.

"I'm sorry I didn't make the connection between you and Vivi sooner," she said.

"That was a little surprising."

"You can come to the Saturday night group instead. Vivi never comes to that one."

"I'll be at the Hive Saturdays."

"Groups are going to be tough if you aren't comfortable enough to open up and talk. Do you think you can get there with Vivi in the room?"

"Why should I be the one to think about switching? She's the one who bullied me. She's the one—"

Betsy put a hand on my arm. "I'll have this same talk with her."

"I'm not switching." This might have been the perfect opportunity to get out of coming to group meetings at all, but there was no way I would give Vivi the satisfaction of thinking she'd chased me away.

“Should we give it one more week then? See how it goes?”

“I might not talk,” I said, wanting to make sure she remembered.

“We’ll see.”

CHAPTER 12

I finally took a look at Betsy's book that night. I looked up *purging* first, and I was right. Sort of. Vivi maybe made herself throw up, but she also might offset her food with laxatives or obsessive exercise. Or a combination of all three.

If she was really bulimic, she also binge ate.

I hated that I felt sympathy for her. Or that we had anything in common. Not that I was like her. I never did anything to purge the food that I ate.

It startled me to feel a twinge of interest. If Vivi looked like—well, Vivi—because she stuck her fingers down her throat, maybe it would work for me, too.

I shook my head, hard, to clear it of those thoughts. Betsy's book talked about binge eating disorder as well. It made me forget about Vivi.

Binge eating disorder involves eating an amount of food that is more than an average person would eat (between five thousand and fifteen thousand calories) within a single sitting or discrete period of time. This happens, usually, twice a week or more for at least six months. There is no compensatory behavior, as there would be with bulimia nervosa or anorexia nervosa. This behavior causes worry for the person suffering from the disorder.

According to the DSM-IV, a person suffering from binge eating disorder must have three or more of the following symptoms:

1. Feels disgusted, depressed, or guilty after binge eating
2. Eats an unusually large amount of food at one time—far more than a non-afflicted person would eat
3. Eats much more quickly during binge episodes than during normal eating episodes
4. Eats until physically uncomfortable and nauseated due to the amount of food consumed.
5. Eats when bored or depressed
6. Eats large amounts of food even when not really hungry
7. Often eats alone during periods of normal eating, owing to feelings of embarrassment about food

Tears pricked my eyes as I closed the book and put it back on my desk.

When I went down for dinner, I was tempted to refuse to eat anything at all. Nauseous and overheated, like I might be getting sick, what I really needed was a cool shower and my bed.

My mother already had my plate filled with an obviously measured portion of chicken breast, salad, and green beans. Her own plate looked about the same.

There were red potatoes on the table, but she hadn't served them to either of us. Dad and Jenna had empty plates. They could be trusted to serve themselves.

"Celly," she said when I sat down. "How was your day?"

My stomach hurt. "OK."

"Jenna?"

I watched my sister fix her own plate and then pour dressing on her salad. "I have extra practices all next week. We're getting ready for nationals."

I reached for the salad dressing, and my mother actually slapped my hand. It didn't hurt, but the sharp sound of it stopped the talking.

Dad stopped with a chicken leg halfway to his plate. "Jesus, Robin."

To her credit, Mom looked stricken. She held her own hand to her chest. "I'm sorry. Celly, I'm sorry."

I have a lot of experience in not letting anyone see me cry, and I clamped down hard on my tears. I wanted to scream at them not to look at me, but I didn't trust my voice. I was afraid speaking would make me lose whatever control I still had over myself.

"I didn't mean to do that," Mom said. "I just—I've told you so many times about dressing."

"I don't like dry salads. Nobody likes dry salads."

"I do," she said. "You can taste the vegetables. You'll get used to it. I promise."

"I don't want to get used to it! I just want to be normal. I don't want you to measure my food or tell me what I can eat. I'm not a kid anymore."

"She's just trying to help," Dad said. "Please, don't overreact."

"I'm not. Do you want to know what your help has done?" I stood up and brushed my hands down the front of my body. "This. Your help has done this. I have an eating disorder. That's what your 'specialist' told me, Dad."

Mom stood up as well. "I don't think you have an eating disorder. It's just discipline, baby. That's all. Eat less—"

"Move more. I know. But you're wrong." I sat back down and so did she.

"It's simple physics," Mom said. "I've helped other women do it. I don't know why I can't help my own daughter. I don't know why you won't just listen to me."

I dressed my salad, slowly, pouring vinaigrette over the lettuce and tomatoes. "I do think I have an eating disorder. Betsy thinks so, too."

"Betsy?"

"The specialist," I said.

"I'd like to have a word with her." Mom picked up her fork. "I don't like how upset she's made you."

I put my own fork down again. "She's not the one who's upset me."

Jenna made a little choking noise. Dad sat perfectly still, like he'd suddenly found himself in the middle of a minefield.

"I'm only trying to help," my mother said again.

"I know that. But you aren't helping me. You're making it worse."

She threw her hands up in the air. "Of course. Blame the mother. Everyone always blames the mother."

I cut a bite of my chicken and chewed it slowly. I was determined not to let myself binge again. Ever. And that meant eating dinner so that I wasn't too hungry later.

At least, I thought that's what that meant.

○ ○ ○

When the most awkward dinner in the history of dinners was finally over, I went upstairs to my bedroom and closed the door.

Betsy's book sat on my desk, but I didn't want to read it. I didn't want to think about it. Instead I lay on my bed, staring at the ceiling.

And I thought about eating disorders.

Finally, I gave up and picked the book up. I rolled onto my stomach and looked at the list of "diagnostic criteria" again.

I definitely felt disgusted, depressed, and guilty after I binged. I felt disgusted, depressed, and guilty almost all the time though, even when I wasn't eating anything at all.

I didn't want to think about it, but I knew that sometimes I ate way more at one time than I'd ever seen anyone else eat. I had the night after the whole Morp fiasco.

That's how I thought of it. The Morp fiasco. Not the day I

almost died.

Sometimes when I gave in and tried to fill the hollow, hungry feeling, I couldn't eat fast enough. I liked to eat alone. It was just easier that way.

I stood up and changed out of my school clothes and into the workout outfit that Jenna had put together for me. Vivi had the same problem with eating that I did, but she wasn't fat.

There is no compensatory behavior, as there would be with bulimia nervosa or anorexia nervosa.

Vivi purged. No way was I going to stick my fingers down my throat or take laxatives. But I could exercise. Hell, my parents were constantly on me to exercise more. It wouldn't be like bulimia. I wouldn't go that far.

But if I exercised more, enough to offset what I ate, then maybe I'd lose some weight.

Maybe I'd be more normal.

I went downstairs and found my dad sitting in his chair, watching Fox News like every night. He turned his head toward me but kept his eyes on the screen.

"Can I borrow the car?" I asked.

"Where are you going?"

"The gym."

He finally looked at me. "Good idea. Endorphins. And you can work things out with your mom."

"Right."

He dug into his pocket and pulled out the keys to his car and handed them to me. His attention was already back on the news, so I just left.

He expected me to go to Belly Busters. It was open for another hour, and my mother was there, teaching a late Zumba class. I kind of expected to take myself there, too, but I turned toward Reno instead.

Fifteen minutes later, I parked in front of the Hive.

Music poured through the open double doors. The Hive looked and sounded more like a club than a gym. Now that I was here, I couldn't make the decision to get out of the car and walk in. I'd never been inside without Jason.

I'd never been in the parking lot without Jason either, and I was starting to feel silly just sitting there. I turned the engine over and put the car in gear. I was just about to back out of my spot when someone knocked on the passenger side window.

Suzy peered in at me. "Hey, Queenie!"

My face heated, and I was glad it was dark enough to hide my flushed skin. "Hi."

She opened the door and sat next to me. "Jason's not here, but if you—hey, are you OK?"

Great. I must have looked even worse than I thought. "Yeah, I'm good. I just—"

I just what? Just thought I'd come by and work out? Just thought I'd see if Jason was here? Just thought, since I was in the neighborhood, I'd stalk the place for a while?

Just thought maybe I'd see if I can shift my binge eating disorder closer to bulimia?

"Are you here to work out? I was about to head in. First chance I've had in like three days. I swear, running a gym isn't nearly as fun as you might think. All work, all the time."

"My parents own one, too."

Suzy nodded. "Belly Busters, right? I've seen it."

"It isn't anything like the Hive." Compared to Suzy and Dirk's gym, Belly Busters was beige and generic. My parents kept adult contemporary music playing on a loop and would have called the police if even a single square foot of graffiti showed up on the walls.

"Want to come in?" Suzy asked. "Be my lifting partner tonight?"

Tears came again before I even realized they were going to. The harder I tried to control my breakdown, the worse it got until I was sobbing full out.

"Whoa," Suzy said. "Marcella, try to breathe with me."

She almost always called me Queenie, and for some reason hearing her use my name made things worse. She didn't think I was a loser. She didn't ever comment on my weight or tell me that I'd lift better if I lost some. And now I was making a fool out of myself in front of her.

"I'm sorry. I'm—"

"Breathe in." I did as she said. "Good, now out. In...out."

Her voice softened to something soothing and calm. I followed her instructions, breathing slower and slower until I was finally in control of myself.

We sat there, quietly, listening to the music coming out of the Hive. When I had some kind of control over my voice, I said,

"Thank you."

"Do you want to talk about it?"

What was I supposed to tell her? "Not right now."

Suzy opened the car door, then turned to me. She was wearing solar-system leggings. Did they make those in an XXL? "I'm going to head on in. You're welcome to come with me. You're welcome here anytime."

"Thanks. I wanted to ask you about joining. I didn't know how much—"

She cut me off. "Anytime, Celly. You come find me if you ever decide you do need someone to talk to."

And then she was out of the car. She didn't try to talk me into coming inside. She didn't look back at me on her way in. I thought about joining her, but in the end, I just started the car and drove back to Sun Valley. I needed to think.

CHAPTER 13

Somehow, I got through to Monday with neither of my parents asking me where I'd really gone with the car Friday night. Or Saturday morning, either. Maybe they figured out that "going to the gym" meant the Hive to me now.

It doesn't rain much in Nevada, but when it does, it comes down in biblical proportions. We were having a Noah's-ark-level downpour by breakfast. I didn't expect Jason to show up in that. Mom drove Jenna to school early for dance practice, and Dad was getting ready to take me when Jason proved me wrong.

He looked like a very long, tall, drenched ferret. A ferret was a woodland creature, right? "Ready?"

"We're not walking in this," I said. "My dad will drive us."

He jerked his thumb toward the curb, and I noticed Suzy's little blue Toyota parked in front of our house. "Want to come with us?"

"Yes," Dad said before I could answer. "She'd love to."

"Jeez, Dad." He was practically pushing me out the door.

"Tell your…tell Suzy I said thank you. I have so much work to do here."

There was a crack of thunder, and suddenly the rain came down in a heavy sheet. If we went out into it, we'd be soaked through before we even made it to Suzy.

"Ready?" Jason asked.

I shook my head. I tried to open the front door again. It was locked. "Nice, Dad."

I rang the doorbell. Then I rang it again. And again. And finally, Dad answered.

"We need an umbrella," I said, sweeping my hand to the rain in illustration. "Do you mind?"

He opened the little closet right by the door and reached up to the top shelf. "Here you go. Have a good day, sweetheart."

He closed the door again. In my face this time. "Seriously, what is going on with him?"

"Who knows?" Jason took the umbrella from me and opened it. "Come on."

He was tall enough to hold the umbrella over both of our heads. We stayed relatively dry as long as we stayed close to each other. I inhaled deeply when I took my first step and my foot went nearly ankle deep in cold rainwater.

"Oh," I said, which sounded kind of stupid.

"You OK?" Jason reached for Suzy's passenger-side door and

opened it for me.

I was OK. I got a nose full of his shampoo, or maybe laundry detergent. Soap? Something. He smelled good, and it caught me off balance. I got into the car without answering him.

"Hello, Queenie," Suzy said.

"Thanks for the ride."

"My pleasure. Can't have you two drowning before homeroom, right?"

"Before what?"

She shook her head as she pulled away from the curb. "Never mind. Dirk said your deadlifts were great Saturday. I'm sorry I missed them."

I shrugged and felt my cheeks burn. "It's not a big deal."

"Oh, hey! Guess what."

"Suzy," Jason said, with some warning in his voice. Now my interest was piqued.

"What?"

"We're going to karaoke tonight. You should come with us."

Jason groaned. I turned enough in my seat to look at him. "You're going to sing?"

"I can't sing in public," he said.

"You can do whatever you put your mind to." Suzy smiled, like she knew something we didn't. "You're going to try at least, right?"

"No."

"Yes," I said. "You have to. You need the practice."

Jason shook his head, his eyes suddenly wide. I closed my mouth.

So, Suzy didn't know about the audition?

"It'll be fun," Suzy said. She'd missed the little bit of tension that passed between me and Jason.

"I'll go if you want me to." I spoke to Jason, and Suzy did seem to pick up on that. She let him be the one to answer.

"I'm probably not going to sing," he said.

"That's OK. I for sure won't, so that'll work out."

"OK then."

"Perfect." Suzy beat her palms on the steering wheel.

"Suzy's singing," Jason said.

"Damned right I am."

○ ○ ○

I was in a great mood before Vivi Hughes ruined everything.

She came out of nowhere when I was walking to my locker between second and third periods. "We need to talk."

This was the second time in a week that a stratosphere-type talked to me in the middle of a crowded school hallway. "About what?"

"You know what. Come with me." She took off without even looking to make sure I followed her. She was so sure of herself. It made me sick.

I just went to my locker to change out my books, and I was so proud of myself.

I spent the first part of third period reveling in the return of the really good feeling I'd had lying on the attic floor. It waxed and waned, and I held on as tight as I could when I had the chance.

It was pretty cool that Dirk had noticed my deadlifts that weekend. And thought they were good enough to mention to Suzy.

Maybe I really was good at this. Weightlifting was an Olympic sport. What if—

The classroom door opened, and Vivi came into my history class, walked up to the teacher like it was completely reasonable, and said, "I'm here for Celly."

I expected the teacher to ask for a note or at least express some sort of hint that she understood that Vivi didn't actually have the authority to call one of her students out of class.

"Celly?" The teacher tilted her head toward Vivi, who stood near the door now. "Pages one-fifty through one-seventy-five for tomorrow."

"Seriously?"

Another sharper head tilt.

I put my book into my backpack and stood up. Vivi walked out of the classroom. I got a little jolt of satisfaction when she looked back to make sure I followed her.

"Does that always work for you?"

She walked into the girls' bathroom and held the door open for me. "Does what?"

"Just doing whatever the hell you want to do."

"Yes." Vivi bent down and looked under the bathroom stalls. "We need to talk."

"About?"

Once she was satisfied that we were alone, Vivi went to the mirror and leaned into it. She smoothed her fingers over her eyebrows. "You know what. Betsy."

"Don't worry. I don't want people knowing I have an eating disorder any more than you do."

She turned sharply when I used the words eating disorder. "I'll know if you start talking about me. It'll be worse for you than it will be for me if people find out, you know."

She was wrong. We both knew that. I didn't have a facade of perfect to maintain the way she did. "Whatever. Anything else?"

"Are you going to Morp?"

That took me by surprise. I hadn't planned on going, but suddenly I didn't want to tell her that I didn't even have a date. My answer came out before I could think it through. "Yep."

"With who?"

I shrugged one shoulder. What was going on with her?

Vivi came closer to me, just like she had in the cafeteria that day. Close enough that I could feel her breath. "You better not be going with Lou."

Where had that come from? I was still trying to figure out how to answer Vivi when she backed up and went to the mirror. She'd given away too much, and we both knew it.

I braced myself. Because I also knew that someone like Vivi doesn't give away too much without making someone pay for it.

"You know," she said, "I'm totally surprised that prank on your locker worked."

Don't ask. Don't ask. But I really wanted to know. "Why's that?"

Vivi turned away from the mirror. "I was sure your sister would give it away."

She left me standing there feeling like the whole world had been tipped over on its axis.

o o o

When the bell rang at the end of fourth period, I still hadn't fully processed my little meeting with Vivi. She'd shown me too much when she told me I better not be going to the dance with Lou. Cutting me down was practically a requirement after that.

What was up with that little warning, anyway?

Wasn't she going to Morp with Lou? I checked my phone, for the twentieth time. No message from him.

At lunch, Jason was sitting at the outside table where we'd fallen into the habit of meeting. I sat across from him.

"Hey," he said. When I didn't answer right away, he waved a hand near my face. "What's up?"

I shook myself. "You wouldn't believe me if I told you."

"Try me."

I told him about Jenna first. His face changed from his regular open expression to one of confusion mixed with a little anger. It had been a long time since I'd had a friend get confused and angry on my behalf. It was nice.

"You're going to ask your sister, right? I mean, Vivi would lie about something like that."

"That's what I thought, too." I truly didn't want to believe that Jenna would have anything to do with that prank. The next thing just kind of popped out, without any forethought. "Do you want to go to Morp with me?" Jason smiled, showing off that little tooth gap. It made him look goofy, in the cutest possible way, and the nerves that should have come with asking a boy out suddenly dumped on me. A little too late.

"I mean as friends."

He lifted his chin and still didn't say anything.

"Vivi asked me if I was going, and I don't know why—I said I was. But, I don't have to. I mean, she probably knew I was lying, right?" Now I was babbling. What the hell, Boucher. Get a grip.

"Yes."

"It's OK if you don't want to," I said. Backpedaling like a pro. "I mean, it'll probably be stupid anyway. You know what? Never mind."

His smile faded. "You don't want to go with me?"

Shit. "Were you going to say yes?"

"I did say yes, Celly."

"Oh. Right." One of us had to stop this train wreck. "Let's do it."

He nodded. "We get to wear costumes, right?"

"Not costumes. Matching outfits." I took a bite of my sandwich. "I was thinking fishnets and tutus."

"Great idea."

o o o

I was supposed to be at Jason's house at seven for karaoke, and I wasn't sure if I wanted to have this out with my sister before or after. Or not at all.

Jenna was kind of like Holly, after all. She had to choose between loyalty to me and the prospect of touching the outer ring of the stratosphere. She even had a chance of breaking through.

I didn't think I'd throw her under the bus in the name of popularity if I were in in her shoes, but that was easy for me to say.

I was still mulling all of this over when Jenna got home from dance practice. I'd pretty much talked myself into being magnanimous. I was proud of myself, too. I'd be the good big sister. The understanding one.

Except when I saw her, what came out of my mouth was: "I can't believe you didn't tell me."

"What are you talking about?"

"You knew about what Vivi did to my locker."

Jenna's mouth opened, then closed again. I watched her face harden, like she was pulling up armor around herself to fend off my anger. Only I wasn't angry. I was hurt.

"I didn't have anything to do with it," she said.

I wanted to believe her. It was one thing for her to know and not tell me. It would be an entirely different thing if she'd helped fill those stupid condoms and load them into my locker. "You knew, though."

"There wasn't anything I could do about it."

"You could have warned me."

"I know." Her armor fell again, and suddenly she was just my little sister, in a way that she hadn't been in a long time. "I'm sorry, Celly. I didn't know what to do, and then it was too late."

"Forget it."

"I should have told someone," she said. "I should have tried to stop Vivi. I just—I didn't know how. And I didn't want to be a snitch, you know?"

She had to choose between being a snitch and a traitor. She'd chosen traitor. I didn't know what to say, so I just said, "I get it."

"I'm really sorry."

"I know."

I expected her to walk away. Instead, she said, "So, you really like Jason, huh?"

Standing there looking at each other was painfully awkward. "We're friends."

"Are you going to Morp with him?"

I tilted my head and looked at her, trying to figure out where this was going. "Why?"

She took a deep breath. "Vivi is all upset that Lou isn't going with her, and that whole thing with the rose and all. I just wondered."

"Wondered what?"

"Are you going with Lou?"

Had Vivi seriously sent my sister to dig for information from me? More importantly: Did Vivi really think Lou was going to Morp with me?

Jenna looked at me, and it hit me like a ton of bricks. That wasn't it. Jenna knew about me and Lou.

I sat down hard on the sofa. “No.”

“It would be bad, you know. If you did go with him.”

“Why would it be bad?”

Jenna fidgeted, standing on one foot and then the other, pulling her ponytail tighter behind her head.

“Jenna, why would it be bad?”

“I’m just worried about another prank, you know. I don’t want a *Carrie* thing happening.”

Laughter bubbled up and out of me. Jenna laughed too and sat next to me. The tension between us eased a little.

“I’m not going with Lou.” I was a little surprised to find that it wasn’t even hard to say it. I wasn’t going to Morp, or anywhere, with Lou Duncan. “And I’m not Carrie.”

“I know.”

CHAPTER 14

Suzy and Dirk couldn't have been more different from my parents if they came from outer space.

They wore matching T-shirts with Pink Floyd's *The Wall* logo. Dirk's long hair lay in a thick braid down his back. Suzy was so buzzed up, I wouldn't have been surprised to find out she was on something. She couldn't sit still.

"She loves this shit," Jason said when he caught me watching her. "Like, *really* loves it."

I wanted to ask why he didn't love it. He was so good. If I was that good at anything, I would love it. "Is Suzy a good singer?"

He laughed a little and said, "Just wait."

The karaoke bar had a restaurant, which meant underage people were allowed. The tables around the stage were suspiciously empty, like people weren't ready to commit to getting up there and making fools out of themselves. Suzy grabbed a black binder from the bar and bounced toward the most front-and-center table available.

"Jesus." Jason sat at the back of the table.

Dirk couldn't keep his eyes off his wife. Not even when he pulled a chair out for me.

"What do you think, Jay? Something classic?" Suzy bounced the palm of one hand off the table. "Oh, God, they have 'Bohemian Rhapsody.'"

"I'm not singing 'Bohemian Rhapsody,' Suzy!" Jason looked truly alarmed. "Come on."

"What then?" She looked up at him.

"What are you going to sing, Banshee?" Dirk asked, pulling Suzy's attention away from Jason.

Suzy was distracted by Dirk's question and looked back at the menu of songs again. "Want to do something together?"

Dirk moved to look over her shoulder. "Sure."

Jason looked so relieved. It was like Dirk had stuck a pin in him and let all the tension out in a slow, steady hiss. I leaned closer to him. "Don't you want to sing?"

He rubbed his eyes with one hand and shook his head. "Stage fright."

"Really? You're so good. What do you have to be scared of?"

He gave me side-eye. "Choking."

"Has that happened before?"

He nodded.

Suzy made a dismissive sound. "You're going to be fine. How

about Michael Jackson? They have 'Billie Jean.'"

Jason was really uncomfortable. Not just with the idea of singing in public, either. He looked like he'd been shoved into a body that was a size too small. I knew that feeling—like you didn't fit anywhere, including in your own skin.

"It's OK." I tried to keep my voice down so Suzy wouldn't hear me over the music. "You don't have to."

Suzy heard me. She stretched her arms across the table toward Jason and wiggled her fingers until he put his hands in hers. "How are you going to audition for that band if you don't get comfortable singing in front of strangers?"

I looked at Jason, and he shrugged. He'd told Suzy about Soiled Dove. That made it real, didn't it?

"Maybe I won't do it."

Suzy's smile didn't waiver. "Oh, yes you will."

Jason pulled his hands back. My heart did a funny little flip-flop when he reached for my hand under the table. Not romantic, I thought. He really needed something to hold on to. "OK, fine. I'll try."

Suzy did a victory dance in her chair. "What will you sing?"

"I don't care," Jason said. "You pick."

That didn't seem like a great idea to me. She was going to have him singing a show tune or something else outrageous, but he didn't seem any more concerned than he had been so far, so I just kept my mouth closed.

"Oh, my God," Suzy said. "We're all doing 'Love Shack.'"

Um. "Wait a minute."

"It'll be fun."

I looked at Jason. He looked even more wigged out than I felt, so I tried to rein it in. All right. I was going to sing. In public. I could do it. I lifted my chin and smiled at him. He looked like he was on the verge of being sick.

Suzy took the binder back, along with a few little white papers she'd filled out. She leaned into Dirk and rubbed her hands together. A girl who looked like she was maybe in her early twenties took the stage, and a Taylor Swift song started.

The bartender brought us a pitcher of Coke and four glasses, and Dirk ordered a plate of chicken wings. I was too afraid of being the fat girl on the stage with wing sauce on my boobs to eat any of them, though.

Something to talk to Betsy about, maybe.

Every time a song ended and someone from behind the bar called out the next name, Jason tensed next to me. He didn't relax in between, so each moment of tension just ratcheted him up until I was afraid he might snap in half when his name was finally called.

Suzy and Dirk turned their chairs around so they could see the stage. That left their backs to us. I leaned over, closer to Jason. "You OK?"

He shook his head. The woodland creature vibe he always had was intensified by his deer-in-the-headlights impression. I moved my chair closer to him, and he took my hand, hard enough to ride the edge of pain.

His fingers tangled in mine, and I wasn't prepared to feel my heart stumble. He must have noticed, because he mumbled something that sounded like "sorry" and tried to take his hand back. I didn't pull back the other way, at least not fast enough, and we had an awkward moment that ended with us still holding hands.

As a trio of forty-something women finished up singing "I Will Survive," Jason opened his hand again and waited until I opened mine, too.

"Be right back," he said.

Suzy turned when he stood up, then looked at me. I just shrugged, and we both watched him walk to the man with the binder. Jason looked through the book, leaning one hip against the edge of the bar. After a minute, he wrote something on a piece of paper and handed it over.

When he came back, he moved his chair a little closer to mine and took my hand again without looking at me. Like it was the way we always sat.

We stayed that way until the bartender finally called, "Suzy, Dirk, Celly, and Jason."

For a second, I really thought I might pass out. But Jason kept holding my hand as he stood up, and I followed him to the little stage.

"Did you change the song?" I whispered. He shook his head.

It took until the second chorus of "Love Shack" for me to relax. It was impossible to be too self-conscious when Suzy and Dirk were both going all out. They sang off key but danced in perfect unison. Despite the lack of harmony, we got applause as we made our way back down to our table.

I felt high. "That was amazing."

"It was awful," Suzy said, although, judging by the smile on her face, she didn't really care.

"Awful fun." Dirk leaned in and kissed his wife.

Jason groaned. "Get a room."

Later, Dirk sang a Fleetwood Mac song, and Suzy and Dirk sang a duet together. I finally relaxed enough to eat a couple of chicken wings and managed to keep the sauce off my boobs.

The bartender called out, "Jason."

Suzy and Dirk both went quiet and I turned to look at him.

"You don't have to do this," I whispered.

Suzy shot me a look that I couldn't decipher. "You're going to be fine, honey."

Jason stood up and walked to the stage. He looked so miserable that I almost wanted to join him up there, just to make him feel better. Before I could decide to do that, though, the music started. I recognized the song from the lyrics that flashed on the screen behind Jason, but he didn't sing them. He opened his mouth when the next line started, but nothing came out.

He was frozen. He called it choking, and that's exactly what it looked like. The words on the screen were stuck in his throat.

I knew that he would've kill this song if he'd let the words out. I could hear his voice in my head. But he just stood there, staring out at the room of people staring back at him.

Suddenly someone behind me started singing the chorus. Loud.

Then someone else joined in. Suzy and Dirk picked it up, and then it felt like the whole bar was having a sing-along.

Jason walked off the stage. Instead of coming back to our table, he went for the door.

I stood up and watched him weave through the crowded bar.

"I'll go," Suzy said, but Dirk put a hand on her arm and kept her in her chair.

It took me a while to squeeze my way through the too-close tables. Maybe it would have been difficult for anyone. I'd just watched Jason turning sideways to get between chairs. It still made me feel like someone had blown me up like a parade float to twice my normal size.

When I finally got outside, I inhaled the cool spring air.

"See why I don't do this?" Jason stood just to the side of the door. "I choke. Every fucking time."

"You didn't choke when you sang for me the other day."

"That was different."

My face heated, for no reason that I could figure out. "Do you even want to perform?"

He slid his back down the block wall behind him, until he was squatting near the ground. "It's all I've ever wanted."

"Have you ever been able to?"

Jason looked up at me. "I used to sing with my sister, before she died."

I tried to imagine what it would feel like if Jenna died. I couldn't do it. So, I just moved a little closer to him. "Was she a musician, too?"

"She taught me to play the guitar."

"How did she die?"

It took so long to answer that I had time to be sure that asking was a major mistake. He finally said, "She was in a car accident."

"I'm sorry, Jason. That's awful."

"I was twelve." He stood up and took a breath. "It was a DUI. Just her and a light post, so I guess it's something that she didn't kill anyone else."

I had no idea what to say, so what came out of my mouth caught me completely off guard. "What about your parents? Why don't you live with them?"

"I don't know. Danielle was fifteen years older than me. I was four when I went to live with her, and I haven't seen our parents since then."

"Oh God. I'm sorry."

"I went to live with Suzy and Dirk after the accident. Suzy was Danielle's best friend. No one really talks about my parents."

"Have you asked Suzy?"

"Asked me what?" Jason and I both spun to see Suzy and Dirk coming through the bar door. "Everything OK?"

"He's fine."

Jason didn't look at me. "I'm ready to get out of here. I have some homework."

That was that. No one talked at all between the karaoke bar and my house.

CHAPTER 15

Jason showed up at my door the next morning. It was Friday, but we had the day off school for a teacher in-service thing, so I was still in my pajamas with my hair pulled back into a slept-on bun.

He said, "Let's go to the Hive."

"It's eight in the morning."

"I know. Let's go."

He had his scooter parked in front of my house, and it slowly dawned on my still half-asleep brain that he wanted me to ride that thing with him all the way into Reno.

A little burst of panic welled up in my chest. Maybe that was how he'd felt standing alone on that karaoke stage with everyone waiting for him to sing.

"I…" *won't fit on that thing with you. Wouldn't fit on that thing alone, probably. I'm too fat. Can't you see, I'm way too fat?* "Let me see if we can take my mom's car."

Jason followed me into the house. It didn't seem like he'd read the thoughts blasting across my brain. I pointed him to the kitchen, where Jenna was eating Lucky Charms before her dance class.

Upstairs, I threw on the same workout outfit that Jenna had helped me pick out. I wasn't in any frame of mind to try to put something together by myself, but it was going to get embarrassing if I showed up in the exact same thing every time. Pretty soon, I was going to need to ask Jenna for some more help.

Mom was in the shower. I knocked on the bathroom door and called out to her. "I need the car."

She turned off the water. "Where are you headed?"

"To the Hive with Jason."

"Can't that Suzy take you?"

"No, Mom. That Suzy can't take us. I can ride on the back of Jason's scooter all the way to Reno, though."

"No." That came very fast. "Take the car. Be home for dinner."

I grabbed her keys off her dresser and went back downstairs to the kitchen. Jason leaned against the fridge with his head tilted all the way to the right. My sister stood on her head in the middle of the floor, her top falling down over her sports bra and her legs stretched straight over her head, toes pointed like a ballerina's.

"What are you doing?" I asked.

Jenna dropped her feet to the floor behind her and she did some sort of back walkover thing to stand up straight again. "Can I ride into town with you? I'm supposed to meet Saralynn."

"Sorry, can't."

"Come on. Please?"

I looked at Jason and he shrugged. "Do Mom and Dad know?"

"Yeah."

She squirmed, though.

"Jenna."

"What? They know I'm spending the night at Saralynn's, OK?" She looked at Jason and he just shrugged, so she turned back to me. "You can ask Mom, if you want."

Jenna wasn't a baby. If she was up to something, she'd have to deal with the consequences herself.

Ten minutes later, Jenna slid into the back of our mom's car with her backpack and Jason took the shotgun seat, his long legs somehow folding under the dash. My sister leaned between the seats and flicked on the radio, then flopped back and buckled up.

"So," she said as I backed out of the driveway. "Are you guys going to Morp together or what?"

"Jesus, Jenna."

"Yes," Jason said at the same time, then looked at me. "Right?"

I nodded and hated the heat that rose over my cheeks. And the way confusion passed over Jason's face.

"Right." I looked through the rearview mirror at Jenna. "Are you going?"

"Just with Saralynn and Laura."

"Did Mom try to get you to buy a rose?" I asked.

Jenna looked at me like I was crazy. "No. Freshmen don't."

She was right. Freshmen could, but they never did. Well, almost never. In fact, I'd only ever heard of it once.

Mom said she invited a junior her freshman year.

I made a mental note to tell Betsy that it made me less angry at my sister to know that she didn't measure up either.

I pulled up to the Meadowood Mall's main entrance, and Jenna got out of the car. She put her backpack on and then knocked on the window. I rolled it down.

"You should come in." She looked at me, then past me to Jason. "I'll help you guys pick something to wear to the dance."

"We're going to the Hive," I said.

"Seriously, though." She took a step back from the car. "I'll help."

I waved at her and rolled up the window as I drove away.

"It might not be the worst thing," I said. "She's good with clothes."

Jason shifted in his seat, so he was looking more squarely at me. "I actually have an idea."

"Yeah?"

"Soiled Dove is playing at the Vagabond tonight."

The Vagabond was a coffee shop near the university that had a stage for local bands and open mics. I'd never been. "They are?"

"You want to go? We could buy T-shirts to wear to the dance."

I did want to go. But before I could say so, doubt reared up. Was this a date? I wasn't sure if I minded if it was, but if he didn't think so and I did, that could be weird.

"I mean." He sat back in his seat. "I'm going anyway. If you don't want to, I can just pick up the T-shirts."

“I want to go, but I have a thing at six. I won’t be home until after eight.”

“They don’t start until nine anyway. I’ll come get you at eight thirty.” I looked at him and he smiled. “I’ll borrow Suzy’s car.”

This felt like a date. Maybe it was a good thing I’d see Betsy at group beforehand. “OK.”

○ ○ ○

By the time we’d finished our workout, everything felt normal again with Jason, and I figured that the whole this-feels-like-a-date thing was just me overthinking things.

I stood in front of my closet. Jenna was spending the night at Saralynn’s house, or I would have asked her to help me figure out what to wear to the concert.

I thought about calling her but changed my mind. That would be a little too extra, considering this was definitely not a date or anything.

A concert at a coffee shop. OK. That was casual. I pulled a T-shirt off its hanger just as my phone buzzed in my back pocket.

Hey.

Just one word. From Lou.

I made myself put on the T-shirt before I texted back.

Hey.

I took a breath and sat on the edge of my bed. I hated that I cared so much that he’d texted me. Before I could decide what to do, my phone buzzed again in my hand.

Can I come over?

Was he asking permission, or did he want to know if anyone was at my house? He wouldn't want to come by if my parents or Jenna were home.

I wondered whether I'd have had the nerve to assume the first and let him show up to see me, right in front of my family.

Sure.

I wasn't being particularly brave. No one was home anyway.

And maybe we needed to just have this out, finally.

I put my phone on my bed and started to braid my hair.

○ ○ ○

When I opened the front door for Lou twenty minutes later, I was startled enough by seeing his car in our driveway that I just stood there and stared at it.

"Can I come in?" he finally asked.

I stepped out of the way.

Will you go to Morp with me? I actually heard his voice in my head. Felt his fingers tug the elastic from the end of my braid, his arms pull me into him for a kiss.

This was happening. Right now. Lou always parked halfway down the block. He wouldn't have parked in our driveway unless something had changed.

"I'm going to a concert with Jason tonight." It came out too fast.

Blurted in a rush instead of smooth and nonchalant. Lou looked at me like I wasn't speaking English and blood rose to my face.

And then he did kiss me. His fingers tugged the elastic from my braid, like they always did, and he untangled my hair. Some part of my brain whispered, *Jesus, Celly, don't do this*. But it was completely drowned out by the part that made me melt against him.

Maybe it was because of his mother's Honda right there in my driveway, where anyone could see it, or maybe it was just that I'd missed being kissed. I don't know.

But when he pulled away and said, "Can we go to your room?" I said yes.

○ ○ ○

Lou had brought a condom with him.

Did he always have a condom with him? Did he bring one this time because he knew if he parked in my driveway, I'd do things with him in my bedroom that I never had on my couch?

Oh yeah. This was too fast. "Wait a minute."

Lou looked up at me. There was a particularly delicious moment where for the first time ever, he was more vulnerable than me. He was more naked. More exposed.

"What?" he asked.

I kept my eyes on his face. "What if my parents come home?"

He shook his head. "They're both working all day. I just left the gym."

"What about Jenna?"

"She went to the lake with Corbin."

I blinked and sat back away from him. "Corbin Hendricks?"

Lou's eyes went back down to what his hands were doing. "Yeah."

"Lou." Corbin Hendricks was four years older than my sister. He had a goatee, for God's sake. "Jenna shouldn't be at the lake with Corbin Hendricks."

Lou looked up at me again. "They're at his family's lake house. Isn't she friends with his sister?"

I exhaled a breath that I felt like I'd been holding for half an hour. "Is Saralynn his sister?"

"Yeah."

He reached for me, and I surprised myself at least as much as I surprised him by standing up. I picked my T-shirt up from the mattress and pulled it over my head.

"What are you doing?" Lou asked.

"Not this."

Lou's cell phone vibrated. He sat on the edge of my bed and reached down to the floor to pick it up.

He read whatever the message was that had come through and muttered, "Damn it."

He stood up again and pulled his boxers over his long legs.

"Vivi?" I asked.

He put his jeans on. "I have to go."

I looked toward his phone, but he shoved it into his back pocket. His unfurled, but unused, condom sat on the edge of my bed. I wondered where Vivi had gotten all of those condoms she'd put in my locker.

I said, "Someone saw your car."

"What?" He pulled his shirt over his head.

"Who was that, on your phone?"

Lou ran a hand through his hair, then stuck one of his feet into a sneaker. "Vivi. I keep telling her . . ."

"Telling her what?"

He put on his other shoe, then knelt to tie them. "That a long-distance thing won't work when she goes to Utah."

"You broke up with her?"

He didn't look at me. He reached into his pocket for his keys instead. "I have to go."

He hadn't broken up with her. He was leaving my bedroom to go to her.

CHAPTER 16

It took me half an hour to settle down after Lou left. I stood in front of my closet for most of that time, staring and not making a decision. I finally settled on the dress my mother had given me for my last birthday.

She'd said the green was the same color as my eyes—but as soon as I'd put it on, she'd decided we'd take it back.

I hadn't realized it had an empire waist. *You can't wear an empire waist, Celly.* She'd actually patted my belly.

But it was the color of my eyes. And I liked it. The one time I'd put it on, I'd liked how it made me feel. Right up until my mother opened her mouth.

And I needed to feel good about myself tonight, even if it was fake.

We'd never gotten around to returning the dress. I took it off the hanger and put it on, then headed out for the bus to group.

○ ○ ○

"Wait a minute," Sharon said. "Aren't we waiting for Vivi?"

Sharon and her daughter wore yellow button-down tops today. The color was OK for Sharon, but it made Brenda look washed out.

"Vivi's not coming tonight." Betsy didn't look at me.

That caused a little ripple around the table, but then Amber took a deep breath. As she exhaled, she said, "I'm going to the hospital tomorrow."

"That's big news, Amber," Betsy said. "Do you want to talk about it?"

She shook her head, but she did talk. "I'm scared."

"What's scaring you?"

"They'll make me eat. I want to eat. I shouldn't want it so bad."

"Everyone eats," Sharon said.

"I know." Amber stared at her hands on the table and ran a fingertip over a blue vein. "Can it be someone else's turn?"

Betsy leaned a little closer to Amber. "Let's talk after group?"

Amber nodded.

"Brenda's selling her hair," Sharon said when things went quiet for too long.

"Brenda can talk for herself," Betsy said.

Brenda chewed at her bottom lip. "It's true. I am. Someone's paying me two hundred dollars for it."

"That's a thing?" John asked.

"Yes, it's a thing. They'll use it to make a wig or something."

Brenda put a self-conscious hand to her dark brown hair, pulled into a thick twist at the back of her head.

Betsy finally looked away from Amber and asked Brenda, "What made you decide to do that?"

"Mom thought it was a good idea." Brenda looked at her mother. "I mean, it's two hundred dollars."

Sharon tipped her chin toward me. "If she had hair like yours, she would have made ten times as much."

I lifted my eyebrows in surprise and wrapped a strand of my light blond hair around my fingers. "Really?"

"What will you do with the money?" Betsy asked.

"What do you think we'll do?" Sharon looked at her daughter. "Pay the bills."

Amber sat beside Betsy, watching with eyes that looked far too big for her face.

She wasn't much smaller than Jenna, I thought. She even looked something like my sister, if my sister lived in some alternative universe where instead of strong and athletic, she was as fragile as a porcelain doll.

Was there such a fine line between perfect and anorexic?

She'd gone to the lake with Corbin.

Something that had been bothering me since Lou left finally snapped into place.

He hadn't found out where my sister was from Saralynn. She was a year younger than Jenna, only in the eighth grade, and even though her older brother was part of the stratosphere, I was pretty sure Saralynn didn't talk to Lou regularly.

I stood up and reached for my bag.

"Celly?"

"I have to go," I said. "I have to go right now. I'm sorry."

"Is everything OK?"

"No. I don't think it is."

I walked out of the room, and Betsy followed behind me. She put a hand on my arm before I could go out into the hall. "What's wrong?"

I didn't know how to begin to tell her. Or whether I should. "I'll come again next week. I promise."

"Celly."

"I'll come to tomorrow's group, if you want me to." She just looked at me. I knew what she was doing, letting the silence stretch out until I couldn't take it. Even knowing, I broke first as soon as a half-lie came to me. "I have a date tonight."

Her eyebrows shot up.

"Not with Lou," I said. "I'm just going to a concert with Jason. So we can get T-shirts for the dance."

It was a stupid excuse. No one rushes out of group therapy for a date they already had planned. But it was all I had. If I told her I was worried about Jenna, she'd call my dad, and things would blow up before I even knew if there was a problem.

I didn't think it fooled Betsy, but she backed off. "I'll see you tomorrow?"

I took another step toward the door. I needed to call Jenna. When

Betsy didn't say anything else, I left her office.

○ ○ ○

I had Mom's car. Thank God. I called Jenna as I took the three flights of stairs down to the street level of Betsy's building.

I'm dancing or sleeping. Leave me alone.

Nice, Jenna.

I called again and got her voicemail a second time. I tried one more time just as I reached the car.

"Damn it, Jenna," I said after the beep when I got the message the third time. "Call me. Right now."

My heart beat so hard between my sudden bolt of worry for my little sister and taking three flights of stairs that I couldn't think over the sound of it in my ears.

I started to text Lou and stopped myself when I couldn't think of what to type. I did the unthinkable instead.

I called him.

He answered before the first ring had finished. He didn't say anything, so I said, "Hello?"

He snorted and said, "Stupid robocalls," only not to me. His voice was distant, like he wasn't holding the phone to his ear.

"Lou?"

The call disconnected.

He was with Vivi. That's why she wasn't at group. She'd seen his car in my driveway, and he was with her, while my sister was at the lake with his creepy friend Corbin.

I punched I need to know where my sister is into a text message and then started the engine.

Before I put my foot on the gas pedal, I added: now.

Then I did what I should have done in the first place and texted Jenna. Where are you?

Her response came first. Y?

Call me.

Wat? No.

Now. It's important.

I might have been overreacting. I tried to convince myself of that as I drove back toward Sun Valley. If I went home then and got our parents involved, I'd get both Jenna and myself into serious trouble. Maybe for no reason at all.

She was good friends with Saralynn. Wasn't she?

How long had they really been hanging out?

I tried to think as I sat at a red light. Maybe just since last summer. I couldn't remember Saralynn Hendricks at our house before then.

They hadn't been friends long enough for me to have connected Saralynn with Corbin.

My phone vibrated and I saw a message from Lou just as the light turned green again. Have you lost your mind? That was all. No worry that maybe there was a reason I'd called him.

I sat at the green light, the car behind me honking, and typed call me before I drove again.

My phone rang thirty seconds later. I answered without looking at who was calling. "Lou?"

"Oh, gross."

I exhaled completely for the first time since Lou left my house that afternoon. "Are you at the lake, Jenna?"

"Yes."

"With Corbin Hendricks?"

It took her too long to answer. Long enough that I almost said something. "With Saralynn Hendricks. Mom and Dad know."

"Corbin's there, too?"

"Yeah, so what?"

"And their parents are with you."

She hesitated again. "Why do you have to be so weird, Celly?"

"Are they?"

"Yes, OK?"

If she was telling the truth, she'd be OK until Mr. and Mrs. Hendricks went to bed. Until Saralynn fell asleep. Until Corbin got bored.

"I'm going to a concert with Jason tonight. To get those T-shirts."

"OK."

"Do you want me to come get you after?"

She was quiet for another minute.

It didn't feel right to leave her there overnight, even if Mr. and Mrs. Hendricks were with them.

I had no real reason to feel that way, except that Holly had gone out with Corbin once when we were freshmen, and she hadn't been the same after that.

That was when she'd stopped talking to me all together.

If I couldn't get Jenna to come home, I'd have to tell Mom and Dad that I was pretty sure she was at the Hendricks' lake house without any adult supervision. That would definitely work. With gusto.

"OK," she said.

I exhaled. "Text me the address."

As I pulled into my driveway, my phone rang again.

"Have you lost your mind?" Lou asked before I could even say hello.

"How did you know my sister was at the lake?"

"What are you talking about?"

"You knew she was with Corbin. You said she's with Corbin, not Saralynn."

"Oh, my God, you're a lunatic."

"What made you say she was with Corbin?"

He stumbled. "He likes her, OK. Don't make a big deal about it."

"She's fourteen, Lou."

"I'm sure she can take care of herself."

I hung up on him and sat in the car for a minute, staring at the phone. *OK,* I thought. *So, this is how it ends.*

CHAPTER 17

Mom and Dad weren't home. They both taught Friday night classes at Belly Busters.

I kicked off my plain black flats and sat down to lace on my combat boots instead. They made me feel kind of badass, and I needed to feel kind of badass.

I went into Jenna's room and found some eyeliner and a can of aerosol hairspray and did my best to make myself look like someone who was going to a concert.

It felt a little like putting on a Halloween costume, but I did it anyway.

Jenna's room had a full-length mirror, so I turned to take in the whole effect. At first, I saw my stomach. Just like Mom said, the dress's empire waist cut right above it and made me look nine months pregnant.

That's all I saw. I ran my hand over the round curve of it.

Jesus. I looked like I belonged in the Thanksgiving Day Parade.

This is why I wore jeans and baggy T-shirts.

No one wanted to see my stomach.

Usually, I avoided looking at myself. If I caught a glimpse, I looked away quickly. I didn't know what made me keep standing there this time. Why I didn't just walk away from the mirror, back to my room, to take off that dress.

But I kept looking.

Your face is so round. It's huge. No wonder they call you Moocella.

Your shoulders are as broad as your dad's.

My skin crawled. God. I was grotesque. A monster.

A beast.

I took a breath, and then another one.

Queen Beast.

You're a beast.

You look strong, Marcella.

My body, in the mirror, snapped back to regular human proportions. I just saw me. Three hundred and twelve pounds, not three million and twelve.

I was big, but I fit somewhere in the realm of human size.

Not a monster. Just a normal fat girl in a green dress that matched her eyes.

Not a parade float. Just me.

"I'm done hiding," I said to my reflection.

And I meant it.

○ ○ ○

"Is that what you're wearing tonight?" Mom asked as I walked through the kitchen.

I stopped, startled. "What are you doing home?"

"Madi took over my class." She sat at the table, still in her Zumba outfit, eating her dinner. "I thought we returned that dress."

"We didn't."

She opened her mouth, maybe to mention the empire waist or to comment on how the green matched my eyes and to tell me she was glad I wasn't wearing black, because it wouldn't make me look skinny anyway.

I didn't know what she was going to say. Whatever it was, she must have thought better of it, because she closed her mouth again. I thought about telling her that I was driving out to the lake to get Jenna later, but changed my mind.

Jason knocked on the kitchen door and broke the awkward moment.

I opened it and he grinned his woodland-creature grin at me, then held up one foot. He wore his own combat boots. "Ready?"

"Bye, Mom."

"Bye, Mrs. Boucher."

"Wait!" She stood up, held up one finger, and went out into the living room in a flash of Old Navy spandex and platinum-blond ponytail.

She came back and put two twenty-dollar bills in my hand. When

I lifted my eyebrows, she said, "Jenna called earlier. She said you were going to get concert T-shirts to wear to Morp. You're supposed to buy them, Celly. It's tradition."

"Oh." My cheeks burned. I hadn't even thought about how we were actually going to buy the T-shirts. I shoved the bills into my phone case. "OK, thanks."

"Have fun."

○ ○ ○

The Vagabond was just a storefront near the university. It served coffee and craft beer, and in one corner there was a wooden box that served as a stage.

The tables and chairs were mismatched, as if the owners had outfitted the place from thrift shops and their parents' basements. Every surface had pages from magazines and hand-drawn cartoons and reprinted photographs of old movie stars pasted to it.

This was a place for college students. I was pretty sure we were going to be carded and turned away.

But just like at the karaoke bar, we were allowed in to the tables. Most of them were full of kids not much older than us with books and laptop computers open, studying while they waited for the concert to start.

"You OK?" Jason asked as we walked toward a card table set up near the front where a guy was selling Soiled Dove T-shirts and CDs.

"Yeah."

There were two T-shirts. A white one and a black one. Both had the Soiled Dove logo ironed onto the front. A broken bird, falling to Earth. Belatedly, my heart beat into my throat as Jason picked up one of the black T-shirts and shook it open.

It would fit him perfectly. Pretty much any size they had would fit him. His biggest worry would be that it might be too short.

I looked down at the neat row of black T-shirts folded in front of us. Medium. Large. Extra large. Double extra large. That was the biggest shirt I saw, and I picked it up and handed it to the man without opening it.

"We'll take these two."

Jason looked at me.

"Please," I added.

"Are you sure you want black?" Jason asked.

"Yes."

What if it didn't fit? What was I going to do then? I should have opened the shirt and looked. Like a rational person. We could have done something else if it didn't fit.

But the man took the money from me. I'd already started down this road and I didn't see how to turn off it.

He put the T-shirts into a clear plastic bag and handed them to me. "Enjoy the show, hon."

I took them and looked up at Jason, who just lifted his shoulders and walked toward the tables.

A waitress came by a few minutes later and gave us menus.

"Are you hungry?" Jason asked. "I haven't had dinner."

"Me either." I didn't look at the menu though. Between worrying about Jenna and those stupid T-shirts, my stomach ached.

I still had the shirts in my lap, my fingers playing with the thin plastic bag. "Do you think someone at the Hive knows where I can get fishnets?"

He lifted his eyebrows. "I'm sure someone does."

A few minutes after we ordered BLTs, the lights dimmed, and Jason's attention shifted to the stage. The guy who had sold us the T-shirts was behind the drum kit. Soiled Dove had a guitar player, a bassist, and a keyboard player as well.

The guitar player spoke into a microphone. "You might know, our lead singer Victor Solo left us recently."

The bassist muttered "bastard" and the guitar player snorted before going on.

"We're auditioning a replacement. Tonight, we have a guest vocalist. Penelope is visiting from Boise, where she's with a killer band called Ozone. Y'all are in for a real treat."

The band went directly into a song, the drummer beating first, and then the guitar player joining as a woman stepped forward and started to sing.

She was good. It was a little like watching a Soiled Dove cover band, even though most of the members were there. Hearing songs I'd heard a hundred times all sung by a woman was kind of cool, I decided.

Our sandwiches came, and I got through half of mine before my stomach started to rebel again. I put the food down and inhaled slowly.

"What is it?" Jason asked. "I know something's wrong."

I shook my head.

"It's Lou, right? You wish you were here with him."

"Oh." I put a hand over my mouth. For a minute I thought my food might actually come back up. "No. That's not it."

"Then what."

We were yelling to hear each other over the band. I looked at him a minute, then picked up my phone and texted him. Jenna's at the lake with Corbin Hendricks.

He picked up his phone when it vibrated, then texted back.

Who's that?

An asshole.

?

A senior.

Jason looked up at me.

I took a breath and tried again. My thumbs hovered over my phone before I typed. I told her that I'd come get her after the concert.

He typed something. I tapped my combat boot and looked up at the band. The drummer caught my eye and lifted his chin. My phone vibrated, and I read Jason's message.

Is she alone with him?

The band finished their song, so I leaned closer to him and said, "Her friend Saralynn is Corbin's sister. His family has a lake house, and they're all up there, but I don't want her to stay overnight. He's a creep."

He looked up at me again, then at the stage for a minute. "What kind of creep?"

I'd never told Holly's secret to anyone. She'd dumped me, and it still hurt, but for some reason I still couldn't make myself tell Jason the exact truth. "There was this girl, our freshman year."

He waited. The band started their next song. The bass player first, thrumming a few notes that I felt in my chest.

"Was it you?" he asked.

I shook my head. "She used to be my friend."

"OK. Let's go."

"Now?"

He pushed his chair back and stood up. "Yeah."

I looked back at the stage, and the drummer gave me a salute before he banged his snare.

○ ○ ○

I typed the address Jenna had texted me into my GPS once we were back in Suzy's car. The house on Lake Tahoe was nearly an hour away.

"I can go get my mom's car," I said. "You don't have to drive all the way out there with me."

"I'm not letting you go to some creep's house by yourself."

I could have told him that I didn't need him to protect me. I didn't. Corbin Hendricks wasn't going to do anything to me. I was definitely not his type. Plus, Jenna had said his parents were there.

But the truth was I wanted to hang out with Jason tonight, so I just put on my seatbelt as he started the engine. Then I looked at him and took it right back off again.

"What?" he asked.

"Stay here. I'll be right back."

The Soiled Dove drummer had left his table set up in a corner of the Vagabond with T-shirts and CDs lined up and a glass jar in the middle. It had a hand-lettered sign taped to it that said "don't steal from us, please." The CDs were in plain paper envelopes. I picked one up and shoved my last five-dollar bill in the jar.

I brushed my hand over the stack of black T-shirts. Medium. Large. Extra large. I picked up a double extra large and closed my fingers around the soft cotton.

There's no way to check if you're being watched at a merch table without looking like you're trying to shoplift. I did it anyway. Everyone was focused on Penelope, belting out "Nobody's Baby" behind me.

I shook the T-shirt out, and my stomach clenched around the half sandwich swimming around in it. No way would I fit into it. Their T-shirts ran so small, even their largest was at least two sizes less than I needed. I didn't have to hold it up to my body to see that.

I folded the shirt as neatly as I could with shaking hands and put it back on the pile and tried to shove the whole thing into a back corner of my brain.

○ ○ ○

When I made it back to the car, Jason still had the engine running. He lifted his eyebrows and I showed him the CD.

I shrugged. "We can finish the concert on the way up."

Jason slipped the CD into the player, and Soiled Dove filled the car.

I leaned back and listened for a few minutes as he drove.

"They'd never pick someone as young as me, you know," he said.

"They would if they heard you."

He shook his head.

"They would."

He turned his head to look at me. "You know, we could have skipped the concert and just gone after Jenna right away when she called you."

"Oh," I said. "She didn't call me."

"Then how did you know?"

"Lou said she was with Corbin and it freaked me out."

The atmosphere in the car changed. It was as if we had our own little Chevy ecosphere going on, and the clouds had rolled in. Somehow, I'd forgotten about Lou at my house that afternoon. Lou with his condoms.

That seemed like a hundred years ago. And wasn't it awesome that I didn't even care that Lou was with Vivi right now? Right this minute? That was something to talk to Betsy about for sure.

But I'd hurt Jason in some slippery way that I couldn't quite grasp. We weren't dating. He wasn't my boyfriend. But the atmosphere in Suzy's car had shifted anyway. And I felt like I needed to apologize, even though I hadn't done anything wrong.

"You were with Lou Duncan after the Hive?" Jason finally asked when I just didn't say anything.

"Just for a little while."

Jason relaxed back into his seat again, and the clouds in the car cleared a little. "Did you ask him to the dance?"

I looked at him, then back to the road. Was he serious? "You know I did. Your first day of school."

"I mean again. Today. Privately."

I shook my head. Soiled Dove kept playing, and I kept feeling like I needed to apologize, which pissed me off. "We didn't do anything."

I kind of hated myself for saying that.

"That's good," he said. "You know, Lou Duncan…"

He didn't finish his thought. When he pulled to a stop at a red light, I turned to look at him. "Lou Duncan what?"

"Lou Duncan deserves Vivi Hughes."

I stared at Jason until the car behind us honked.

"He deserves a perfect cheerleader?" I meant it to be sarcastic. Biting. Instead, it sounded true. The car honked again, then roared around us and went through the intersection.

Jason sat back in his seat and propped his foot on the dash again. "He deserves a honey badger."

"Oh my God."

"What?" he said. "She looks just like one."

"Yes. I know." We had to sit through a second red light. The woman in the minivan behind us didn't look very happy when I looked over my shoulder and I held up an apologetic hand that she probably couldn't see anyway. "I didn't think anyone else noticed."

"Really? With that mean streak?" He ran his hand over his own head, where Vivi's blond streak was.

The light turned again, and this time he drove through it. Jason sang along with the CD. No choking when it was just me listening. That did something to the pit of my stomach.

Soiled Dove would pick him. If he auditioned, they would pick him. They'd be so stupid not to.

A few minutes later we were in the mountains, completely out of the city. There was no blurring of the line between town and mountains around here. After the last street of houses, there were just pine trees and winding roads leading up toward Lake Tahoe.

The sun had already set, and there were only sporadic streetlights. Maybe it was the dark that made me say it. Or the rhythm of the road mixed with music and Jason's voice.

"I almost slept with Lou today."

Jason stopped singing but didn't say anything.

"He had a condom with him. It was like the ones that Vivi put in my locker and I just...I didn't do it."

"But you wanted to?" he finally asked.

"I thought I did. For a long time, I really thought I did." I inhaled slowly. Telling Jason the truth felt like purging—but in a good way. A way that might actually get me out of counseling, not into it. "Turns out, I really didn't, though."

The song hit its chorus, and Jason sang with it. *Love knocks you over, baby. Every time. Every time.*

Even in the dusk, Lake Tahoe was unreal as it came up in front of us. Like a painting. Jason sat up a little taller to see it.

"Will you come with me?" he asked.

"Where?"

"To the audition."

Turn left in eight hundred feet. Your destination is on the right. He flicked on the blinker.

"Of course I will."

"I'll probably choke."

"No, you won't."

He lifted his eyebrows and exhaled. "So, are we going to have to use our shitkickers?"

The Hendrickses' lake house filled the entire block to our right. Lit up like a Christmas party, it looked like something from another time. There were only four Hendrickses, but their weekend mansion could easily hold a hundred people.

"I doubt it." I couldn't imagine that anyone who lived like this would cause a scene in front of their parents.

Jason craned his neck to look out the front window as he pulled through the gates into the driveway. "Jesus."

When he cut the engine, we both sat there a minute. I picked up my phone and tapped in a message to my sister. I'm here.

We both watched the massive front door.

When it didn't open, I tilted my head to look up at the top of the house through the windshield. Three stories. It might take her ten minutes to make it out. She could text though.

Jenna.

"Are you sure they're here?" Jason asked.

"Every light in the place looks on."

"Do your parents leave every light on?"

Too late, I looked around and realized that there were half a dozen cars in the huge driveway. No one was in the yard or on the porch, but something wasn't quite right.

There was a party happening here tonight. The kind parents aren't part of. "Oh, Jenna."

I opened my car door and stood up out of my seat just as light finally poured through the front door. And music. My little sister came through it, followed by Corbin Hendricks. He loomed a full foot taller than her, crowding her from behind, one arm around her waist, pulling her against him.

Jason got out of the car, and Jenna looked over at us. She said something to Corbin, who pulled her closer to him, turning her around, and leaned in to kiss her.

I started toward the porch. "Jenna!"

She stumbled back as well as she could with a football player attached to her top half. His hold on her pulled up her dress so the skirt lifted completely over her bottom.

Jason got to them before me. Somehow, he managed to maneuver Jenna out of Corbin's arms and into his own, like they were dancing. She stumbled, and he lifted her right off her feet, honeymoon style.

"OK," he said, like it was an everyday thing, and carried her toward the car.

"What the fuck, asshole?" Corbin started toward them.

Then Jenna leaned over Jason's shoulder and vomited onto the Hendrickses' driveway. Corbin looked truly startled and stopped in his tracks.

I missed what he did next. I was distracted by Lou's mother's Honda parked in front of the garage.

Jason tucked Jenna into the back seat of Suzy's car after she'd emptied her stomach of whatever she'd been drinking. I leaned in and asked, "Where's Saralynn?"

She blinked up at me. "What?"

"Jenna. Where's Saralynn?"

Jenna's splotchy face crumbled. "She didn't want to come with me."

"She stayed home?"

She shook her head. "I made her come. I made her. She didn't want to, and I made her. I'm a bad friend, Celly."

Jason looked at me over the top of the car. "Can we leave her here?"

It was her parents' house. And Corbin was her brother. I bent back down to the car. "Where do Saralynn's parents think you guys are?"

Jenna was curled against the back seat like she used to on road trips when she was a little girl. "Our house."

I said to Jason, "Saralynn's only in eighth grade."

He tilted his head, like he'd be in if I said the word. "I'll go find her."

"Do you know her?"

He shook his head.

I looked at the house, then at Lou's mom's Honda. "I'll go. Stay with Jenna. Don't let her choke on her vomit or anything."

I bent to look into the car again. My sister was asleep. Or she'd passed out. I reached in and put my hand on her wrist. Her pulse was steady at least.

Music beat through the front door, and now that I was on the porch, I heard voices inside. Party noises. Before I could knock, it swung open, and I had to stumble back to avoid being knocked over by the people coming out.

Layla Anderson stopped cold and looked blankly at me, then up to the boy standing beside her.

"Belly's here," she said, her voice slurred. "Mike, why is Belly here?"

Mike and Layla were a stratosphere couple. Too high in the social order to bother with people like me, usually. But I didn't normally show up in their space, so Layla's confusion seemed more genuine than mean-spirited.

"Dunno." Mike looked at me, too. "Why're you here, Belly?"

"Celly."

"Huh?"

"My name is Celly." I shook my head. "I'm looking for Saralynn Hendricks."

"Oh, right." Like it made perfect sense. Mike looked back down at Layla. "She's looking for Saralynn. Is that Corbin's little sister?"

"Isn't Saralynn still in middle school? Are there middle school kids here?"

Mike pulled a confused face, then looked back at me. "We don't think any middle school kids are here."

"How about Corbin?" Both Mike and Layla turned to look at me with a kind of astonishment in their perfect faces. As if they were at the zoo and the elephant had asked them a question. I would have laughed if I'd had the bandwidth. "Corbin. Do you know where he is?"

Layla shook her head slowly.

"OK," I said. "Lou, then."

Mike lifted one heavily muscled arm and scratched the back of his head. "Lou and Vivi are out back."

"Thanks."

Layla was taken so by surprise that she snorted on her laughter, falling into her boyfriend. Then the two of them stumbled past me and down the stairs toward the cars.

"You're not driving, are you?" I called after them.

Layla looked back at me. "No, Belly. We won't even be in the front seat."

That's exactly how Robin Delaney had ended up pregnant at her graduation, I wanted to warn her. But I didn't bother.

I took a breath, stealing myself, and walked into the massive house.

It was a fairly small party. Mostly only stratosphere. Somehow, I had launched myself completely out of my own orbit. At first no one seemed to notice me. I didn't know where to start, so I just stood tall and looked around, trying to spot Saralynn. I saw Holly instead. She sat on the arm of a chair, with Stephen Northrup's arm around her waist. Holly had broken through, but she wasn't part of the stratosphere. Stephen was. My ex-best friend was collaterally popular. At least, she was that night.

Something unclenched in my chest. Holly and I weren't friends anymore, but she would help me find Saralynn so I could get out of here.

Holly's head came up when I was still halfway across the huge room. Something flashed on her face. Panic?

She shook her head once, and I stopped. Holly met my eyes again, and I tipped my head to the side, toward the sliding glass door and the backyard beyond it. I tried to telegraph *meet me out there* to her. I widened my eyes, and she nodded, barely. But she didn't get up.

The backyard was dominated by a swimming pool filled with half a dozen kids swimming in their underwear. The heated water steamed in the cooling night air.

My eyes were drawn to Lou, whether I wanted them to be or not.

He was stretched out on a lounge chair, one long leg wrapped around Vivi Hughes's small body. He was dressed, still in the jeans and T-shirt he'd had on at my house earlier. She was stripped down to a pink bra and panties—she must have been in the pool, because her ponytail was damp down her back.

For a moment Lou looked at me over her head.

And then Vivi turned around.

"Are you serious right now?" She sat up, curling against Lou in a position that looked so comfortable, she might have been his pet cat. "What are you doing here?"

"I'm looking for Saralynn Hendricks. Have you seen her?"

"You came all the way up here for Saralynn?"

"No. I came all the way up here for Jenna. I'm not leaving without Saralynn, though."

"So, do you just not want anyone to have fun? Not even your own sister?"

"My sister is fourteen," I said.

Vivi rolled her eyes and looked back at Lou. "Tell her Jenna is fine."

"Jenna's upstairs."

"God, Lou." Vivi smacked a hand against his chest.

"Actually," I said, "my sister was on the front porch drunk and about to be molested by Corbin. She's in the car now. I'm looking for Saralynn. Do you know where she is?"

Lou untangled himself from Vivi, whose face darkened. "Corbin wouldn't do anything to Jenna."

"That's bullshit and we both know it." When he just stared at me, I said, "Did you catch the part about the groping? And that she's fourteen? How about this. She vomited half a pint of peach schnapps

Lou stood up and shouted, "Saralynn? Saralynn Hendricks!"

When it was clear she wasn't by the pool, he moved toward the house. Vivi followed him, wrapping a towel around her body and keeping herself between Lou and me. When he went into the kitchen through a sliding glass door, he called out for her again, "Saralynn!"

She still didn't show herself. Holly stood in the center of the kitchen though. She must have been watching me talk to them through the window. Lou moved past her like he didn't even see her. She made a strangled little sound as I followed Lou to the stairs. He took them two at a time, calling Corbin's sister's name.

"Jesus, Lou," Vivi said. "You're going to scare the shit out of the poor girl."

He looked at me and then started opening doors. That caused some scuttling. I caught glimpses of half-recognized, half-naked bodies in some of the rooms.

What if I hadn't said something to Jason? What if I'd waited until after the concert? "Did you know Corbin was coming on to my sister?"

Both Lou and Vivi turned around and looked at me and I realized I was asking them both. Vivi looked up at Lou.

"He wouldn't do anything to her," Lou said again.

"Jesus, Lou," Vivi said again. She wrapped her arms around herself.

I opened another door. This one led to a room with yellow walls and white curtains. A girl's bedroom, with band posters and anime drawings tacked up on the walls. Saralynn Hendricks was curled in a chair by the window. She wasn't as small as Jenna, but with her eyes red from crying and a stuffed dog hugged to her chest she looked about ten years old.

I inhaled sharply. At least there wasn't some high school boy in here with her. "Are you as drunk as my sister?"

She shook her head. "I don't think so."

Jenna's backpack and another one sat on the foot of the bed. I picked them both up. "Let's go."

"I'm tired," she said.

"Get up." I moved to the door. "Now. Because if I go back to my car without you, I'm calling your parents."

That brought her to her feet. She wobbled, then stuck out her arms and found her footing. Maybe she wasn't quite as drunk as Jenna, but she was pretty close.

Vivi had managed to find a T-shirt to put on over her underwear. She stood in the hallway with Lou, the two of them watching us like we were a circus sideshow. I couldn't read either of their expressions and, really, I didn't care. I hustled Saralynn ahead of me toward the stairs.

She turned to look at me when she reached the landing. "I have to pee."

"OK," I said. "This is your house. I'm sure you know where the bathroom is."

She went the rest of the way down, then around the corner and through a door that led to a bathroom directly under the staircase.

I stood by the bannister and waited, like the world's most awkward butler. A couple of kids looked at me as they went by, their heads turning as they did a double take. I was as out of place as a teacher or a parent would have been.

"Celly."

I turned toward the voice that was still familiar, even though Holly hadn't really spoken to me in more than a year. "Hey."

"What are you doing here?"

"I came to pick up Jenna."

"She in the bathroom?"

"No. That's her friend. Saralynn."

"Corbin's sister?" Holly bit at her bottom lip and looked around, then back at me. "You shouldn't let Jenna…"

I waited for her to finish. I knew what she had to say. *You shouldn't let Jenna be alone with Corbin.* But she didn't say it.

"Well, I wasn't here." But Holly had been. Her cheeks went as red as mine do sometimes. "I got here as soon as someone told me."

She inhaled through her nose, then turned and went back where she'd come from.

The bathroom door opened and Saralynn stumbled out. "I puked."

"Wonderful."

CHAPTER 18

"Are you going to tell your parents?" Jason asked quietly as we drove back into our neighborhood.

I would have laughed if I hadn't felt so sorry for Jenna, knowing what was about to descend upon her pretty little head. "I won't have to."

"No?"

"No."

Jenna moaned from the back seat. "Just take us to Saralynn's house."

"No," I said again.

"Please, Celly."

"Where does Mom think you are?"

"She thinks I'm at Saralynn's. Just take us there."

"And the Hendrickses think you're at our house? Smooth."

"They don't care," Saralynn said without opening her eyes. I believed her, too.

I didn't particularly want to turn my drunk little sister over to our mother in her current condition. But there was no way that I was taking her to the Hendrickses' house either.

She was never going there again. She just didn't know it yet.

There would be no sneaking Jenna and Saralynn into our house, either. Our mom was a notoriously light sleeper. Especially if one of us wasn't home.

Jason drove Saralynn home first. The Hendrickses' Sun Valley house was almost as opulent as their lake house. Only it was dark. Saralynn stumbled up the stairs and used her keys to go in the front door.

No front porch light flicking on or Mrs. Hendricks coming down the stairs asking what was wrong and who'd been in a car accident.

The huge house just ate the girl up.

Jason headed for our house next.

"Well, this was an adventure," he said after we were out of the car.

"Yeah." I looked at Jenna. She looked more sober, at least. Not completely sober, though. "I'm sorry about this."

"Is she going to be OK?"

I nodded. "Oh, yeah. She'll be all right.."

He got back in the car and waved at me before he drove off toward his own house.

My sister stared up at the house like she'd never seen one before.

"What were you thinking, Jenna?"

"That he liked me."

"Of course he liked you. Everyone likes you."

Her eyebrows lifted. "Everyone does not like me."

"Jenna." I reached out and pushed a strand of hair off her forehead. It was sticky with hairspray. "Do you want to talk about it before we go in?"

She shook her head, but she talked anyway. "You…you got there in time."

I exhaled. "Lou was there. You could have asked for help."

She nodded a little. Neither of us said out loud that Lou had known she was there with Corbin, and he'd been in the backyard with Vivi. Forget whatever relationship he had with me, or that he'd worked for our parents for almost two years. She shouldn't have had to ask for his help. "I'm sorry, Celly."

"Don't do that again."

"I won't. Celly?"

"Yeah?"

"Thank you for coming to get me."

A soft light flicked on behind the window to our parents' room. Mom's nightstand light. Then the curtain shifted. "I'll always come to get you, if you need me."

If Mom had just seen me coming home, she would have gone back to bed. But when she saw Jenna was with me, there was no chance of that. The porch light lit up before we made it to the steps.

Jenna exhaled and looked up at me. "I'm in trouble."

I stepped back from her bad breath. "Yep."

She wiped a hand over her mouth and tried to pull herself

together. "Do I stink?"

A lie wouldn't do her any good. "Yep."

We walked slowly toward the house like a couple of death row inmates on the way to the gallows in some old Western movie. We made it about halfway before Mom tore the front door open.

She looked us up and down for a minute. As soon as she was satisfied that we weren't bleeding and there were no broken bones, she asked, "Do you know what time it is?"

"Past midnight," I said. "I'm tired."

"You're tired."

"And Jenna's sick." Not a lie. And not likely to work, but worth a shot.

Mom came to the edge of the front porch and waved us toward her. "What's wrong?"

"I threw up," Jenna said. "Celly came to get me."

All of that was true. And if Mom didn't get any closer…

She came down the stairs and put a hand on Jenna's clammy forehead at the same moment her face recoiled back from the strong smell of vomit and fruity booze that rolled off my little sister.

The former Robin Delaney would recognize that smell, I thought. I was pretty sure she knew it well.

"Are you drunk?" she asked. "Celly, has your sister been drinking?"

Jenna's small face crumbled, and tear-streaked mascara ran down her flushed cheeks. "I don't feel good."

"I bet you don't, little lady." Mom looked back at the house, like she was wondering where Dad was, then back at me. "Where was she?"

The last thing I wanted was to get pulled into the middle of this in the front yard in the middle of the night while Jenna was still half drunk and swaying on her feet. "You can ask her in the morning, Mom."

"What?" She looked back at the house again.

"Jenna needs a shower and to lie down."

"I need to know what's going on," Mom said.

Jenna looked at me, panicked. I chewed on my bottom top lip, then inhaled slowly before invoking The Rule. As far as I knew, this would be the first time either of us had called The Rule into action.

The Rule was simple. We could ask for help—in particular, a ride home—without worrying about getting in trouble in the moment. We might hear about it later, but we wouldn't be punished for asking for help.

"Jenna asked me to come get her," I said. "She used The Rule."

Mom's eyes narrowed, and for a minute, I thought she might argue. Maybe tell us that The Rule only worked if we called her or Dad. But she looked us each over again and then stepped back into the house and finally let us come inside.

"Go take your shower. And get some sleep." She stopped Jenna as she started past her, toward the stairs, and brushed her hair away from her face. "I love you."

"I know, Mom."

"We're talking about this tomorrow."

"I know that, too."

Mom kissed Jenna's forehead, then let her go. I started to follow her, suddenly so tired I wasn't sure how I was still upright. Mom caught me by my sleeve though. "I'll make us some tea."

"I'm tired, Mom."

She just nodded and walked toward the kitchen. Damn it. I followed her and plopped on a kitchen chair while she filled the kettle at the kitchen sink.

After she'd lit the burner, she sat across from me and said, "Were you drinking?"

"No."

"Because if you were drinking and driving—"

"I wasn't."

She seemed satisfied with that. "What happened?"

"Mom."

"What happened?"

"That's not fair. The Rule—"

"Bullshit." My eyebrows shot up into my hairline, and Mom waved a hand at me, dismissing my shock. "Something happened. I need to know."

I squirmed a little in my chair. I needed to think without my mother staring at me in her pajamas. "You'll have to talk to Jenna tomorrow."

The stove click-click-clicked and then whooshed into flame. Mom sat the kettle on the burner, then turned back to me. "Is she OK?"

This night felt like it had lasted at least a week already. "I think so."

"I'm so grateful I don't have to worry about you this way."

Jesus. "Right, Mom? Because who would invite me to a party anyway?"

Mom looked so startled at my outburst that for a second I was startled, too. She blinked, her dark lashes fluttering. "Celly, I—"

"I'm going to bed."

She put a hand on my arm before I could walk away. "That's not what I meant."

"Then what did you mean?" I tilted my head and waited. *This should be good.*

She opened her mouth, but before she could speak, the teakettle went off, whistling loud enough to make me jump. Saved by the bell, Mom turned away from me and poured hot water into her cup.

"Good night," I finally said. I'd let her off the hook, for the sake of my own aching brain. And because she was going to have enough on her hands tomorrow with Jenna.

"I meant," she went on as if I hadn't spoken, "that you make good choices."

"Right."

"I mean it, Celly. You aren't like me when I was your age."

"I'm very aware of that." How could I not be?

"When I was your age—" She turned and just looked at me for a long time. "When I was your age, I let other people make decisions for me. I didn't think I could say no."

"No to what?"

"To anything. If people didn't like me..." She inhaled deeply before going on. "I wasn't anything."

"Mom."

"I mean it. I wasn't strong the way you are."

Was she really confusing my social awkwardness with strength? It's not hard to avoid being drunk at a lake party, when no one is inviting you to the lake party in the first place. "I'm not that strong."

"Yes, you are. Suzy sees it."

Just *Suzy*. Not *that Suzy*. I'd dropped into an episode of *The Twilight Zone*. Nothing else made sense. "Suzy thinks I can lift weights."

Mom pulled her tea bag out of her cup. "Jenna is like me. That's all I'm saying."

Small. Pretty. Popular. Talented. "I know."

"I don't know how to stop her from making the same mistakes I did."

I rubbed my fingers over my eyes and winced at their gritty dryness. It was strange that they were so dry when I was so close to tears. "You mean me."

"Celly." When I didn't say anything more, she put her mug down and came to me. Sitting, I was nearly as tall as she was standing. She took my face in her hands and turned me to look at her. "I love you."

"I know."

"I don't want your sister to get pregnant in high school."

I blinked several times, taken back by her bluntness. "I don't think she—"

She bit her bottom lip, and her eyebrows furrowed together.

"She's not as sensible as you are."

Is that what we're going to call it? My brain instantly replaced *sensible* with *fat.* "Right, Mom. I get it."

She squinched her face and took a deep breath. "Jenna isn't as smart as you are. She doesn't make good choices, the way you do."

She whispered the word *smart* and looked past me, toward the kitchen door, as if hoping Jenna wouldn't appear there. "I know what you mean, Mom."

"Do you?" She exhaled and slumped back against the kitchen counter.

"Yes. I do. You don't think anyone will want to sleep with me, so you don't have to worry."

She dragged a hand through her hair, pulling it back from her face. "That's what you got out of what I just told you?"

"That's what I get out of it every time you say it."

The tip of her tongue darted out over her top lip, and she reached under her glasses with her fingertips to rub her eyes. "That's not fair."

"We both know it's true." It was so close to the surface to tell her about Lou. To let her know she was wrong. Lou would have slept with me just that afternoon.

Except. I was smart.

We looked at each other and she finally said, "Go on to bed, baby. I'll talk to Jenna in the morning."

○ ○ ○

It wasn't all that late. Not quite midnight. But I was so tired, every muscle in my body ached. It occurred to me as I opened my bedroom door that the ache was probably from all the work I'd been doing at the Hive. I really was tired, but it was a good ache.

I stopped just inside my door. Jenna was curled on my bed. She'd taken a shower. Her hair was still wet. But she'd put her dress back on. The hem had pulled up to her hips in a way that reminded me of Corbin raking it up earlier that night. I crossed the room and tugged it down again.

"I really hope you didn't puke on yourself," I said.

"I didn't." She didn't open her eyes, but her voice sounded mostly clear.

"What are you doing in here?"

She did look at me then. I almost never thought about how small she was, except when I was upset about how unfair life was. But lying in my bed, her face free of makeup, she looked like a little girl playing dress-up. She was less than half Corbin's size.

What if I hadn't come for her?

"Can I stay with you for a while?" she asked.

I reached into one of my drawers and tossed a T-shirt on the bed. "Get out of that dress first. I'll be right back."

I grabbed my own pajamas and went back into the hall. I meant to just go to the bathroom, wash my own face, and get undressed. But as soon as I had my bedroom door closed, I couldn't breathe.

Lou had known that Jenna was at the party, and he'd thought she was there with Corbin.

He'd told me as much. Even Vivi had been surprised by that.

I finally made it to the bathroom and locked the door behind me. The ache was worse, and my skin crawled. I turned on the shower and tried to wash away thoughts of how Holly went out once with Corbin when they were both fourteen, just after she'd had a glow-up that pushed her toward the stratosphere.

And how she'd never been the same after that.

When I made it back to my bedroom, Jenna had my T-shirt on like a nightgown and was under the covers. I climbed in next to her.

When Jenna was born, I was four years old. She was my favorite thing, then. A perfect doll baby with soft brown curls and huge blue eyes. She'd grip my finger when I put it in her palm, and I couldn't wait for her to grow up enough to play with.

When Jenna was four, I was in school. Kids were calling me Moocella. I was as tall as our mother and outweighed her by twenty pounds. And my little sister was still a perfect doll baby.

Now she was in my bed. Fourteen, drunk, and faking sleep. And I was still her big sister. It was my job to take care of her.

"Do you want to talk about it?" I asked.

She opened her eyes. "Maybe."

She didn't say anything else. Neither did I.

"Was it my fault?" she finally asked.

I didn't know what *it* was. It could be so many things, and I was afraid to know which of those things she was talking about. But if she was talking about Corbin, I knew one thing. "No. It wasn't your fault."

"How do you know?"

"I know because you're fourteen," I said. "And he's not."

Her eyes fluttered closed. "I wanted him to like me."

"Look at me." She did, although her eyelids only came halfway up. "In the morning, Mom's going to ask you what happened."

"I know."

"You should tell her."

I was prepared for a fight, but Jenna's eyes closed again and, after a couple of minutes, I realized that this time she was really asleep.

CHAPTER 19

Jenna's snoring woke me up at dawn. She'd rolled onto her back and somehow managed to make her small body take up two-thirds of my queen-sized mattress.

It was Sunday. That meant the Hive. I smiled as I stared up at the ceiling, then shook myself. I should try to sleep a little more.

But Jenna shifted and smacked an arm down across my face.

"Jesus, Jenna."

She mumbled something in her sleep. I gave up and let her have my whole bed. Might as well let her rest as long as she could. She had a hard morning ahead of her, between the hangover she had waiting for her and the loving wrath of Mom.

The sun was barely up, and anything I could think of to do this early—making breakfast, taking a shower, watching television—would wake someone up. In the end, I grabbed one of my dad's protein shakes and went out the front door.

A walk while everyone else slept felt like something an athlete might do.

Does that really sound like you?

I stopped in the middle of sidewalk. When had Vivi Hughes become my inner critic?

You know it doesn't, though. You're not an athlete.

Maybe I did know. I mean, it wasn't like Vivi actually did live in my head, right? I'd been to the Hive a bunch of times, and I was learning about weightlifting. But I wasn't a fucking athlete for God's sake. Not like Lou was. Or Jenna. Or Vivi, for that matter.

And I was probably the fattest person in the Hive every time I went. I stopped walking about a hundred yards from the school bus stop.

Was I the fattest?

I suddenly realized that I didn't know. Somehow, I hadn't noticed. I never didn't notice that. Every time I was around any other people, I took an inventory.

Was there anyone who weighed more than me?

I hadn't done that at the Hive since the first time Jason brought me there.

Suzy was small. Not as petite as my mother, but slender.

Midge, the woman who'd taught me to move my stomach out of the way when I stretched, probably didn't weigh as much as me, but she was a lot shorter, so we were similar in size.

I stood there, thinking through all the people I knew at the Hive.

Categorizing them.

See. You are the fattest.

"Maybe," I said out loud. "But it doesn't matter."

I walked again. I couldn't have stayed still if I tried. Cool spring air filled my lungs, and I thought I felt it flowing through my muscles, too.

I didn't mean to go to Jason's house, but next thing I knew, I was standing in front of it. I was pretty sure I could find his bedroom window. I'd been over a couple of times.

The sky was lightening. Not quite morning, but almost.

Close enough.

I picked my way through the toys on the front lawn and went around the right side of the house. I had to go through a gate, and it didn't occur to me to wonder whether Suzy and Dirk had a dog until I had it open.

They didn't, but the thought made my heart yank against my ribs. What in the hell was I doing?

I'd only been inside Jason's house twice, and now that I was trespassing for real, I wasn't certain which room was his from the outside.

I realized as I walked along the side of the house that I could just as easily wake up one of his foster brothers as him.

Or a neighbor. Who, if they were decent human beings, would call 911 and report a possible cat burglar. Or something like that.

The houses were close enough together that I could have stood near the fence and put a hand on each one. Someone was definitely going to call the police.

The moment I came to my senses and decided to turn to leave the side yard and go home like a rational person, I caught a flash of dinosaur wallpaper through an opening in the curtains covering a window halfway down the length of the house.

I made a mental note to myself: never leave home without my cell phone again.

If I'd had my cell phone, I could have just texted Jason. Or called him. Something other than what I did, which was to take a deep breath and then knock on the glass—just barely, with the tip of one knuckle.

He'd have to have been half awake to hear me. That's what I told myself. I waited what felt like an eternity but was probably only ten or fifteen seconds and then finally did something that made sense.

I turned to leave.

"Celly?"

I inhaled in a gasp that came out like a hiccup. Shit. I was trapped against the fence. Obviously, he'd seen me.

"Marcella."

Moocella. My head filled with a chorus of mooing.

"Sorry," I whispered as I opened the gate to leave. The adrenaline that had flooded my body earlier left it all at once.

Nobody wanted me at their house at six in the morning.

Nobody wanted me to wake them out of a dead sleep, knocking on their window.

Nobody wanted me.

I walked quickly. The cadence of my steps was an earworm. I

remembered it on some kind of visceral level. It was the same pace I'd set when I'd walked home from school with hand soap all over my shirt.

I was so caught up in my thoughts that when I felt a hand on my shoulder, I nearly came out of my skin. I spun and backed up at the same time, only managing to stay on my feet because Jason reached out with both arms to steady me.

He lifted his arms in the air when I yanked away from him. "Celly, what's wrong?"

"Nothing."

He tilted his head. "Yeah. That's not true."

I sniffed and ran both hands over my face, my lack of sleep suddenly catching up with me. My palms came away wet with tears. I never cry in front of them. Ever.

Jason was not one of them. Tears flowed faster. "I don't know."

"Did something happen?"

I shook my head. "I'm fine."

"No," he said. "You're definitely not fine."

Didn't Jason know that when someone says *I'm fine* you're supposed to just nod and go along with it? *I'm fine* is code for *I don't want to talk about it.*

I should have been annoyed. But for some reason, it helped to know that he wouldn't let me get away with that. Holly would have, even when we were still so close we were practically sisters. Lou definitely would have. I was pretty sure everyone else in my life would have.

But Jason didn't.

"Jenna slept in my room last night. I woke up early and didn't know what else to do, so I went for a walk." I took a breath.

Jason ran a hand through his hair, pulling the messy curls back from his face.

"I'm sorry I woke you up."

"You scared the shit out of me." He let his hair go and it flopped right back over his forehead. "I've been awake for like ninety seconds I think."

"I'm sorry. I won't do it again." I needed to move. Standing here, on the sidewalk, was a mistake. That feeling—the one I hadn't felt since I fired up Google after getting home on Morp rose day—was flirting around my edges and I needed to get away from it.

I started to walk away. Not from Jason, exactly. From that dead lack of give-a-damn that I never wanted to fill me up again. But from Jason, too, though. He could go home, get some more sleep, forget all this happened.

Only, he didn't. I walked two steps and then Jason took my hand. He was one of the only people I knew whose legs were long enough to easily keep up with me.

He didn't say anything else. Just walked with me, holding my hand. He was in his bare feet, but it didn't seem to bother him. There wasn't anything romantic about the way he held my hand. It was like he knew that I needed an anchor right then, and he just gave it to me.

"What's Ratt?" I asked.

He looked down at his T-shirt, then at me. "Really?"

"Are they good?"

"Let's go back to my house. I'll show you."

○ ○ ○

Ratt was an eighties hair band. After we picked our way quietly through the house to his bedroom, Jason fired up his laptop, handed me an earbud, and showed me a video.

"You're going to love this," he said. "Watch."

We sat side-by-side on the edge of his bed. "OK."

"Look!" He pointed to a girl sitting at a fancy dining table with her weird, aristocratic family. She had dark hair and delicate features. "Just trade the tiara for a blond streak."

He was right. The girl in the video looked just like Vivi Hughes. Gorgeous. Perfect. Skinny. "You thought I'd love that?"

"Just keep watching."

He bobbed with the music. Ratt was almost a caricature of the 1980s—perms and full faces of makeup—jamming in the attic and upsetting the family dinner below them.

The song was good. I'd never heard it before, and maybe I would have listened to it again if it wasn't completely tied to Vivi now in my mind. The girl in the video was clearly chosen for her perfection.

Toward the end of the song, the Vivi look-alike stood up and headed for the attic. On the stairs, she went through some kind of metamorphosis, shedding her ball gown and smooth brown hair and even her glowing skin.

She emerged as what I could only imagine was a 1980s hard rock goddess, creeped up on the band, and then danced to the final notes of the song.

Jason looked at me when the song was done. Being yanked out of bed at the crack of dawn did nothing to lift the woodland-creature thing. If anything, his eyes looked wider. His hair was definitely wilder.

And he definitely expected me to have gotten something more from the Ratt video than I did. I finally said, "I guess people have idolized girls like Vivi for generations."

He closed his computer and shook his head. "Celly. Don't you get it?"

"I guess not."

"She was wearing a costume with her family. Then she had to completely change for the band to like her. Another costume." He waited a beat, looking at me. "She isn't ever herself."

I sat up a little straighter. And I thought about Vivi with her blond streak. Vivi in her cheerleader uniform. In her underwear at the party the night before.

Draped all over Lou. In front of everyone. No rules there.

Only, was that true? Was it really?

"Right?" Jason asked. He must have seen my wheels turning.

"Yeah."

He leaned down and set his computer on the floor, then lay back on his pillows and yawned. "We're supposed to sleep in on Saturdays, you know."

Heat rose up over my face and I stood up. "You should go back to sleep. I'll see you later."

"Are you OK?"

Why did he have to see me so clearly? Anyone else would have just let me go. Anyone else would have let me go on the sidewalk. Actually, anyone else wouldn't have even come down to the sidewalk. Suddenly, I was very aware of how much space I took up in the little bedroom.

It was on the tip of my tongue to say I was fine, so it took me by surprise when what came out of my mouth was, "Not really."

"Me either."

That took me by surprise. "What's wrong?"

He slid over in his bed, so that he was stretched out along one side. "I miss my sister. I don't think I'm going to be able to actually do this audition. School sucks."

I sat on the edge of the bed. "School totally sucks."

"Right? But we went on a rescue mission last night, and that was pretty badass."

I lay down next to him, suddenly so tired my bones ached. "We were like the Avengers or something."

"Is Jenna OK?"

"I think she will be."

He turned on his side, to face me. "I like being your sidekick."

A snort of laughter escaped me. "I like being yours, too."

His eyes drifted closed and I had the idea that I should leave. In a few minutes. I was so tired.

○ ○ ○

"This is going to be hard to explain to your mother."

"What?" I startled awake and for a panicked moment had no idea where I was.

"That's my question," Suzy said. "How long have you been here?"

My brain finally caught up to my body and I sat up.

The bed shifted as Jason climbed off the end of it. "An hour."

"Come on out for breakfast. You need some carbs, Celly." Suzy left the door open as she started down the hall. "Big day."

"Big day?"

I definitely wasn't at home. My mother hadn't uttered the words "you need some carbs" once in her entire life. I wanted to tell Suzy that I needed to go home, but the words couldn't quite swim up over my embarrassment over being caught asleep on Jason's bed.

He sat next to me on the edge of the mattress. "Morning."

This really would be hard to explain to Mom. Hard enough to take my breath away.

"Oh my God," I finally said, softly.

"She made pancakes. She always makes pancakes before—"

I held up a hand to stop him. "I can't believe that just happened. Is she going to call my mom?"

"What?" Jason shook his head. "No. She was just teasing you."

"I can't go out there."

"Celly." He was already at the door, as if the smell of pancakes filtering in was drawing him out. "We fell asleep. Come eat breakfast."

My brain was at least two full steps behind. "Before what?"

"What?"

"You said she always makes pancakes before..."

"Oh." He stretched, his long arms above his head so his hands were flat against the ceiling. "You definitely need carbs."

"I don't know what you're talking about."

"Suzy wants you to deadlift this morning."

"But, the Hive isn't even open on Sundays."

"I know." He smiled that wide woodland-creature smile. "It's tryout day, Celly."

My eyebrows shot up, and my heart skipped a beat, then pounded hard as that registered. "I've only been to the Hive a few times."

"Doesn't matter. She decided last night that you can, if you want to, even though the roster's been set for weeks."

"I won't make the team, Jason."

"Who cares. Tryout day is fun." He shrugged one shoulder. "And you might be wrong. Let's get some pancakes."

I didn't have much choice, unless I planned to go out the window. I made a stop in the bathroom first and washed my face and wrestled my hair into something that didn't look like I'd just woken up.

"Morning, Queenie," Dirk said from the kitchen table when I finally gathered my nerve up enough to join them there.

I was one hundred percent sure my face was beet red. "Morning."

He held up a fork full of pancake, dripping with syrup. "Ready for the big show?"

Jason tilted his head toward an empty chair beside him and I sat down. This was so weird. My parents would not have served him breakfast if they'd found him asleep in my bed. That was for sure.

"I think so," I said.

"We're leaving in an hour," Suzy said as she set a plate in front of me.

"I need to go home and change."

"Eat first. Your mother doesn't strike me as the type to understand the importance of carbs."

That was the understatement of the century. I took a bite.

CHAPTER 20

I didn't have to worry about my parents. When I got home half an hour later, everyone was still asleep. Even Dad, who was a notorious early bird.

Then again, it wasn't even eight on Saturday morning.

I went into my bedroom and grabbed my gym clothes as quietly as I could. Jenna was sprawled out on my bed, flat on her stomach, snoring.

Before I got in the shower, I piled my hair on top of my head. I wouldn't have time to dry it if I washed it that morning. The hot water felt good. I closed my eyes and imagined doing a deadlift today, in front of everyone.

No way I'd make the team. But Suzy wanted me to try out, and that did something unusual to my insides. I'd never been on a team before. I stood under the stream and thought about whether I'd ever really felt part of anything before.

After I was out of the shower, I pulled on my black shorts and gray T-shirt and looked at myself in the mirror.

"You don't look like the Queen Beast." And I didn't. I looked like Celly. All 312 pounds—but no more than that. Maybe seeing Betsy was starting to work.

I wanted to look like Queen Beast today. I wanted to feel like her. And black gym shorts and a gray T-shirt weren't cutting it.

I went back to my bedroom and flicked on the overhead light. Jenna moaned softly and pulled the blanket over her head. "What are you doing?"

"I need your help."

"Right now?" She stretched under the covers and then peeked out at me. "What kind of help?"

"I'm trying out for the Hive's competition team this morning."

That perked her up some. She understood competition teams—she'd been auditioning for dance teams since she was six years old. "Really? That's a thing?"

"Yes."

"Well. That's cool." She sat up and hugged a pillow against her chest. She'd fallen asleep with wet hair, and it was a tangled mess now. Her face was puffy, and she looked a little green around the edges.

"Are you OK?"

"I think so." She eased back down though, until she was lying on her back. "What kind of help?"

"This doesn't feel like how I feel when I'm at the Hive." I tried to put together words to make her understand. "I'm way more badass than this. Inside."

"Badass?"

I sighed and bent down to pick up my sneakers. "Never mind. This is fine."

Jenna sat up again. "No, wait. Tell me."

"I want to look like—" Damn it. This was harder than I thought it would be. "I want to feel like…oh, really, never mind."

Jenna stood up, gingerly. She blinked and stood still for a minute, arms out for balance, like she wanted to make sure she wouldn't either fall over or puke. "Oh my God."

"Yeah? Try to remember that next time someone offers you schnapps."

"Not helpful." Once the color came back to her face, Jenna went to my closet. She flipped through my hangers, then looked back at me. "You definitely need to go shopping."

I picked up the bag I'd thrown on my desk the night before and pulled out the Soiled Dove T-shirt and shook it out. It was at least a size too small, and my stomach sank. "We're supposed to wear these to Morp, but it won't fit."

Jenna held out a hand. "Let me see."

I handed her the T-shirt and she turned it over, stretching the fabric like she was testing it. "Do you trust me?"

"Um." I mean. What was the worst that could happen? "I guess so."

She went back to my closet and pulled out a pair of jeans and the flowery workout pants I'd worn a few times to the Hive already.

"Stay here."

She left the room and I sat on the edge of my bed. My phone still sat on my nightstand, plugged in. I picked it up and opened up my text messages.

There was nothing from Lou, and I hated myself a little for the gutshot of disappointment that left me with. He was probably still at Corbin's lake mansion with Vivi.

My pity party was interrupted by an incoming text from Jason. We'll be there in twenty.

I picked up a brush from my nightstand and pulled the elastic from my hair. As I worked through the tangles, I thought about how the Queen Beast should wear her hair.

Not a messy bun. Way too basic.

Not a braid, either. Way too Lou's-favorite.

I didn't have a lot of time. I settled on a pair of buns high up on either side of my head. When I had them in place, I looked at myself in the mirror over my dresser and decided that they looked appropriately crown-like.

I looked at the plastic box that held my small collection of make-up. Most of it was what I'd bought at the beginning of the school year, after I'd lost some weight and had the delusion that I could pull off what Holly had in the ninth grade.

Some of the women at the Hive went all out with makeup. Not glamour makeup. That would just melt off their faces. These were athletes, sweating their way through heavy workouts.

Warrior makeup. Beast makeup.

I picked up a lipstick and opened the tube. The brightest color I had was an orchid pink. Not red, which would have been better. But I ran a line of it along each cheekbone, then filled in my lips.

I finished with mascara. The tube said it was waterproof, so that was probably a good thing.

"All right," I said to my reflection. "Not bad."

The bedroom door opened as I reached for my eyeliner, and Jenna came in, then stopped and looked up at me. I expected her to make some kind of crack, but instead she nodded, then handed me the pile of clothing she held in her hands.

"Put it on," she said, then went back out and closed the door behind her.

She'd reduced the volume of the clothes she took out of my room by at least half. The floral leggings were cut to thigh-length, and she'd hacked the legs off my jeans and somehow managed to fray the raw edges.

When I unfolded the Soiled Dove T-shirt, it barely even resembled the original. She'd opened the sides from the armpit to the hem and cut pairs of holes along the length.

Somewhere, she'd gotten more black jersey. Maybe she'd sacrificed one of her own T-shirts. A long strip was woven through the holes on each side, expanding the width of the garment by several inches.

She'd also cut out the neckline and hem at the bottom and around the sleeves.

She'd butchered my Morp shirt. Anger rose up first but died out quick. I couldn't have worn it anyway. I pulled off my gray T-shirt and pulled on Jenna's creation.

It fit perfectly. And somehow, she'd managed to keep it from looking like my little sister's arts-and-crafts project.

I pulled off my black gym shorts and tugged on the cutoff floral leggings. The raw edges around the leg openings looked a little off, so I tucked them under.

I was buttoning the jean shorts when the door opened again and Jenna stood in the opening. She looked me up and down and said, "I'm a genius."

"Don't get too full of yourself." I lifted one arm and looked in the mirror. I felt exposed. The lacing along the side exposed a two-inch wide swath of my skin from the bottom of my sports bra all the way down my side. "Maybe I should put on a tank top."

"Don't you dare." She poked my upper arm. "Say it. Jenna is a genius."

I looked at myself in the mirror. I had to admit it, I looked like the Queen Beast. I looked like someone who might have a chance at the competition team.

I looked like how I felt when I was at the Hive.

"Jenna can be a genius, sometimes." She smiled behind me, and I don't know what possessed me, but I asked, "Do you want to come with us?"

Her eyebrows shot up. "Really?"

"Sure."

"I do," she said. "Honestly, I'd want to go with you if you were going just about anywhere that wasn't here. But I have a feeling that Mom's not going to let me out of the house until graduation. From college."

"Go get dressed." I slipped the orchid lipstick into my pocket and turned to her. "Let me see what I can do."

○ ○ ○

"Mom." I touched her shoulder. "Mom?"

Her blue eyes flew open. "What's wrong?"

"Nothing's wrong." I took a step back from the side of her bed.

"What time is it?" She blinked as her brain caught up with her eyes. "What are you wearing?"

"I'm going to the Hive this morning."

"Is that a costume?"

"No." I wasn't about to try to explain the Queen Beast to her this morning. "Can I bring Jenna with me?"

"Absolutely not." Mom sat up. "If she's awake, tell her to meet me in the kitchen."

"Please, let her come with me. Maybe she'll talk to me." I was surprised by how badly I wanted her to say yes. It came out in my voice. "We'll be home by two."

She looked up at me. "No later than two?"

"I promise."

"Is that Suzy driving you?"

Back to that? "Mom."

"Well, is she?"

"Yes. That Suzy is driving us."

Mom lay back down on her pillow. "If you're not home by two, I'm coming down there."

I leaned down and kissed her cheek. "Thank you."

CHAPTER 21

"We aren't at Belly Busters anymore, Toto," Jenna said softly as we walked into the Hive.

She wasn't kidding. On a normal day, the Hive was nothing at all like Belly Busters. But today? The place was swarming with people. The bleachers were full. Women were warming up all over the place.

It was so strange to feel so in my element and see her so outside of hers. I'd never even considered that there might be a place where Jenna didn't fit in. Anywhere, on Earth. But she looked as out of place here as I felt at school.

It would have upset me to be so out of my element. A lot. The first time I was in the Hive, I'd almost left. But it didn't seem to faze my sister. I added that to my list of things to talk to Betsy about at my next appointment.

"Where should I go?" Jenna asked.

"You can hang out with us." Jason pointed to Dirk, who stood near the bleachers. He had a clipboard tucked under one arm and was loading water bottles into a cooler.

I looked around at the women surrounding me and wished I'd just stuck with my black-and-gray gym clothes. "I'm going to go wash my face."

Jason turned back to me, then pulled his phone out of his back pocket and, before I realized what he was doing, held it up to me and took a picture.

"What the hell, Jason?"

He turned the screen around and showed me the shot. My head and shoulders, a couple of Hive women whose names I didn't know behind me. "That is the Queen Beast."

He was right. I lifted my chin a little. "Will you send that to me?"

Jenna came to stand beside me. "You look like a badass."

"Is that the T-shirt we bought yesterday?" Jason asked.

I squirmed a little, tugging at the sides. "Jenna fixed it."

"You should fix mine, too."

Jenna was at least a foot-and-a-half shorter than Jason. She had to tilt her head back to look up at him. "Sure."

"Cool."

"Queenie!" I turned and saw Midge waving at me. "Come spot me?"

"Go ahead," Jason said. "Jenna can help me at the merch table."

"It's kind of crazy there's this many people here just for the tryout."

"Yeah. Wait until you see the actual competitions. It's insane. Go help Midge. We'll see you at the deadlift trial."

I had a serious case of imposter syndrome, but I went to help Midge anyway. I could do that much.

Her salt-and-pepper hair was teased out into a wild halo around her head and she had dark circles colored around her eyes. She wore an eighties-style rainbow-striped leotard over a pair of hot-pink tights.

She didn't do a single thing to hide any part of her body.

My mother would've passed out if she was here.

Midge lay on a bench as I came closer. She settled her hands, wrapped in fingerless gloves, around the bar above her head. The bar was loaded with more weight than Lou usually bench-pressed.

"This is your warm-up?" I asked as I stood behind her, ready to help if she needed me.

She grunted something that sounded like "yep" and then hefted the barbell off its rack and over her head. She lowered the bar to her chest and pushed it up, then lowered it again before replacing it on the rack.

She did it again. And one more time. Then she sat up, straddling the bench, and looked over her shoulder at me. "Are you warmed up?"

"I just got here."

She turned so her legs were both on one side of the bench. "Get stretched."

I went through the warm-up stretches Suzy had taught me, stretching my arms, my legs, my back and neck, my torso.

"Feeling good?" Midge asked. When I nodded, she grinned at me. "Then it's your turn."

Lou had taught me to do bench presses over the summer. But I'd never lifted the amount of weight Midge just had. It hadn't ever even occurred to me to try to lift more than Lou had loaded onto the bar for me. "I'm just here for the deadlift."

"This will help you really warm up." She stood up from the bench and took some of the weight off the bar. Not much, though. "I'll spot you."

I sat on the bench and swung my legs around to straddle it. I didn't want to hurt myself and have to forfeit the deadlift. "This is still too much weight."

"I won't let you hurt yourself." Midge stood behind the bench and looked down on me. "Put your palms on the grips, just like when you deadlift."

I wrapped my hands around the bar, my fingers against the scored grip marks.

"Wait." Midge took off and left me lying there.

I blinked up at the ceiling and tried not to imagine what I looked like. I was about to sit up when something plopped in the center of my chest.

A pair of fingerless gloves. I picked them up.

"You can borrow them," Midge said. "But you'll need to buy your own when you make the team. You'll tear your hands apart otherwise."

When I make the team. I sat up and put the gloves on, wiggled my fingers a little, then lay back down.

Midge adjusted my fingers a little. "Good, now breathe in, and lift when you exhale."

"How much does this weigh?"

"A hundred and seventy pounds. You can do this. Breathe in, and lift when you exhale."

I breathed in and out a couple of times without trying to lift and then inhaled one more time. On my next exhale, I hefted the bar upward and made a small, triumphant sound when it pulled out of its rack. "Oh my God!"

"Lower it slowly on the inhale," Midge said.

I did what she said. The barbell was heavy, but not too heavy. I had control over it. I lowered it until I felt it touch my breastbone.

"Now exhale as you lift it again, slow and easy."

I exhaled and lifted the bar three or four inches and then stopped. I couldn't get it past the point where my upper arms were perpendicular with the floor. "Midge."

"I'm here." She leaned over so I could see her and put her hands under the bar but didn't lift. "One more breath. You can do this."

I inhaled again, and when I exhaled, I pushed the bar up. For a second it almost felt stuck, but then I made my way past that point and was able to lift it smoothly all the way up and back into the rack.

I tipped my head back so I could see Midge. "Can I do it again?"

She grinned at me. "That's our Queenie."

I put my hands back on the bar's grips and lifted on an exhale, then lowered the bar back to my chest as I inhaled again. This time

I was able to lift the bar up again without hesitating. It was as if my brain just needed proof that my muscles could do it.

Before I put the bar back on the rack, Midge said, "Go ahead. One more time."

I lowered the bar and lifted it again. Then one more time. By the time I finally put it back in its place, my arms were shaking a little, but they felt loose and ready.

"Jeez, Celly. That thing must weigh as much as I do." I sat up as Jenna came to the bench and put her hands on the bar from behind it. She tugged once, twice, and it didn't budge.

"More than that," Midge said.

My face was already heated, from the lifts, so I couldn't tell if I blushed or not. "Well, it's a weightlifting tryout."

"I'd never be able to lift something this heavy, no matter how much I worked out."

"Sure you could." Midge pointed toward the floor mat. "See Dolly over there? The little one?"

Jenna and I both followed her finger and nodded.

"She can lift twice her body weight."

"No kidding?" Jenna tugged at the bar again. "You really think I could?"

Midge wrapped a hand around my sister's upper arm and squeezed. "It'd take some work. But sure."

Jenna lit up from the inside, and her excitement threw me a little off balance. "Do you think Mom would let me come here with you?"

"Let's see if Mom lets you survive the day first." That put a hole in her excitement, and I winced a little as she deflated. "Plus, you're probably too young."

My sister shook her head. "This is your place, anyway."

"Don't sweat it, Pip," Midge said. "The Hive will be here when you're a little older."

"Pip?" Jenna asked.

"Let me guess," Jason said. "Short for Pipsqueak."

Midge put a finger to her nose. All three of us groaned and she laughed.

○ ○ ○

There were only three events: squats, bench presses, and deadlifts. Suzy stood with two other women, all of them holding clipboards and taking notes, while Hive women warmed up all around them.

She looked up and caught my eye, gave me an excited little thumbs-up, then went back to paying attention to the bench press happening in front of her.

The five women with the best lifts in each category would be offered spots on the competition team for the upcoming season.

"Fake it until you make it" was one of my dad's go-to sound bites. I'd always hated it. Who wants to be a fake? Maybe it would be better for me to wait until next year. When I wasn't faking it so much.

I searched the Hive for Jason. He'd know what I needed to do to take my name off the deadlift list. Maybe he'd tell Suzy for me, because the idea of doing it myself made me feel a little queasy.

Next year. I'll get some more experience, and I'll do this next year. I practiced my getaway speech as I made my way toward the merchandise table where Jason and Jenna were selling Hive T-shirts and bumper stickers.

"Hey, I really don't think—" I stopped when I finally got a good look at them.

Jason wore the Soiled Dove T-shirt that I'd bought him for Morp the night before. Jenna wore a T-shirt, too. Different, but featuring the same band.

Hers was far too big. It must have belonged to Jason. She had the front tied up around her waist and the collar slipped over one shoulder.

When Jenna saw me, she waved, then elbowed Jason and said something to him. He looked up and his woodland face lit up as he lifted his arms over his head, thumbs locked and fingers flapping like a dove's wings. Jenna did the same.

"We're Team Celly," she said. "Cool, right?"

"Team Celly?"

"Yeah." She pointed at her T-shirt, then mine and Jason's. "Jason drove all the way back to Sun Valley to get them."

I hadn't even noticed he was gone. Jenna turned away to take money from a man, and Jason asked, "You really don't think what?"

I shook my head. "I don't know."

"I won't blame you for chickening out," he said.

"I thought you were Team Celly." That sounded stupid coming out of my mouth. Stupid and whiney.

"I am."

"Who's chickening out?" Jenna asked after she was done with her customer. "Celly, you have to do this."

"No, she doesn't," Jason said.

"Queenie!" someone called from behind me.

Jenna came from around the table. "It's your turn."

"I'm going to humiliate myself."

"Trust me," Jason said. "Choking is no picnic either."

"I'm not choking."

He smiled and lifted a shoulder. If I wasn't choking, then I was doing this. I breathed the way Betsy had taught me. In for four, hold for five, out for six. Then did it again. I couldn't control much, but I could control whether or not I at least tried.

"Queenie, you better get out there." Dirk walked around the table. "I'll watch the shop."

Jason and Jenna both looked at me, waiting. Well, shit. I had a freaking team. "Fine."

We walked to where Suzy and the other judges waited. My stomach ached. The bar was already loaded with weight plates. The first woman lifted to her capacity. Each woman took a turn after her, adding weight if they could lift more. Anyone who couldn't lift the bar was eliminated from this round.

If more than five were left, there'd be a second round.

If there weren't five left, the eliminated women would get a second round. I was late to join the tryouts and the last one on the list for deadlifts.

"Ready for this?" Suzy asked me.

I shook my head. "How many people have already made the team?"

"Don't worry about that." Suzy put a hand on my back. "I'm rooting for you, Queenie."

"How much does it weigh?"

"Devilette lifted three hundred and fifty pounds."

"Jesus." I'd never lifted more than two-fifty.

Suzy went back to the other judges, and I walked over to the deadlift bar. I meant to keep my head down. Seeing people watching me wouldn't help. But I looked up anyway, scanning for Jason and Jenna.

They stood near the judges. When Jenna saw me looking, she nudged Jason, and they lifted their arms and made the Soiled Dove sign over their heads again.

I only needed to lift this thing once. And if I couldn't, I couldn't. *It won't be the end of the world, Boucher.* I bent my legs, my feet under the bar, and wrapped my hands around the grips the way that Suzy had taught me.

I heard Nana's voice in my head: *Like a gorilla about to sit in a chair.*

Back straight, ass out, I pulled. Nothing happened. Frozen, I didn't let up. I wrapped my hands tighter around the bar and imagined all the muscles involved in lifting this thing off the ground.

"Come on," I whispered. "Come on."

I belonged here. I was the Queen Beast.

I inhaled and pulled harder.

CHAPTER 22

Jenna chattered like a squirrel the first few minutes we were in Suzy's car. Jason was behind the wheel, taking Jenna home to face the music.

"I can't believe you lifted that thing off the ground, Celly," she said. "Aren't you excited? You made the team. Why aren't you more excited?"

"I am." I wasn't the type to squeal and bounce like my sister, but I was walking on air. I'd made the freaking team.

"Well, I'm excited."

The closer we got to Sun Valley, though, the less enthusiastic she became. Mom loomed on the horizon like a dark cloud. I did not envy my little sister the conversation she was about to have.

"I'll be right back," I said to Jason as I got out of the car with Jenna.

We stood together on the driveway, looking up at the house.

"What do I tell her?"

"Honestly?"

Jenna looked at me and nodded.

"The truth."

"I was afraid you'd say that."

The front door opened, and Mom was there, waiting for us. I had meant to go in and wash my face, but changed my mind. "Can I go get some lunch with Jason?"

Mom nodded, without taking her eyes off Jenna. She didn't look angry. She looked worried. I couldn't decide which was worse, and I was glad I wasn't on the receiving end of it, either way. Poor Jenna.

I got back in the car and Jason put it into reverse. It felt like escaping.

"Thanks for hanging out with her today," I said.

"I think she had fun. The Bees treated her like a little mascot."

"Bees?"

"You know…Hive? Bees?"

"Cute." My late night and early morning caught up with me as the adrenaline rush that came with hearing Suzy say my name when she read off the list of deadlifters on the competition team wore off.

"When do you see that therapist again?" Jason asked.

It took a minute for my sleepy brain to process his question. "What? I mean, I mean, I have a makeup group tonight and then my regular appointment on Thursday. But why?"

"You freaked me out this morning." He kept his eyes on the road as he drove back toward the Hive and a post-tryout potluck party.

"I didn't mean to." The truth was, though, I'd freaked myself out, too.

"Do you want to talk about it?"

I shook my head.

"You're OK, now?"

My instinct was to shoot back *I'm fine* without thinking about it. There was something about the way that Jason held himself as he drove, though, that made me return his question instead. He'd mentioned his sister that morning. And at karaoke. I hadn't had a chance to ask him about her. "Are *you* OK?"

"I am now."

"Do you want to talk about it?"

He kept his eyes on the road. "I had a hard time after Danielle died. Suzy saved me. Her boys were babies, and she took me in anyway. For a long time, I didn't think I deserved that."

"Of course you deserved it."

He took his eyes off the road long enough to look at me, then turned back away. "I know that now."

His sister drove her car into a streetlight. I couldn't make myself ask him if he thought Danielle had killed herself. Maybe I didn't want the answer.

When I was in the attic, standing on that chair, it was the thought of my sister finding me up there that finally kicked in my give-a-damn. So instead, I said, "I'm sorry I freaked you out."

"Will you talk to your therapist about it?"

"It's on my list."

He laughed and the tension in the car broke some. “You have a list?”

“Definitely.”

○ ○ ○

I felt pretty good when I made it to Betsy’s office for Saturday’s group. I would have skipped it, but I’d promised. I got there early, even, so I wouldn’t have to explain my fast exit the night before in front of anyone else.

Even climbing all those narrow stairs didn’t bother me this time.

“You’re in a good mood,” Betsy said as she moved to open the group room.

“I made the Hive’s competition team.”

Her round face broke into a wide smile. “Good job, Celly! That must be exciting.”

“It is. It was, I mean. I was nervous.”

“I want to hear all about it, but first can we talk about what happened yesterday?”

“I’m sorry about that,” I said. “My sister was in trouble, and I had to help her.”

“What kind of trouble?”

I looked at Betsy, weighing whether or not to tell her the whole truth. “She was just in a bad situation. Jason and I went to pick her up.”

Betsy nodded slowly. “Jason’s a good friend.”

Warmth spread over my face. Not the heat of embarrassment. Just a nice glow. "Yes."

"Is your sister OK?"

"Well, she had to talk to our mom about what happened. I think that was probably at least as traumatizing as—" I stumbled over my words, then decided to just be honest. "As being groped by her friend's older brother at a party she shouldn't have ever been at."

"You went and picked her up at the party?"

"Yeah." First item on my list of things to talk to her about. "Lou and Vivi were there."

"I can't talk to you too much about Vivi," Betsy said.

I waved that away. This wasn't about Vivi. "Lou's friends with the guy who got my little sister drunk and… well, I got there in time. Thank God. But Lou knew. I don't even know how to process that."

"Do you think he knew this other boy was dangerous for your sister?"

I shook my head. "I hope he just didn't think it through."

"Because you care about him."

"Because I don't want to have been that wrong about him."

Betsy put her bare feet on the floor. I wondered if she ever wore shoes. "That was a lot to have happen before your tryout."

Yeah. Item two on my list. "It kind of caught up with me."

"What do you mean?"

I'd promised Jason I'd do this. I felt so much better now that it almost seemed silly to bring it up at all, though, and for a minute I balanced in that place where I could still choose not to say it out loud.

"I woke up really early this morning and couldn't sleep, so I went for a walk and ended up at Jason's house."

Betsy listened while I told her what happened. Once I started talking, the whole story just came out.

"Were you having suicidal thoughts?" Betsy asked, her voice even.

"No." I didn't want to end up back at Doctor Harrison's office and in some kind of psychiatric hold. But also? It was the truth. "I don't know how to explain it. Maybe I had some kind of anxiety attack."

"Have you had anxiety before?"

"I don't know. I don't think so. I don't think I've ever let myself care as much about anything as I do about the Hive and—" Jason. I wasn't ready to say that out loud yet. Not until I figured out why his name was on the tip of my tongue.

"Vivi's going to be here tonight," Betsy said. "Are you OK with that? If you would rather move to Saturday permanently, I'm OK with that."

I had a longtime policy. I never let them make me run away. And Saturdays were for the Hive. "No. I'm good."

○ ○ ○

I knew before I saw her that Vivi would be at Saturday's group. She'd been at Corbin's party, same as me. Different reasons, but same result.

During both Friday groups I'd been to, she'd had her cheerleader uniform on. Tonight, she wore jeans and a T-shirt. Like a normal person.

Her hair was pulled back into a messy bun, and she didn't have any makeup on. She looked tired.

Vivi sat in the same chair she always did. She didn't look at me when she asked, "Is your sister OK?"

I lifted my eyebrows. "Since when do you care about my sister?"

"I didn't know she was there. Or Corbin's little sister, either. They shouldn't have been there."

"Right." Any idiot could say that after it was too late.

"Really. I didn't know."

"Lou did."

Vivi ran her tongue over her chapped bottom lip. "How did you know that he knew?"

I looked at the door, half hoping someone would come in and save me from this awkward conversation. No such luck. *All right, Queenie. If she wants this, let's do it.* I sat in a chair across from her. "He came to my house yesterday."

She nodded slowly, and it occurred to me that she wasn't tired. Or not just tired anyway. She'd been crying. Well, crap. I opened my mouth to say…something. I didn't even know what.

The group room door opened before I could figure it out, and a woman came in. She stopped in her tracks and looked at me and then Vivi as if maybe she was afraid she'd walked into the wrong therapist's office. "Hi."

I lifted a hand in greeting, but Vivi stood up and pushed her way out of the room.

"Damn it." I argued with myself for the space of two breaths. *I should just stay here. I absolutely should not chase after her.* But I was already coming around the table. I looked at the woman apologetically. "Sorry."

I was nearly out in the hall when I was stopped by the sound of someone retching behind me. I went back into Betsy's jungle room and knocked on the bathroom door.

"Vivi?" If she was in there barfing up her dinner because Lou had been at my house the afternoon before, I really didn't know how I was going to handle that. "Come on, Vivi. Don't do this."

She didn't answer, except with another gagging retch and a moan. I tried the doorknob and it opened in my hand.

"Oh God, just go away," she said without looking up. She had one hand on the edge of the toilet tank and the other arm wrapped around her stomach.

The office door opened. I went all the way into the bathroom and closed the door. "Are you seriously purging in your therapist's bathroom? That has to be the most meta thing I've ever heard of."

"I'm not purging."

Before I could argue with her, she moaned again and leaned into the toilet, dry heaving. No fingers down her throat. I picked a hand towel from a basket on the sink and ran it under cold water, rang it out, and handed it to her. "What's wrong?"

"Nothing."

"Oh, yeah? How stupid of me. You're obviously stellar."

Vivi straightened, held perfectly still for a second as if she was making sure that her stomach was going to behave, and then closed the toilet lid and sat on it. She patted the wet towel against her cheeks.

"I'll get Betsy," I finally said.

Vivi shook her head. "I'm OK now, I think."

This was a pretty extreme response to the idea that Lou had been at my house. It was on the tip of my tongue to apologize and tell her that nothing had really happened. It almost had, but it didn't.

Did I owe her that?

No, I decided. Lou probably did. But I didn't owe Vivi anything.

I had a flash in my mind's eye of Jason when he realized that I'd been with Lou just before we'd gone to the Soiled Dove concert.

Fuck. Why did this have to be so hard?

"I'm sorry about your locker."

I blinked at Vivi. "What?"

"I shouldn't have done that. I—" She threw the toilet seat up, and heaved again. Her stomach must have been empty, because as dramatic and awful as the sound was, nothing came out of her.

She must have the flu or…the truth hit me all at once, and my own stomach flopped over. "Oh, Vivi."

"Don't you dare," she said, still leaning over the toilet, one hand on either side of the seat. "Don't you dare feel sorry for me."

She really was the Robin Delaney of her generation. "Does Lou know?"

"I told him yesterday."

"At the party?"

She stood up again and sat on the toilet lid again before she looked up at me. "Yesterday morning."

He'd known. When he'd come to my house, when he'd pulled out that condom, he'd known that Vivi was pregnant. I leaned back against the sink. "What an asshole."

She nodded gently, as if she was afraid the movement might kick off her puking again.

"What are you going to do?"

She shrugged. "Marry the asshole."

"What?"

She stood up, flushed the toilet, and, when I moved out of the way, turned on the sink to wash her hands. "It's not like I have a ton of good choices."

"You have some choices, though."

She went out into the office and closed the door behind her, leaving me alone in the bathroom. I pulled my phone out of my back pocket and checked my texts. Nothing from Lou.

I was still used to waiting to hear from him first, but I typed a quick message and left the bathroom, too.

○ ○ ○

The Saturday group was oddly similar to the Friday group, only different. Like turning on a sitcom and seeing the same setting, the same story, with different actors.

I sat down next to Vivi without really thinking about it.

She looked up at me and didn't say anything nasty.

Betsy lifted her eyebrows at us and said, "Ready to get started?"

I nodded.

"Good. Why don't you introduce yourself, Celly."

Me first? Jesus. "Um. Hi, I'm Celly and I'm a fatass."

The younger girls sat across from me and they both giggled, on cue.

"How was your week, Celly?" Betsy asked, without taking the bait of my weird mood.

"It was actually—" I took a breath. How was my week? My mood lifted, suddenly. "Not too bad."

Betsy waited until I went on.

"I made the competition team at my gym," I said. "For deadlifts. And I had a lot of fun with my sister for the first time in forever."

"And you almost slept with my boyfriend," Vivi said, without sitting up from her slumped posture or uncrossing her arms from over her chest.

The breath went out of me, and I focused on a spot on the table in front of me. I hadn't told her that. Lou must have.

"Vivi," Betsy said.

"What? It's true."

Betsy pushed her chair back and stood up. "Step out here with me a minute?"

Vivi rolled her eyes, and I thought she was going to refuse, but she stood up and followed Betsy out to the hall.

"Drama," Sharon said. "Vivi is always so damn dramatic."

A painfully thin man sitting near the door with a meticulously groomed mustache snorted. "It's always drama when Vivi comes to our meeting."

It seemed like this day would never stop making me feel the need to defend my straight-up nemesis. "She's having a hard day."

"Are you friends with her?" one of the girls asked.

It was my turn to snort. "Not hardly."

The door opened again and Betsy and Vivi came back in. I expected some seat rearrangement, but Vivi just sat next to me again and said, "I'm sorry."

I didn't know what to say to that, but I didn't have to say anything. The man with the mustache started talking, taking his turn to update about his week.

"I'm Adam," he said, for my benefit. "My week was OK. I gained twelve ounces."

"No weight talk," the two girls said at the same time. He threw up his hands. "Fine. I had a date this week. It actually went pretty well. We went out to dinner, and I actually ate in front of him."

Everyone had a turn until it was finally Vivi's turn.

"I had a shit week," she said. "Yeah, it was pretty much one hundred percent shit."

My face burned and I hated knowing that everyone would see that her words affected me. Her bad week wasn't my fault. I mean it was hardly my fault that she didn't protect herself. She clearly had access to condoms.

My ungenerous thoughts made my face burn even hotter. Damn it.

I wondered if she was actually going to say the words *I'm*

pregnant out loud. She didn't. Instead, she said, "My boyfriend is an asshole. I lost my scholarship. And I've been puking all week."

CHAPTER 23

Dad was home alone when I walked in after the longest group-therapy session of all time.

"Where is everyone?"

"Mom and Jenna went to a Zumba class."

That was their way of making up. And Mom's way of keeping Jenna close and occupied on a Saturday night when my little sister's judgment was suspect.

"OK." I was suddenly bone tired. "I'm going to go lie down, I think."

Dad muted Fox News and turned to look at me. "Jenna said you made the competition team at the Hive."

I lifted my eyebrows. Did he even know what the Hive was? We hadn't spoken much since I'd started seeing Betsy. "For deadlifts."

"How much did you lift?"

For no real reason, my cheeks burned. "Three sixty."

His eyebrows shot up. "No kidding?"

I nodded.

"When's the competition?" he asked.

"There's a whole season. But the first one is in June."

"Can I come?"

Dad and Mom were good at being sports parents. Just not for me. Not because they wouldn't want to be, but because other than one season of soccer when I was ten, I'd never joined a team. I hadn't ever really given them a sideline to sit on.

They'd been to every one of Jenna's dance recitals and competitions. Somewhere along the way, I'd stopped tagging along.

"You can't bring your cowbell," I said. I wondered if he still had that thing. He'd embarrassed the hell out of me on the soccer field, ringing it every time one of my teammates got a goal.

"What? Everyone loves the cowbell."

Maybe spending hours watching on the sidelines was just what parents thought they were supposed to do when they had a kid involved in something. "Are you sure you want to come?"

He looked up at me, a little more intently than he had before. As if he was trying to see into me. And then he changed the subject. "How are things going with that therapist?"

"You're not supposed to ask that."

"I'm asking anyway." He moved his feet off the ottoman in front of his chair and sat up straighter, kicking it a little farther away from him so I'd have room to sit.

I hesitated a minute, but he waited me out, and I finally sat. "It's fine, Dad. I'm fine."

"You should have called me when Jenna needed a ride."

I opened my mouth, then closed it again. He was right, and there wasn't anything I could say to negate that. It hadn't even occurred to me. I started my next "Things to Talk to Betsy About" list with wondering why I went after Jenna on my own, instead of telling our parents.

I finally settled on, "I know."

"It sounds like Jenna's OK."

Anger bubbled up in me, and I wasn't sure where it was coming from.

"Are you going to make her go to therapy?"

"If we think she needs it," Dad said slowly.

"You won't."

"Therapy isn't a punishment, Celly."

I ran a hand through my hair. "Yeah, I know."

"What's bothering you?"

Damn it. What I wanted to do was muster up the nonchalance to say "nothing" and have him believe me. What came out when I opened my mouth was, "Do you ever regret having me?"

His eyebrows shot up. "Absolutely not."

If he'd hesitated even a second, I would have fallen apart. He hadn't, though. The answer was definitive and strong. "OK."

He leaned forward, his hands on his knees, and looked at me a heartbeat too long before he spoke again. "Are you trying to tell me something?"

It was my turn to shoot my eyebrows up into my hairline. "I'm not pregnant, Dad."

"Jenna?"

I shook my head. "Jesus, Dad. No one in this house is pregnant."

He sat back and exhaled. "Whose house then?"

"What?"

"You said no one in this house. What's going on? Is it that boy you've been walking to school with? Did he get some girl pregnant?"

I held up a hand, as if to ward even that thought away.

"No. It's not him. It's—" I snapped my mouth closed before Lou's name came out of it. Or Vivi's, because Dad might know her name from Lou. I wasn't ready to talk about this. "It's just some girl at school."

"I'm putting a box of condoms under the bathroom sink."

Heat rose up my cheeks, and I watched a matching flush climb his. "Jesus, Dad."

"I'm serious. I don't regret a single thing about you, Marcella Jane, but seventeen was too young. It is too young."

I stood up. "Well, I don't need a box of condoms. No one has to worry about me. Just ask Mom."

"Your mother sees herself in Jenna, so she worries about her more." Dad stood up, too. "I see myself in you."

And they had both been there when Mom got pregnant with me. He didn't say that part. I added "deal with being relieved my dad thinks some guy might want to sleep with me someday" to my

Betsy list.

I was going to be in therapy forever. Seriously. "I need a shower."

He pulled me into a hug and after he let me go again said, "Your mom doesn't understand what you're doing at the Hive, but she'll come around. And she'll be there."

I thought about Saralynn slipping into her dark house—her parents totally unaware about what was going on with her, or with her brother for that matter. "I know she will."

○ ○ ○

My phone's text message alert woke me from a dead sleep.

I was fully dressed, lying the wrong way in my bed, my head at the foot of the mattress.

For a minute, I couldn't swim all the way up to consciousness. I was disoriented, not sure what day it was or even where I was as I fought to sit up.

My muscles ached. I should have taken a shower before I lay down. The heat would have eased things. In fact, I decided, a shower now would help.

I dug my phone out of the blankets and looked at it, expecting to see some middle-of-the-night hour. It was only nine thirty. I'd only been asleep an hour. It felt like days.

As I stood up and started toward the dresser to grab pajamas to take into the bathroom with me, I checked my text messages.

Can we talk?

I hated, *hated*, that Lou's name and those three words together made my heart tighten. I hated that they meant anything to me at all. What I really wanted to do was ignore the message.

Or to type back: No, asshole, we can't.

What I typed was: About what?

I stood there, but he didn't answer right away, so I went down the hall to take my shower. I let the hot water run over me, trying hard to not keep one ear on my phone and failing miserably.

Maybe I just needed to hear him tell me that he was going to be a teenage father. Maybe that would give me the closure I needed to move past this thing. The fact that just knowing Vivi was pregnant wasn't enough made me feel a little sick to my stomach.

Who was really the asshole here?

I was out of the shower, in my pajamas with a towel wrapped around my wet hair, when my phone pinged again.

Meet me in your backyard.

You're in my backyard?

Yes.

I went to my window and pulled back the curtain. Lou sat at the picnic bench, staring at his phone. He didn't look up at me.

I got dressed and braided my hair. It would be a mess in the morning, but I wasn't going out there with a towel around my head. The house was quiet. Too quiet, really, for nine thirty on a Saturday night.

Jenna had been spending a lot of time in her bedroom, since she was grounded for the foreseeable future from everything but school and dance practice. I was sure she was in there now.

I heard the television on in our parents' bedroom.

Lou had no way of knowing my family was in bed so early. Did it mean something that he was there and didn't care who saw him?

Or maybe he did care. It wasn't like he had knocked on my front door like a normal person.

I pulled open the sliding glass door and walked out. Lou looked up at me without moving. He didn't flinch. God, he was so absolutely positive that it couldn't be anyone but me coming through that door.

What was it like to go through life so sure that you'd get just what you wanted?

"What are you doing here?"

He shrugged his shoulders. "I honestly don't know."

Might as well get this over with. "I saw Vivi this afternoon."

That got his attention. He looked up at me, sharply. "Where?"

I kept my mouth closed. When he didn't say anything else, I finally asked, "Why don't you just get it over with, Lou?"

"She told you."

I didn't bother to answer. Lou pulled his cigarettes out of his hoodie pocket and tapped one out of the pack. I looked toward the house, but everything was still quiet and dark inside.

He lit his cigarette with a cheap plastic lighter and inhaled. "I can't believe how much this sucks."

Was he here for sympathy? Seriously? "I'm sure it's no picnic for Vivi either. Pregnant cheerleader is about as cliché as it gets."

"She's giving up her scholarship."

I mean. "Pregnant cheerleader actually sounds pretty impossible."

He took another drag from his cigarette. "I broke up with her, you know?"

My heart betrayed me. It jerked against my ribs and then my brain followed suit, kicking up an image of Lou telling me that Vivi's baby wasn't his and that I was all he'd ever wanted.

Fuck. What was wrong with me?

"No," I said. At least as much in answer to his question as to my own ridiculous inner monologue. "I didn't know."

"After that thing with your locker. That was so out of line."

"You were at Corbin's party with her."

"She wants to get back together." He looked at me. "I had no idea what she was planning for those condoms."

So, they were his. "I can think of something better they could have been used for."

He inhaled sharply and then flung his cigarette into the grass. How many had I picked up after he'd left? "I don't want any of this."

Welcome to the real world, Lou Duncan, where people have to do shit they don't want to do. "What are you going to do?"

"I'm not giving up my baseball scholarship. I'm not turning into your dad."

I narrowed my eyes. "What's that supposed to mean?"

"I'm not going to wind up in Sun Valley for the rest of my life, working at Belly Busters."

"He owns Belly Busters," I pointed out. "And he's happy."

"Are you sure about that? He talks all the time about how he missed out on the NFL."

One: My dad did not miss out on the NFL. He missed out on playing football in college. Not the same thing. Two: "I can think of something my dad could have done with a box of condoms in high school, too."

Lou grunted. "I don't need you to judge me, Celly."

It bordered on absurd, that this stratosphere boy was sitting in my backyard, trying to make me understand him. He'd come to me. "What do you need?"

Lou untangled his long legs from the picnic table and came to his feet. "Sympathy, I guess. I don't know."

"Have you told your mom?"

His face crumbled, and I blinked back surprise. He was on the verge of tears. "I don't want her to ever know."

"Hiding a grandchild forever might be a little hard."

"Yeah."

"Like, kind of impossible."

He ran a hand through his hair. "How am I going to tell her?"

"Hey, Mom, I knocked up Vivi Hughes and you're going to be a grandma."

"Not helpful."

My first thought was at least it isn't me. I hated the chaser though, because I couldn't even decide what it meant. Why isn't it me?

I absolutely did not want to be jealous of Vivi Hughes right now. But I couldn't help it. I was an expert at daydreaming about Lou Duncan, and I saw so clearly the two of them getting married, living in a cute little house with their baby.

Just making their way, like some fucking sitcom.

And why isn't it me? That thought made me an idiot.

"I don't know what you want from me," I said. "I told you that you should break up with her months ago."

"I'm going to."

I tilted my head as he tapped another cigarette out of his pack. "You're going to what?"

"Break up with Vivi."

"You just got done telling me that you already broke up with her."

He closed his eyes and put the cigarette in his mouth. Didn't even bother to acknowledge that I'd caught him in a lie.

"You waited until she was pregnant to decide to really leave her?"

He lit up. "What am I supposed to do? She wants to get married. I'm not going to marry her."

It wouldn't be helpful to point out that he might have thought about that before he slept with her. "I doubt she actually wants to marry you, Lou."

He looked up at me. "What?"

"I mean, she wants to go to Brigham Young. She wants to be a cheerleader."

He took a draw on his cigarette and held the smoke a long time before exhaling. "Then she should."

I opened my mouth, then closed it again. The only way she could go to Utah and be a cheerleader was if she wasn't pregnant anymore. If she had an abortion, which took this way, way outside my business.

I really wasn't getting into this part of this conversation with him.

He tossed his second cigarette into the grass, half smoked, and reached across the table to pull my braid over my shoulder and tug the elastic from the end of it.

"What are you doing, Lou?"

"We were supposed to go to Las Vegas together."

I was aware of that. I'd been holding on to it pretty damn desperately for months. I had some experience with disappointment, though. Lou was acting like this was the first time he'd ever had to deal with something not happening the way he wanted it to.

"I guess even you can't always get what you want," I finally said.

He pulled his hand back from my hair. "Bullshit."

I mean. I didn't disagree. Right out here in my backyard, not very long ago, he'd reminded me of the rules. Vivi must have already been pregnant when she loaded my locker with school-bathroom hand soap and Lou's condoms.

Tears surprised me, welling up too fast for me to do anything about them. I inhaled sharply, trying to stop them before they fell, but it was no use.

"Christ, Celly." Right, he was here for me to comfort him. Asshole.

I stood up and wiped at my damp cheeks. I never let them see me cry. That was my rule. And it included Lou. I did what I should have done months ago.

"Pick up your butts," I said.

And then I walked away.

CHAPTER 24

By the time my next one-on-one session with Betsy came around, my list of things to talk about with her had grown.

"I've had a crazy week," I told her.

"I want to hear about it, but we need to talk."

My stomach sunk. Those words almost never meant something good. "About what?"

"I'd like to talk to you about seeing another therapist for your one-on-one sessions."

"You're firing me."

Her round face registered surprise. "Those aren't the words I'd use."

"But it's true. You don't want to be my therapist anymore."

"This isn't about what I want, Celly. It's about getting you the best possible care."

"You said there aren't any other local therapists who specialize in eating disorders."

"That's technically true."

Technically. What she'd meant when she told me that was *I'm the only childhood obesity specialist around.* Vivi wasn't obese. Why did I always have to accommodate her? "Maybe Vivi can get referred to someone else."

Betsy inhaled slowly. "I can't talk to you about another client, Celly."

"This isn't fair."

"It's a fine line," Betsy said. "I can't talk to you about Vivi. But, because there aren't other choices, I can keep treating you both in a group setting. And I can find someone else to treat you one-on-one."

"Someone for me. Not her," I pointed out.

Betsy didn't answer that. Instead, she said, "Let's try on some rules."

I rolled my eyes and leaned my head back against the sofa. Rules were going to kill me. "Whatever."

"I can't talk to you about Vivi. I can listen today and going forward, in group. And I have someone in mind who is a good fit and doesn't have a conflict."

I didn't want another therapist. It was hard enough getting to where I could talk to her. "Forget it. I don't have to talk about it at all."

"Tell me what's bothering you, Celly."

I thought for a moment, wondering if I could find a way to not make this about Vivi at all. "Remember the boy?"

"I remember two boys," she said.

"The first one."

"Your boyfriend."

I tilted my head side-to-side. "He's not my boyfriend. But yeah, him."

"I remember."

"He's having a baby."

I wasn't sure what I expected. Not a small, sympathetic nod and no sign of revelation at all. She knew already. "How does that make you feel?"

"I have no idea."

"Are you sure?"

Pretty sure. My feelings about Lou were so fucked up. He was an asshole. I'd been in love with him for what felt like most of my life but was really less than a year. "He makes me feel like an idiot."

She didn't speak, just waited me out.

"I mean, pretty stupid of me to think that there was some world where I'd be with someone like him for real."

Boys like Lou Duncan didn't screw up their lives with girls like me. They didn't.

Ugh. Get a grip, Boucher.

I refused to be jealous of Vivi Hughes right then.

"You aren't stupid, Celly. And it makes perfect sense to me that he likes you. You're smart and funny and—"

"And fat," I finished for her, whether she was going there or not.

"And fantastic," she finished for herself.

"He came to my house last night. He wanted me to make him feel better about not giving up his scholarship the way my dad did after high school."

"Your father gave up a scholarship?"

"Because my mom was pregnant with me."

She stayed quiet and just let me talk.

"Have I told you that before? My parents are pretty much a Lifetime movie. Mom was pregnant with me when they graduated. They gave up their athletic scholarships and stayed in Sun Valley, got married, and here we are."

"How did things turn out for them?"

"Well, their baby is now a fat teenager who tried to hang herself in the attic and needs therapy." I breathed hard and my heart felt strangled by my ribs. That was the first time I'd said that out loud. "Not on purpose. I didn't really try to."

"I have a suggestion," Betsy said, slowly, like she was choosing her words with care.

"OK."

"I'd like you to see Ursula."

"Who's Ursula?"

"She's a graduate student I've been working with."

I looked at the ceiling. "Of course you would. Why upset Vivi's perfect little world?"

"I don't want to upset anyone's world," Betsy said. "That's the point."

"But if you have to, of course it's mine. It makes perfect sense." I stood up. "Lou thinks he can just go about his life and do whatever he wants. Vivi expects everyone to bend over backward for her. And why not? That's exactly what's always happened."

"Please sit down, Celly."

"Or what? You're going to tell my dad? I'm going to end up in the hospital on a psychiatric hold? I don't care. I'm not suicidal. So, bring it on. I'm so over this."

"I've already told you—"

"Right, it only works if I want to be there. Well, I don't want to be Ursula's patient." I flopped down on the sofa again. "She's not even a real therapist."

"Yes, she is. And she's very good."

"So, send Vivi to her." Betsy didn't respond. She also didn't look like she was considering it. Maybe she already had. Maybe she'd done this with Vivi already. Did they sit around talking about me? That thought made me want to gag. "God. You know what? Fine."

"You'll see Ursula?"

"I can't talk to you anyway."

At least that got a reaction from her. She winced. "If you're more comfortable at the Saturday—"

"No. I'm at the Hive Saturday nights. Except this Saturday. I'll be at Morp."

She looked at me like I'd suddenly started speaking French.

"Reverse prom?"

"Oh. Right." Betsy pulled her legs up, cross-legged, and leaned toward me. "You're going with Jason, right?"

"Yes."

"How do you feel about that?"

I lifted my eyebrows. "We're still doing this?"

"If you want to."

I leaned back and looked at the clock on the wall behind her. For the next twenty minutes, I stared at my hands in my lap.

Usually the silence would have gotten to me, but this time I just thought about Vivi sitting in my place and Betsy letting her know that the conflict was resolved. I'd been removed from the equation.

I needed Betsy, and she'd pawned me off on someone else. And of course Vivi wouldn't have expected anything else.

When the clock ticked over to the last minute of my time, I came to my feet.

"I'll set your appointment with Ursula for the same time next week," Betsy said.

"Sure."

"I know you're upset. I promise, I'm not abandoning you. You'll meet with her here, in my office. I can be there for the first session, if you'd like. And I'll see you at group tomorrow."

"Do I have to still come to group?"

Betsy stood up, too, and looked at me with so much pity in her face. "I really hope you will."

I shrugged. "If I don't have to, I'd rather not. You and Vivi will be talking about me, and I don't really want to be in the same room with that."

"No," Betsy said, her voice sharper. "I can't discuss another client with you, but that isn't something you have to worry about."

"Right." As if Vivi wasn't going to talk about her pregnant teenage client's baby daddy's down-low girlfriend. I was so out of this whole nightmare. "Anyway."

"At least come tomorrow," Betsy said. "Don't make a decision without all the facts."

"Facts?"

"See how you feel in an actual group tomorrow."

I just needed out of the room. "Fine."

○ ○ ○

I left Betsy's office and drove to the Hive to meet Jason and Suzy for a workout. I was an official part of the competition team now. That meant showing up to train even if I felt like the aftermath of a trainwreck.

My head was so full of thoughts I wished would go away, it actually hurt. I couldn't stop thinking about Lou and Vivi. They mixed up with my parents in my imagination.

My parents were happy together.

Sure, my mother had some issues. She'd probably benefit from one of Betsy's groups. And my father apparently waxed nostalgic over some professional sports career that probably wouldn't really have been a thing anyway.

But overall, they were happy.

Lou and Vivi probably would be, too. Once they got past the whole "pregnant in high school" thing. A year or two from now, they'd be a family, and all this drama would be over.

I wasn't part of the equation. At all.

Thankfully, the Hive worked its magic on me. The music pulsed and chased out visions of Lou and Vivi's domestic bliss. They didn't belong here.

"Hey." Jason waited for me when I came out of the locker room. "Ready?"

I nodded, and we started to walk around the track marked around the perimeter of the warehouse. Eleven trips around was a mile. I had to walk slightly faster than strictly comfortable to keep up with Jason's longer stride.

"Is everything OK?" he asked when we were about half a mile in.

I started to say that everything was fine, but the words caught in my throat. To my horror, tears were suddenly right at the surface. They didn't fall, but it was close. Apparently, I was going to cry in front of both Lou and Jason in the same twenty-four hours.

What the actual hell?

"Celly?" Jason slowed his pace but didn't stop. "What's wrong?"

"Nothing," I finally got out. "I'm fine."

"Bullshit."

I grunted and walked off the track, to the bleachers just to our right. In a perfect world, Jason would have kept warming up and left me alone for a minute. Instead, he followed and sat next to me.

"Vivi Hughes is pregnant," I said.

Jason's woodland-creature thing was enhanced when he was surprised. That had to be some kind of survival mechanism. It was impossible to be pissed off at someone who was so damned adorable.

"That's—" He cut himself off. I didn't blame him.

I was making a fool of myself. I wiped my face with the back of my hand and sat up straighter. "It's stupid."

"Among other things. So, Lou?"

I nodded, not trusting myself to speak. This really was stupid. I never cried. Ever. It seemed important to me, suddenly, that Jason know that it wasn't Lou I was upset about. "I need a new therapist."

"What? Why?"

I looked at the floor between my feet. I hadn't told Jason that Vivi was seeing Betsy, too. Why was I so hell-bent on protecting her? "I just do."

"OK." Jason shook his head. "That sucks."

"I actually think I'm going to try to talk my dad out of making me do any of this anymore."

Jason opened his legs enough that the outside of one of his thighs bumped against mine. "You sure?"

I nodded. "I mean, what's the point. The new therapist is a student. She's probably going to suck."

"But, maybe she won't."

I huffed a half laugh. "Right."

Jason stood up. He didn't start walking again until I did. And then he stayed right beside me.

CHAPTER 25

In the end, I went to Friday night's group because I didn't want to let Vivi chase me out of it. Or Betsy either, for that matter. I never cried in front of them, and I never let them make me run.

I'd cried twice in twenty-four hours. I wasn't going to run, too. I'd go, I decided. Prove to myself that it was useless, then talk to Dad about it.

What I didn't expect was to find Vivi Hughes leaning against the wall outside Betsy's office building, hyperventilating. She had her hands on her knees and gasped in breaths like she was a fish out of water.

I couldn't get into the building without passing by her. I meant to just pretend like Vivi wasn't there. I was good at that. But when I walked in front of her, she stood up straight and said, "Why are you doing this to me?"

I stopped and looked at her, trying to put her words into some sort of context. "What are you talking about?"

"I was fine, you know?" She walked toward me, and I took a step back. She had that honey badger thing turned up to eleven.

"Right, fine. Clearly."

"I was. Things were good with Lou. And I had a scholarship for next year."

"I know you're not blaming me for losing your scholarship."

She snorted and shook her head. "Of course not. Nothing's your fault, right? You're the victim here."

"You filled my locker with—"

"You fucked my boyfriend."

I stared at her until I could form a coherent response to that. "Did he tell you that?"

"Not that it was you." She leaned against the wall again. "He wouldn't tell me who. I can see why, now."

Ouch. "Don't worry. He didn't fuck the fat girl. Your world is intact."

I started past her, toward the door, but she moved in front of it to stop me. "Are you telling me you didn't sleep with Lou?"

"This is so beyond none of your business."

Her face softened and suddenly she looked like just what she was—a scared, pregnant, teenage girl. "Please, Celly."

"No, all right? I didn't sleep with Lou."

She moved away from the front of the door, back to where she stood earlier. I really hated the surge of sympathy I felt toward her.

What I wanted to do was just go inside and get this group session over with. But before I could stop myself, I asked, "Are you OK?"

Vivi looked up at me. "No. I'm not OK. I don't know how I'm supposed to do this without Betsy."

I swept a hand toward the door. "Betsy's right through there, waiting to let us up to the group room."

"She's pawning me off on another therapist. Because of you."

Wait. What? "You're not seeing Betsy anymore?"

"As if you didn't know."

"I didn't know." I looked at the door again, then back at Vivi. "If you want, I'll tell her—"

"Bitch, you've done enough, haven't you?"

I stepped back, away from her. "I wouldn't be here at all if you hadn't turned the whole school against me."

"You wouldn't be here at all if you hadn't asked my boyfriend to Morp in front of the whole school," she said. "And my life would still make sense."

Well. Shit. "I can't believe we're even having this conversation."

"Betsy's been my therapist since the seventh grade," she said. "Why did you have to come here?"

"Because, you narcissistic honey badger, I tried to hang myself in my attic and I didn't have a choice."

"You were sleeping with my boyfriend!"

"No. I wasn't."

She rolled her eyes. "Well, you wanted to."

I opened my mouth, but nothing came out. It wasn't true. I didn't want to sleep with her boyfriend. I wanted him not to be her boyfriend. I couldn't think of a way to say that without sounding like a bitch.

What came out of my mouth, finally, surprised me as much as it seemed to surprise her. "I'm sorry."

The biggest surprise was that I meant it.

She took a deep breath and straightened up again. "So am I."

I opened the door and felt her take it from me so that she could follow me inside.

○ ○ ○

"You look like a Viking princess," Jenna said.

I highly doubted that. I sat at my desk chair and my sister stood behind me, doing something to my hair. Something that felt like it was taking a thousand years. "This seems like overkill."

"No way."

I wore my upcycled Soiled Dove T-shirt with a black tank top under it, because even if I was inclined to go to a school dance with side boob showing, it wouldn't be allowed. Jenna had paired it with a long black skirt and my combat boots.

"Seriously," she said as she sprayed my head with an aerosol can. "You look killer."

I turned in my chair to face her and she handed me a tube of lipstick. Deep purple. It must have belonged to her, because I didn't recognize it.

I stood up and turned to look in my mirror, to apply the lipstick, and froze. She'd weaved my hair into an intricate series of braids, pulled tight back on one side and arranged nearly into a crown. She was right. I looked like a Viking princess. Not precious. Fierce.

I opened the tube of lipstick and added the final touch.

"I told you so," she said.

I turned to face her. "Yeah?"

"Oh, yeah."

The doorbell rang, and my stomach did a funny flip. Silly. It was only Jason. Jenna bounced on her toes and waited for me to go answer. I just stood there.

"What are you doing?" she asked. "Come on!"

"Maybe I should just wear my hair down."

"Don't even think about it."

"I look—" I just shook my head. I didn't know how to finish that sentence. I looked like someone who wanted attention. I could dress like this at the Hive. And with Jason. But at school?

"You look amazing." We both turned toward my bedroom door. Mom stood there with her cell phone in her hand, ready to take pictures. "Jason's here. But, wait. You need one more thing. Don't move."

Jenna and I stood in my room for a minute while Mom disappeared and then came back. She handed me a white rosebud with the stem trimmed to a couple of inches long. All of the thorns were removed.

"Is that from the front yard?" I asked.

She gestured for me to bend down a little and, when I did, she pushed the rose stem into my hair behind my left ear. "Gorgeous."

I turned to look, the scent of the rose filling my nose. She was right. It was perfect. "Thanks."

"OK. Jason's waiting. He brought Suzy's car."

Just *Suzy*. Not *that Suzy*. Progress.

Jason stood with Dad in the living room. He wore a black fedora and a white tuxedo jacket over his black jeans and Soiled Dove T-shirt. White brocade, I corrected myself as I got closer. It was over-the-top fancy. "Did you raid the wedding shop?"

"The thrift store." His face cracked into a wide smile. "Am I Morp appropriate?"

"Definitely."

"You look fantastic."

I waved that off but stopped when he reached for the coffee table and a box I hadn't seen there before. A corsage centered around a deep-purple flower I didn't recognize. I wondered if Jenna had known he was bringing it. The color matched my lipstick perfectly.

"You didn't have to do that."

"I wanted to." He opened it and held the elastic so I could slip my hand into it.

Without taking time to think it through, I pulled the rose from behind my ear and slipped it into the buttonhole in his crazy jacket's lapel.

"Now we're both snazzy."

He grinned his woodland-creature grin and Mom snapped a picture.

She made us pose in the living room and on the front porch and finally let us go to Suzy's car.

○ ○ ○

Prom would be held in a few weeks in the ballroom of a casino in Reno. Morp was smaller and less important. We drove the familiar route to Twain High School, where the gym was decorated with streamers and twinkle lights.

Two theater kids ran the music and lighting. The student government served punch and cookies. This was the dorkiest event of the whole year. And it was packed, wall-to-wall, with kids from every level of the social atmosphere dressed to match their dates.

In my bedroom, I thought I'd stand out. But once we were there, I realized I didn't have to worry. No one stared. Or mooed. Or even looked at us, really.

Jason took my hand and led the way into the gym after I handed over our tickets. There wasn't any romantic undertone to the gesture. More like a joining of forces. There were a lot of people packed into a small space.

We were herded toward a picture-taking station where someone had set up a background that looked like a Hawaiian waterfall. Jossue Cruz stood in front of it with his arm around a girl I didn't recognize. He caught sight of Jason and lifted his chin, his eyes narrowing.

"Have you had more trouble with him?" I asked.

Jason lifted his shoulders and shook his head. "Not really."

We moved forward as the photographer snapped shots. A group of half a dozen girls all wearing matching plaid shirts went after Jossue, posing in a sort of pyramid. A pair of stratosphere couples took their photo together next.

When it was our turn, Jason and I stood next to each other and I suddenly felt awkward. All we needed was pitchforks and we'd be that weird old couple in front of the farmhouse. I turned to look at him just as the photographer started to count backward from three.

Jason took my face in his hands, popped one long leg back behind him, and kissed my cheek just as the flash popped.

"Cute," the photographer said, then waved us off so the people behind us could have a turn.

"Want to dance?" Jason asked me.

The theater kids were playing a song with a pulsing beat. The center of the gym was filled with kids all bouncing to it, arms lifted. My gut instinct was to go sit in the bleachers and watch. But Jason was already bouncing.

We were going to stick out like a sore thumb. The freakishly tall new kid and the fat girl.

"Sure," I finally said.

He took my hand again and made his way through the crowd. Not to the edge of the dance floor. He kept moving until we were in the center of it. A familiar heat rose from my chest over my face, but when Jason lifted his arms and started bouncing on his toes, I took a breath and did the same.

By the time the first song was over and the next started, it was clear that no one cared that I was in the middle of the dance floor with Jason. It didn't trigger a round of mooing. No one even looked at us at all, as far as I could tell.

I heard Lou before I saw him. His voice cut through the music and the noise of a couple hundred kids singing along.

"Jesus Christ, Vivi!"

I turned toward him. He stood a few yards from me, at the edge of the dance floor. Close enough that I was surprised that I hadn't already noticed him. His white button-down shirt was soaked.

Vivi stood in front of him, a matching shirt tied at her waist, holding an empty cup.

The crowd had parted for them. It was normal for them to have that effect, but in this case, it was probably to avoid whatever it was she'd thrown all over him.

Lou pulled his wet shirt away from his chest. "What's wrong with you?"

"I can't believe you gave me alcohol," she yelled back at him.

Lou looked around, as if noticing for the first time that there other people in the room. "Shut the fuck up."

"Why? You don't want people to know I'm pregnant?"

Oh. Wow. The noise level dropped instantly. So did the dancing. Vivi, maybe belatedly, seemed to notice the rest of us. She pushed Lou with both hands on his chest and then stalked off, away from the dance floor.

Lou stood there a minute. The room erupted. *Vivi's pregnant? There's alcohol? What just happened?* And laughter.

"Hey, Lou!" one guy called out. "At least it's not Belly!"

And then he mooed.

I tensed, waiting for a replay of the day that Shannon Peterson read out "Lou Duncan from Celly Boucher." My heart beat faster and I felt a kind of ghost nausea.

"Shut the fuck up," Lou shot back, this time at the kid who mooed.

The chaos lost momentum almost immediately. I doubted that it would have any consequence for either Lou or Vivi, socially.

Hell. It might elevate them.

The most stratosphere of all stratosphere couples at Twain High School were having a baby. How cute.

Lou caught my eye, then went after Vivi.

The music switched abruptly. I saw the vice principal talking to one of the theater kids as the hard-hitting dance music softened to a slow song.

No hesitation on stopping this particular train wreck. Good bet that no one would end up in ISS for their own good.

I looked up at Jason, and he lifted his eyebrows. He tilted his hat back on his head and held his arms open for me. The dance floor emptied by half when the music slowed. Self-consciousness made me awkward, but I moved close and wrapped my arms around his neck.

"I don't really know how to do this," I said.

He shrugged. "Me, either."

I laughed a little and then rested my head on his shoulder. His arms went around me, and we swayed together to the music as the lights dimmed.

Seemed a little ridiculous to me that the vice principal thought the answer to a scene caused by a pregnant teenager and her boyfriend was to dim the lights and encourage more teenagers to snuggle up.

Jason's fingers tugged at the ends of my hair a little and I looked up at him. For the second time, I knew for sure that he was about to kiss me. In the middle of the dance floor at Morp.

I chickened out and put my head back on his shoulder. He stiffened, but only for a second, and then relaxed and just danced with me. Kissing Jason would have consequences. I wasn't ready to face them, yet. Especially not in the middle of a school dance.

○ ○ ○

Jason leaned down in the middle of the last dance of the night, so I could hear him. "We need pancakes."

"We definitely need pancakes."

His woodland face broke into a grin and he tilted his head toward the door. The gym was already less crowded, but fresh air and less noise suddenly seemed like a great idea.

Once we were outside, I rubbed at my ringing ears. "That was fun."

Jason nodded. "Way more fun than I expected."

I looked at him over the top of Suzy's car as he unlocked the doors with the button on the key fob. "You didn't think we were going to have fun?"

"I mean, it's a school dance." He got into the car and waited for me before he finished. "Did you expect to have fun?"

Actually, I had. Not because of the dance. I'd expected it because I always had fun with Jason. I filed that away though, to think about later.

The start of my Ursula list, I guessed.

"Where should we go?" he asked when I didn't answer his question.

"Edith's. Definitely, Edith's."

Edith's had the best pancakes in Reno. It was worth the drive into town. Apparently, we weren't the only people who thought so, because by the time we got there, half the tables were filled with Twain students.

The waitress sat us at a booth and handed us menus. "Cool T-shirts," she said. "I love Soiled Dove."

"Are you ready for your audition tomorrow?" I asked Jason as she walked away.

"Not even a little bit."

"You're going to kill it."

He leaned back in his seat, one long leg extending across to my side of the booth. "It's going to kill me."

"I don't know why you're so nervous. You're incredible."

"I just get up there and I can't make myself sing. It's like there's a big cork in me."

"You've never been able to sing in public?"

The waitress came back with ice water. "What can I get you?"

"Pancakes," we said at the same time.

"And coffee," Jason added.

She smiled and made a note on her pad as she walked away.

"I used to sing with my sister all the time," he said when she was gone again. "It's been really hard to do it without her."

It was so weird to think of Jason insecure. He always seemed like he fit comfortably in his own skin. "You have to know how good you are."

He brushed that off with one hand. "It's not about confidence."

"Then what?"

"All those people looking at me." He took off his hat and sat it on the seat beside him, then ran his hands through his curly hair. "I open my mouth, and nothing comes out."

"Maybe you could close your eyes."

Jason took a sip of his coffee. "That was weird with Lou and Vivi, huh?"

Smooth. I let him change the subject, though. "Super weird."

He shook his head. "Crazy kids. I wonder if they'll make it."

"People like them have a way of landing on their feet." There was more bitterness in my voice than I meant to let through.

"Are you OK?" he asked, more serious.

I shrugged. "Why wouldn't I be?"

"Well," he said, slowly. "Last week you almost slept with him."

The waitress came back with our coffee before I could respond to that little bit of friendly reminder. After she left, I poured two sugar packets and a little plastic cup of fake creamer into my cup. "It doesn't have anything to do with me."

"Danielle had a baby the year our parents took off."

It took a minute for my brain to change tracks. "Really?"

He nodded and sipped his own coffee. Black. "The year our parents—"

I waited for him to finish, but the silence got to me. "You're an uncle?"

"I guess so?" He put his cup down and poured milk into his cup. "She put the baby up for adoption. I was only four when the baby was born. She was nineteen."

I stirred my coffee slowly as I processed that. "She gave up her baby and then raised you?"

"Yeah." His spoon tinked against the side of his cup. Not randomly. A rhythm, like he heard a song in his head and it was coming out through his hand. "Pretty fucked up, huh?"

"Yeah."

"After all that, our parents dumped me on her."

"You really don't know where they are?"

He shook his head. "She never talked about them. They've never tried to find me, as far as I know. Suzy says Danielle never told her anything about what happened, either."

I couldn't imagine my parents disappearing on Jenna and me. My brain just refused to compute how awful that would be. I couldn't handle a vandalized locker and a bunch of asshole kids mooing at me. I couldn't manage to stop daydreaming about a guy who'd gotten another girl pregnant.

How was Jason the most together person I knew?

"Your sister must have loved you so much," I said, quietly.

"She did."

I bumped my leg against his under the table. He smiled across the table at me, then shook himself, like he was shaking off sad memories.

Our pancakes arrived, and we both sat up straighter.

"Enjoy," the waitress said as she sat a syrup dispenser between us.

My mother would fall over if someone sat this many carbs in front of her at ten thirty at night. I didn't think she'd eaten as much as a crouton after lunch in a decade.

"You must think I'm ridiculous," I said.

Jason stopped his fork halfway to his mouth. "What?"

"All of this stuff. With Lou and Vivi and those stupid kids at school. You must think I'm ridiculous to let it upset me so much."

"I don't think that."

I took a bite of syrupy pancake. "I think it."

Jason turned to the tiny jukebox sitting at the back end of our table. Every table in Edith's had one with the songs displayed on menu-like pages that slid along a track. When someone made a choice, it activated the big jukebox at the front of the store and played the song over the speakers throughout the restaurant.

Jenna and I used to love taking turns feeding the thing quarters and making old songs play.

Jason dug in his pocket and came up with a coin after flipping through the choices. He finally punched in some numbers. "I love this one." I recognized the song right away. No preamble, just a slow, sort of sad voice singing.

Sitting in the morning sun, I'll be sitting when the evening comes.

Jason leaned back and closed his eyes. His leg moved against mine as he tapped a foot along with the song. After the first verse, I sang along. Jason hummed at first, his eyes still closed, then sang, too.

His voice was beautiful. Clear and deeper than I'd expect it to be. It took my breath away. Whatever his stage fright was, he was going to have to figure out a way to break it. That's all there was to it.

He still had another choice left on his quarter. I reached for the jukebox when the song was done and typed in some numbers from memory. This was the song I always picked, every time my parents brought us here.

Jason grinned and opened his eyes. He sang this one from the start.

I laughed as he beat his fingers against the table and really getting into it. He reached for my hands and leaned in toward me.

Everyday seems a little longer, every way, loves a little stronger, come what may, do you ever long for true love from me?

He looked at me so intensely that I actually opened my mouth to answer. But before I could say anything, he got silly again, jutting his chin out and exaggerating the lyrics as he sang along.

Me—ee, ee, ee, ee, ee.

"See," I said when the music faded. "You can do this."

"I can sing to you." He took his hands back and forked up a bite of pancake. "I'm pretty sure you don't want to spend the rest of your life going around with me so that I can actually get a song out of my mouth."

I shrugged. "I mean, not the rest of my life. But I'll be at your audition."

"I'm really thinking I might just skip it."

"What? You can't do that."

"I can too."

"The flyer said they're going to Sacramento next week. If you miss this, you won't get another chance."

"I mean, they're not going to hire a kid, right?"

"They sure will, when they hear you."

"And anyway, I'm going to UNLV in the fall. Am I seriously going to skip college to—"

"Wait." I held up a hand to stop him. "You're going to UNLV?"

How had we never talked about this before? I clapped my hands, because I had to do something with the pure joy that filled me up.

"You're going to Las Vegas?" he asked.

I nodded.

"But if Soiled Dove actually picks me…"

If Soiled Dove actually picked him, then I'd be back to going off to college by myself. I screwed up my face, trying to be funny, and said, "Maybe I won't go with you tomorrow after all."

He narrowed his eyes. My joke missed the mark. "You think it would be better for me to go to college?"

I shook my head. "That's not what I meant. I just think it'll be cool if we're together next year. Don't you?"

"Yeah." He sat back in his seat. "I do."

"Like, really cool."

He smiled. "Agree."

"You have to go to that audition tomorrow, Jason. Or else you'll never know."

"I'm going to humiliate myself."

"No, you're not."

"I'm eighty-seven percent sure I am."

"Well," I said, "then you're going to surprise yourself."

When Soiled Dove picked him—and I knew they would—he'd stay here next year. They were based in Reno. I'd already been accepted to UNLV, but UNR wouldn't be so bad. A little close to home, but I'd have Jason and the Hive.

I didn't even think about how that would mean not going to school with Lou until I was in bed that night. And even then, it didn't really bother me.

Interesting.

CHAPTER 26

Jason and I worked out at the Hive the day after Morp.

I was on my way to home to change and get ready to hang out with him before his audition and hopefully keep his nerves from taking over.

When my phone rang, I answered without looking at who was calling. "I'll be there in twenty minutes."

"Celly?"

The car in front of me slowed for a red light, and I almost rear-ended it. I stepped hard on the break, and my seatbelt tightened as the momentum flung me against it. "Jesus."

"It's Lou."

"Yes, I know." I took a breath. "Why are you calling me?"

"I just wanted to hear your voice."

Are you fucking kidding me? "Just hang on a second."

The light turned green. I turned on my blinker and pulled into the parking lot of the McDonald's on the other side of the intersection.

I could not drive and do this at the same time.

"Are you OK?" I asked, after I stopped the car.

"Not really."

"What's wrong?"

I heard him breathing, but the silence dragged on long enough for me to wonder if there was something wrong with the connection. "Lou?"

"Can you come over?"

My eyebrows shot up. "To your house?"

"Yeah."

"You want me to come to your house?"

"Celly."

What alternate universe had I stumbled into? "I don't think so."

"You won't come over?"

"Why don't you call Vivi?"

"Because you're my best friend."

Of all of the things he could have said to me—that was the one that drove a knife into my heart. The idea that Lou and I were friends mattered to me.

It meant that I wasn't just the fat girl who went further than his girlfriend would. Because, clearly, I wasn't even that.

"I have something to do tonight." I made a real effort to leave it there, but I couldn't stop my mouth from moving. "I can't stay long."

"Thank you, Celly."

I waited, expecting him to add some kind of direction, like *Will you park down the street?* But he just disconnected the call.

I looked at myself in the rearview mirror. "Plot twist."

I texted Jason, I have to do something before the audition. I'll meet you there.

As I started the car again, I wrote the queasy feeling in my stomach off as nerves. I'd never been to Lou's house before. He'd never even called me before. Maybe something had happened with Vivi. Maybe he couldn't live without me.

Fuck.

I wanted to shower. And braid my hair. I shook that off. I didn't have time if I was going to see what Lou wanted and get to the audition on time. I was going to have to see Lou all post-Hive sweaty and go to Jason's audition the same way.

I turned the car off. At least I could wash my face in the bathroom at McDonald's.

○ ○ ○

The smell of french fries and chicken nuggets was a physical wall when I pushed open the restaurant door. I inhaled and realized I hadn't eaten since breakfast.

It would be easier to deal with whatever was happening with Lou if I wasn't hungry. In fact, now that I thought about it, I was a little shaky after my workout.

I needed to eat something.

You don't need to eat this junk, though. Right. Nothing like my mother's voice in my head on my way to talk to the asshole who broke my heart. *Get a salad, Celly.*

I went into the bathroom and splashed water on my face, then looked at myself in the mirror. My hair was pulled back in a ponytail. A braid would look better.

I pulled out the elastic and wished I had a hairbrush with me.

None of this is for him, I told my reflection. *You are not fixing yourself up for Lou Duncan.*

Right. That was believable.

When I'd done the best that I could with myself in a McDonald's bathroom with nothing but water and a single hair tie, I left.

I meant to just go right back outside. But there was no line at the order counter. None at all. In fact, the only visible people were an elderly woman behind the register and a kid behind her, literally flipping burgers.

There must have been more people back there, out of my view. Someone working the drive-through. A manager. But for some reason, the grandmotherly lady with her visor set at a jaunty angle over her steel-gray permanent wave made it OK to walk up and place an order.

I didn't binge anymore. I also didn't have a thing with Lou anymore. But here I was.

"Two number sevens." The order that I'd placed dozens of times came out of my mouth, even though what I meant to say was *grilled*

McChicken and a Diet Coke. McDonald's doesn't even have salads. "Large. With barbecue sauce and Diet Coke."

Ordering two whole meals let me at least pretend that the person taking my order thought I was ordering for two people.

I stood there, breathing in the fryer fumes. I couldn't deal with Lou on an empty stomach. I couldn't do this hungry. A cavern opened up in the center of my belly, and while I waited, it grew until it encompassed all of me.

I couldn't do this hungry. Even Betsy would agree with that, right?

And I had just worked out for two hours. Chicken nuggets weren't the worst thing I could do. This isn't like standing over the stove and shoving spaghetti down my throat.

I stood there and rationalized while the woman who'd taken my order filled two paper cups with Diet Coke and the kid behind her went to the fryer station to fill two boxes with nuggets.

I didn't have to eat it all.

"Can I add two apple pies?" I asked the woman when she came back with my bag.

○ ○ ○

The ache of being overfull was a comfort.

That was something to put on my list of things to talk to Betsy about at the next group meeting. Or Ursula, I guessed.

It was like solid ground under my feet that made everything else easier to handle.

I sat in my mom's car, parked in front of Lou's house, and ate the last apple pie, even though I was so full I felt a little sick. Then I tilted the rearview mirror so I could make sure I didn't have barbecue sauce on my face.

My cell phone pinged, and I picked it up, expecting a text from Lou wondering where I was. Instead, there was a message from Jason.

Are you sure you can't come over now?

I looked up at Lou's house. Heading over to Jason's would be the smart thing. The safe thing.

It would be the right thing.

But all of those Cinderella daydreams—months worth of them—came rushing back all at once. Lou had picked me. He wanted me.

I typed I'm sorry.

And I meant it.

The little bubbles that meant Jason was typing something back to me popped up. I opened the glove box and put my phone into it before his message came through. Then, I took one more look at myself in the mirror.

You're a bad friend and a cow, Moocella.

I shook that off and got out of the car.

Lou's house was nearly a clone of mine. A pretty standard three-bedroom, two-story ranch house with a small front porch and a two-car garage.

Just like me, he'd lived in the same place his whole life. His mom is older than my parents by more than twenty years, though. She was closer to my grandmother's age. His oldest brother had been a freshman the year my parents graduated from Twain.

Lou was her baby. A surprise baby who was about to make her a surprise grandma.

I wondered where she was that Lou could ask me to come over.

It was awkward, standing on his front porch, knocking on the door. I looked over my shoulder, wondering if anyone would see me. I'd wanted Lou to just acknowledge our relationship for months, but now that I was here knocking on his front door, I didn't feel great.

He was having a baby with Vivi.

By the time Lou finally opened the door, I'd backed up to the front stairs, ready to turn and go back to my car.

We just looked at each other for a minute. A few weeks ago, this would have been the part where he kissed me. At least I thought so. I'd never actually done this on his front porch before.

Since kissing wasn't happening today, there was a weird kind of formality between us.

"Want to come in?" he asked.

"Sure." I mean, that's why I was there, right?

He opened the door wider and I followed him inside.

The similarity to my house ended at the front door. My parents' style was comfortable and modern. Not quite minimalist, but my dad liked everything where it belonged, and my mom had expensive taste.

Lou's house was cluttered and oddly Victorian. Ornate. The sofa was velvet and carved wood. Where we had a ceiling fan, his living room had a hanging lamp with a stained-glass shade. And there were things everywhere. Pictures, books, little knickknacks.

I turned to Lou, my mouth open to say something, and was cut off when he pulled me into his arms and hugged me close to him. I froze for a second, then patted his back.

"Are you OK?" I asked when he finally pulled back away from me.

"It's been a hard week."

I bet. "Have you told your mom yet?"

He shrugged one shoulder. "I don't want to think about it."

I was struck, again, by how deeply rooted the idea that Lou never had to do what he didn't want to do seemed to be. "I'm pretty sure you're going to have to, eventually."

He was like a bull in this weird china shop of a living room. How had he been raised here? He had three brothers and a dad, but there wasn't even the slightest hint of male influence in the room.

It was like a woman's magazine had exploded all over the place.

"I don't want any of this," he said.

To my credit, I didn't point out that it was a little too late to think about that now. "I don't blame you. Vivi probably doesn't, either."

"Yes, she does." He flopped down on the sofa. "She gave up her scholarship. She told her parents."

I lifted my eyebrows. "To be fair, it would be a lot harder for her to keep it a secret."

He looked up at me.

"Don't you think her parents will tell your mom?"

"Probably."

"It would be better coming from you."

If Jenna or I told our parents that we were pregnant in high school, I was positive the next step would be a call to the parents of whatever boy had knocked one of us up.

"Where is your mom?"

He shook his head, then blinked hard, as if he was trying to clear his vision. "In Boise, visiting my brother."

I sat next to him.

He took a breath, and then his head lolled back for a second before he straightened up. For the first time, I noticed that his eyes had a weird glazed-over look to them.

"Lou?"

"I should have taken your rose." He reached for the end of my braid, but just tugged on it a little without taking off the elastic. "I wanted you to know that."

Something wasn't right. It was like he was winding down. Running out of steam. "Are you OK?"

He shook his head. "Will you tell her for me?"

"Tell who, what?"

"My mom. Will you tell her about the baby?"

"Have you taken something?"

"Just some of my mom's valium."

Crap. "How much?"

He brushed his fingers over the side of my face. "Just two. Don't worry."

I stood up. "I have to go."

"Don't leave me." His fingers slid around to the back of my head and he pulled me closer to him. I had time to inhale before he kissed me.

He picked me. I leaned into his kiss. He couldn't pick me for long. I knew that. But right now, in this moment in his weird living room, he picked me, and I let myself have it.

He pulled the elastic from my hair and shifted his weight, deepening his kiss. His hand caressed the side of my face, and he pulled away just far enough to look at me.

"I love you, Celly."

"Wait." I pulled back from him, brushing his hand away when he didn't move it. "What?"

"We're supposed to go to Las Vegas together. Fucking Vivi ruined everything."

I rubbed my hands over my face and turned to sit straight on the sofa. He loves me? My daydream maker went into high gear, and I couldn't stop it.

The words *I love you, too*, were on my tongue, but I didn't let them out of my mouth.

If I said it, maybe there'd be a big scandal. The kind of thing bad movies are made of. Vivi would be devastated. Of course she would. The fat girl never gets the cheerleader's guy.

But who cares?

Lou and I were both headed to Las Vegas for college in a couple of months anyway. Maybe we'd get an apartment together, instead of living in our dorms. We'd never move back to Sun Valley, that's for sure.

I dropped my hands and turned my face to look at him. I'd fantasized about that face for so long. It never felt real that he was into me at all. And it still didn't.

"Vivi's going with you to Las Vegas, isn't she?" I asked.

"No."

I lifted my eyebrows, still watching that face.

He sighed. "I don't want her to."

"But she is."

"This is such a fucking mess, Celly." It was his turn to flop away from me on the sofa, so that we sat side-by-side. He reached for my hand and I let him take it.

"She applied to UNLV. She thinks she can go to school in the fall, even with a baby."

"Maybe she can. Between the two of you—"

He shook his head, his mouth twisting. "I don't want to do this."

A little late for that, Lou Duncan. "She probably doesn't, either."

"She doesn't have to." Silence stretched out as his words landed like a boulder in the middle of the room. Lou threaded his fingers between mine, his thumb moving against my skin.

"I should go," I finally said.

He kept hold of my hand. "Please stay."

Seriously. Why couldn't I be the one who got what she wanted?

I wasn't stupid. I knew that there couldn't be anything real between us. Not now. He would figure out what to do about Vivi—and it would involve their baby.

They would end up together.

But right at that moment, he wanted me there with him. And that was like some kind of drug. If I walked out, the moment would be gone forever. Next time I saw Lou, the whole school and his mom would know about the baby, after Vivi had made a scene at the dance.

I turned to look at him again, and he leaned in to kiss me.

This time, I didn't pull away.

○ ○ ○

It was dark by the time I finally left Lou's house. Pitch dark. I stood at my mom's car and just stared at it for a minute, trying to get my bearings. And then I finally got in.

I opened the glove box and pulled out my phone. What was wrong with me? I hadn't even thought about Jason while I was in the house.

Not once.

God, I really was a terrible friend.

Suzy was with him, I told myself. *He's fine. He nailed it.*

As evidence that I was the worst friend ever, I was already formulating a lie as I unlocked my phone. *My car broke down.* Or maybe *I got sick.*

Anything other than *I blew you off because Lou Duncan told me he loved me, and I wanted to make a bad decision with him.*

It was even later than I thought. After ten.

Jason was probably home by now.

Fuck. Guilt hit like a wrecking ball. Hard enough to make me feel sick.

I wanted to check my text messages and see celebration. He killed it. He kicked ass and Soiled Dove was definitely picking him. Maybe some pictures.

Where are you?

You promised me.

Celly!

Oh, God. I thumbed through a few more increasingly panicked messages.

And then: I choked.

Oh, Jason. Rationally, I knew that me being there probably wouldn't have made a difference. He always choked. He said so himself. But I'd promised him. I'd let him down.

I typed I'm so sorry.

I was still formulating my lie. Because at least he would never know why I'd abandoned him tonight. He'd never know what I was doing instead.

I typed with my thumbs while the little dots that let me know he was typing too blinked.

His message came through first. I saw your car.

My stomach fell, and the world actually swayed. I'd parked right in Lou's driveway.

He couldn't know this was Lou's house. Could he?

Maybe I could tell him that it wasn't me. That it was Jenna.

No. No. Jenna was fourteen.

Could I figure out some way to make him believe one of my parents was at Lou's house?

I turned the key in the ignition and drove the three blocks to Suzy's house without any thought about little things like being aware of the other cars on the road.

I had to make this right.

Now. Tonight.

What had I done?

I got out of the car and stood in front of Jason's front door for a long moment, trying to gather myself.

I was a mess. Still in my workout clothes. My hair was a tangled disaster, and I needed a shower maybe more than I'd ever needed one in my life.

And I was on the verge of tears.

Jason wasn't my boyfriend. I hadn't cheated on him. But he was my friend, and I had hurt him. I finally forced myself to raise my arm and knock on the door.

It occurred to me, after I'd knocked, that it was after ten, and Suzy and Dirk had little boys. I should have texted Jason to let him know I was there. I pulled my phone out of my pocket to do that now.

Maybe no one had heard the knock.

The door opened before I could thumb in a message. Suzy stood there, her face tight as she looked up at me.

I really thought I might be sick. "Is Jason here?"

She lifted her eyebrows and somehow managed to radiate absolute disappointment in a single look. That must be a mom skill they handed out in the delivery room. "This isn't a good time, Celly."

That last word let me know how much trouble I was in, and my stomach turned over. She'd never once called me by my real name. I would have done anything to hear her call me Queenie.

I wasn't only in trouble with Jason, then.

"Please, Suzy." I used her name, too. Not Banshee. "I have to talk to him."

She came out onto the porch and closed the door behind her. "Jason's been through a lot."

"I know."

"I know that you know."

I winced. That hit like an actual gut punch. "Please, Suzy. Ask him to talk to me."

"You're the first person he's let himself get close to since Danielle died."

Tears burned behind my eyes and down my throat. "I just wasn't thinking straight."

She shook her head. "We almost never do."

"I'm sorry." My face crumbled, and there was nothing I could do to stop the tears from falling down my cheeks. "I'm so sorry I hurt him."

She nodded, her face softening some. "Just give him some space."

"Will he be at the Hive tomorrow?"

She lifted her glasses to the top of her head and rubbed her eyes. "Maybe it isn't a good idea for you to come by the Hive for a while."

My chest hurt, and I wondered for a second if I might actually be having a heart attack. "But the competition—"

She shook her head.

"You're kicking me off the team?" I hated how pathetic that sounded.

Suzy was quiet. She had to choose Jason. She had to. His own parents hadn't. I sure as hell hadn't.

I took a breath through my nose, trying to control the tears that welled up behind my eyes. I never cry in front of them. That's my rule.

Somehow, I made it back to my mom's car.

I pulled out my phone and read through Jason's texts again. Then I typed I'm sorry. Again. Weak.

I couldn't get a good breath. And I couldn't drive like this, but I managed to pull away from Jason's house and park again down the block so I could cry in private before I went home.

CHAPTER 27

Mom was waiting up for me. It hit me, as I walked into the house, how tired I was. Just bone tired. Everything hurt. I had about a thousand things to process.

In the last couple hours, I'd managed to lose my best friend, the Hive, and my virginity. The last thing I wanted was to talk to my mother about any of that.

But she had some kind of radar.

"Celly?" she called out as I tried to sneak past and up the stairs. "What's wrong?"

How did she do that? "Nothing."

She came out of the living room and looked up at me. "What happened?"

I shook my head. "I'm fine."

Her eyes narrowed, and I was pretty sure she was looking into my soul. That thought made my chest ache. No one wanted to see into my soul at the moment.

I am a terrible person. She'd say it wasn't true. Of course she would. What else was she going to say?

But it was true.

"Come with me." She took my hand, led me to the kitchen, and sat me down at the table. I expected her to sit down, too, but she went to the stove instead and turned on the burner under the teakettle.

"I'm tired, Mom." I stood up again, but she shot me a look that sat me back down again.

She opened a plastic box of blueberry muffins and pulled one out. My eyebrows shot up as she used a butter knife to cut it in half and put it on two plates. She put tea bags into two mugs and poured water over them when the kettle whistled.

When she'd moved the tea, the muffins, and a little bear-shaped honey bottle to the table, she sat across from me.

"What are you doing?" I asked.

"We're having a snack."

"You don't eat carbs at night." She broke off a bite of the muffin top and put it into her mouth. "Seriously, what's happening right now?"

"I read that book."

It took me a minute to realize she meant Betsy's book. *Healing Childhood Obesity from the Inside Out.* "You did?"

"Did you?"

I shook my head. "Only the part about eating disorders."

She took a breath and poured honey into her tea. I'd never seen her do that before. "I read that part, too."

I took a bite of my muffin and, when she was done with the honey, sweetened my tea. This was surreal. This whole night was surreal. The tears I'd been holding back since leaving Jason's house surfaced again, too quick for me to stop this time.

Mom put her mug down. "Celly, please talk to me."

"I can't." I wiped at my eyes with the back of my hand. "Anyway, I'm fine."

Except I had the same kind of disconnect going on that I'd felt the day Vivi filled my locker with condoms. I was just so tired. If I could just sleep.

Mom took my mug from my hand and set it down. "Look at me."

I did. Her hair was in a ponytail on top of her head. Her cheerleader ponytail. She'd already washed her face, but it was easy to draw the line between Robin when she was like Vivi—pregnant at graduation, having a baby with the most popular boy in her class—and Robin today.

"I slept with Lou Duncan." The words escaped before I could sensor them and I took a wobbly breath when I heard them. Shit.

She sat back in her chair. "Oh. Celly."

Oh, Mom. There's more. And I couldn't stop it from coming out. "He's having a baby with Vivi Hughes."

"Lou's having a baby?"

I looked at the table, trying to figure out what exactly I wanted to say. "He said he loved me."

"They do that." She brushed the hair from my forehead. "They always do that."

I swallowed hard. "I didn't believe him. I know he doesn't love me. Boys like Lou don't fall in love with girls like me."

Mom tilted her head and held up a perfectly manicured finger. "First. Boys like Lou are assholes."

I blinked at her language. My mother never cursed. Ever.

She held up a second finger. "Second, you are an extraordinary girl. It's a curse that boys like Lou will always fall in love with you. You'll have to learn how to weed them out."

Right. I'm cursed with beautiful, popular boys falling in love with me all over the place.

She held up a third finger. But I shook my head and reached for her hand, pushing it down. I couldn't take whatever her third point was. "I'm tired. Can I just go to bed?"

She stood up and shifted her hand so that she had hold of mine and pulled until I stood up too. She wrapped me in her arms for a hug. She didn't let go until I hugged her back.

"Are you OK?" she asked.

I meant to say I was fine, but I just shook my head instead. I couldn't even begin to tell her how I felt, but fine wasn't part of it.

It wasn't Lou that was tearing me up.

I couldn't tell her about Jason. I didn't even know how to put that into words. I'd hurt him badly enough that he didn't want to be my friend anymore. I didn't know how to be a friend.

That thought brought tears again.

"Take a shower," Mom said. "It'll make you feel better."

○ ○ ○

She was right. A shower did make me feel better. Cleaner, anyway, which was something. I checked my phone after I was in bed. No messages from Jason or Lou.

Did I expect Lou to text me?

Yeah. Pathetic as it was, I kind of did.

He'd told me he loved me. Either it was true or he'd just said it so I'd sleep with him. That idea made my stomach turn over.

I opened a message to him and typed in Do you really love me?

And then just stared at it for a minute. It would be pathetic to send it. I really should not.

What would I do if he said yes?

And what if he said no?

Maybe worst of all, he might just ignore the question entirely.

I made a little noise, like someone jumping off a cliff, and hit *send* before I could stop myself.

I watched. It took ninety seconds for him to respond to my message.

My phone let me know he was typing a response. Then nothing. Whatever he'd typed, he didn't send it. Then he typed some more. And again, nothing actually showed up on my end.

One more time. I watched the little icon flash at me, telling me that he was typing.

I'm sorry.

All of that for two words?

Sorry for what? That he loved me? That he didn't love me? That he'd slept with me while his pregnant girlfriend was at home contemplating how her life was about to blow up? Oh, God. I was a horrible person. An honest-to-God bad person.

My response was only one word. Sorry?

Today was a mistake.

I went through the stages of grief, one breath at a time.

He can't mean that. Breath. *He doesn't mean it.* Breath. *What if I agree to the rules, until we get to Las Vegas?* Breath. *God, I'm a loser.* Breath. *And he's an asshole.* Breath. *No one will ever love me.* Breath. *Maybe that won't be so bad.*

Breath.

What I finally typed was: You're right.

○ ○ ○

I dreamed about orange nylon rope, slippery and soft against my skin. In my dream, I practiced tying square knots.

I woke up in the dark and lay there for a long minute, taking an inventory of myself. *I'm alive. I'm clearly a mess, but the tug-of-war in my brain hasn't yanked me back over the "Do I want to die?" line.*

It was trying though.

I was too afraid to go back to sleep. I checked my phone—for the last time, I told myself. It was 5:32 in the morning.

Jason had not messaged me.

I wanted to say something to him. Some magic thing that would make him forgive me. Not *I'm sorry*. I'd already said that. Something else. Something perfect.

I'm an asshole. That slipped off my fingertips too easily. It was true.

I don't deserve a friend as good as you've been to me. Also, true.

I'm such a loser. I deleted that one. It was true. But this message was starting to be all about me, and I didn't want to do that.

I tried again. I don't blame you for hating me.

I thought about telling him my heart was broken. I thought about begging him to forgive me. I didn't do either one. I sent what I had written and tucked my phone under my pillow to keep myself from just staring at it, waiting to see if he answered.

He wouldn't. I knew he wouldn't.

Silent tears fell down the sides of my face as weak early morning light filtered through my curtains.

I had no friends.

I hadn't had many friends before I met Jason. But this was worse. Because I'd had the Hive. And I'd had him. And now that I didn't, their absence was like a boulder on my chest.

I couldn't breathe.

CHAPTER 28

By the time the sun came up, I hadn't slept, but I'd made a decision.

My phone let me know that Jason had seen my message from the night before. But he hadn't responded.

He was probably asleep. Maybe he just needed to think about things. Maybe later he'd come over and yell at me and tell me what a horrible person I was.

That would be better than this.

Anything would be better than this.

I had to do something, or I was going to spiral into a place I really didn't want to go again. I threw on some clothes and went downstairs as quietly as I could. I took my mother's car keys from the bowl near the front door and left.

I was going to be in so much trouble, but I didn't care. At least I'd be around to be in that trouble. The drive to Reno happened on autopilot. Because it was so early, I was able to park in the spot directly in front of Betsy's office building.

I didn't have any change for the meter, but I didn't care. I was already going to get busted for car theft. What was a parking ticket?

I sat in Mom's car and watched the door to Betsy's building, waiting for her to show up. The wait was long enough for me to decide half a dozen times that this was a mistake.

Just go home, Boucher. There was nothing Betsy could do for me. I should just go home. Get some more sleep. Figure out how to live with myself.

I'd just about talked myself into doing that when Betsy finally walked down the sidewalk toward me.

Well, toward her office, but whatever.

I opened the car door and stood up. "Betsy?"

She turned, and for a moment, she looked at me like she had no idea who I was. Then she squeezed her eyes shut and opened them again. "Celly?"

"I need to talk to you."

"We don't have an appointment."

"I know," I said. "But I really—"

"It's important that you make an appointment. With Ursula. Please, give her a chance. I think you're going to like her."

"It's not about that. I just—"

Betsy held up a hand. "Come inside with me. We can make an appointment for you to meet with Ursula."

"Never mind," I said. "I'll call."

"Celly."

I turned away, back toward Mom's car. I'd gotten myself into a lot of trouble for absolutely nothing.

"Marcella."

I turned back to her. "I messed up, Betsy. Really bad."

"Everything will be OK."

"How can you say that? You don't know."

"I know that it takes time to get better. And you are the one who gets to decide who you are." She put her hand on the door again. "You already know what to do, Celly. You just have to listen to yourself."

Who the fuck did she think she was? Next thing, she was going to tell me to tap my heels together three times and say *there's no place like home*. "You don't even know what I wanted to talk to you about."

"It doesn't matter." She looked up at me. "Come in with me, and we'll make you an appointment to see Ursula today."

I snorted and got into the car.

She stood there for a moment. And then she was gone, inside the building, and I was left sitting alone.

I sat back in the car and checked my phone again. Nothing from Lou or from Jason. I was such an idiot. Was I going to spend the rest of my life waiting on text messages from them?

You know what to do.

Like hell. I had no clue.

I'd slept with a pregnant girl's boyfriend and broken my only friend's heart. No. My best friend's heart. Who in the hell could know what to do about that?

I pressed my head against the headrest and squeezed my eyes shut.

I wished I could take it all back. All of it.

And then I did know what to do. "Damn it."

○ ○ ○

By the time I got back to Sun Valley, it wasn't quite so miserably early. I pulled up on the street in front of Vivi's house and just sat there for a minute.

Who cared if someone who flew so close to the sun got burned?

I took a deep breath and left the car.

Here goes.

I walked straight to the door and knocked before I could talk myself out of it.

I expected Vivi to open the door. I was ready for that. I wasn't prepared for a woman who looked like Vivi would in thirty years, with red-rimmed eyes.

"Hello?" Vivi's mom said. It had to be her mom.

"Um." This was a bad mistake. Bad.

"Can I help you?"

"Yeah. Is…is Vivi home?"

"I'm sorry, but Vivi can't come out right now."

"Oh," I said. "OK, well—"

"Jesus. What are you doing here?"

Vivi's mother turned to look at her daughter. "You are not hanging out with friends this weekend."

"Does she look like my friend, Mom? Come on."

Mrs. Hughes looked back at me and at least had the grace to look embarrassed.

"We have a…um…a school thing," I said.

Vivi's mom nodded and actually looked relieved. "OK. Ten minutes."

I wouldn't need half that. After Vivi came out to the porch and closed the door I said, "I just wanted to check on you."

Vivi wrapped her arms around her body. "Whatever."

"I really thought that Lou…" Loved me. Not a great apology. Had broken up with you? A lie. "I just wanted to check on you."

"OK. Well, good for you." She turned to the door, then spun back toward me. "That might mean more, you know, if you hadn't slept with him last night."

I blinked. The wind sucked right out of my lungs.

"Oh. Didn't think I knew that? Yeah. I drove past Lou's house last night on my way home. Saw your piece of shit car in his driveway. Right in his goddamned driveway for anyone to see."

What the hell? Had everyone in Sun Valley driven by Lou's house last night? "Look. I just wanted to apologize."

So much for listening to myself. Maybe Ursula was a good idea.

I expected Vivi to scream some kind of nastiness at me. Instead, she sat down hard on the top porch step. And she cried. She took a few hard breaths after a minute and looked up at me again.

"Don't you dare feel sorry for me."

That wasn't the problem. Not at all. I didn't feel sorry for her.

I'd been feeling so sorry for myself. For so long. I'd thought Vivi was perfect. That Jenna was perfect. That I didn't fit anywhere. Except I fit with Jason and Suzy and the Hive. And I'd fucked that up.

I sat next to Vivi.

She kept her eyes on the step between her feet. "I thought he loved me."

"What are you going to do?"

"Have a baby."

I inhaled and then blew out my breath slowly. "I thought he loved me, too."

I expected her to laugh. What kind of idiot would actually think that? But she just stood up and said, "I'm pretty sure that makes us both idiots."

It was a weird thing, for me to have to tilt my head to look up at Vivi. But she moved up to the top step and that was the only way I could see her.

And then I did what felt like the most honest thing I'd done in days. I said, "I'm sorry."

○ ○ ○

When I finally made it home, I went to Jenna's room instead of my own. She was in bed still, but awake, lying on her stomach typing something.

My sister wouldn't end up like Vivi. Or our mom. She was smarter than either of them. I would have backed out of tryout day without her. She hadn't let me hide the Queen Beast behind Moocella at Morp. I was going to have to do something big to make things right with Jason. Something huge. "Will you help me with something?"

Jenna looked up at me. "With what?"

"I need to do something and I'm not sure I can do it by myself." I took a breath. "I think you're going to love it."

"What is it, though?"

"Get dressed. You'll see."

She rolled her eyes, then sat up sat up, cross-legged, on the mattress. "OK."

I went to my room and pulled out my phone. I didn't look at my messages this time. I pulled up an internet browser, searched for what I needed, then made a phone call.

Then I searched for one more thing. The very next thing. I didn't get any kind of feeling like it was a bad idea, so I just went for it.

o o o

"Really," Jenna said half an hour later as I parked at the mall. "What are we doing here?"

"Well, you're here to make sure I don't change my mind."

"Change your mind about what?"

I turned to look at her. "I'm selling my hair."

She leaned toward me, shock changing her face. "What?"

"They're giving me two thousand dollars for it."

"Whoa." She put a hand to the back of her own head. "Who is?"

Would my sister cut off all her hair for two thousand dollars and the hope of making things right? Hers was light brown and only shoulder length. She didn't have the option. Brenda had only gotten two hundred for her brown hair, and it was long.

"There's a wig shop." I tilted my chin toward the mall entrance. "I need you to make sure I don't back out."

"But why are you selling your hair?"

I had no idea how to explain that to Jenna, so I just got out of the car.

She caught up to me by the time I was at the mall's front door. "Celly, are you sure you want to do this?"

I stopped in the middle of the parking lot and turned to look at her. Was I? "Yes. I think so."

"Why?"

Because I want to let go of the one thing that Lou liked best about me. Because I needed a change. A big one. Because I needed to do penance, somehow. "I need the money."

"What for?"

I walked past her, toward the mall, and didn't stop when she caught up and put a hand on my arm.

"Celly," she said. "Are you OK?"

I did stop then. "Not really. But I will be."

"Why do you need two thousand dollars?"

"I want to buy a scooter."

Jenna blinked at me while that sank in. "A scooter?"

"A Vespa. Like Jason's."

She made a little *huh* noise and looked up at me. And then she just said, "OK."

I went into the mall, and she walked with me. The refrigerated air had a strange canned quality to it, mixed with combating scents of cinnamon buns and hair dye from the bakery and the salon just inside the door.

I didn't have to go any further. Not yet, anyway. I had to bring my hair, gathered in a ponytail, to the wig shop. I'd sent an awkward selfie to the owner earlier, and she had been almost obscenely excited to get three feet of platinum-blond hair.

I inhaled deeply before turning to the salon.

"Mom's going to kill you," Jenna said. "Twice, maybe."

She was right. Once for cutting off my hair. And once for buying a Vespa. Giving up my one beauty and then doing something she considered dangerous were like a double face slap. But I couldn't think about her right now.

This wasn't about my mother. "She'll get over it."

"Why do you want to buy a Vespa so bad?"

I couldn't explain that to her. Not right now. That was the second part of my plan, and I wasn't ready to think too hard about it yet.

Jenna looked at me, then just walked past me, toward the salon, so that I was the one following her. Then she waited for me to talk to the woman behind the cash register just inside the door.

My hands and feet tingled, as if all my blood had rushed to my insides. I tried not to think about what I was actually doing. Just needed to take the very next step.

The wig shop had told me to go to a salon and have my hair cut, with the length in a ponytail, to keep it all together. It had to be at least thirty inches for the price they'd quoted me.

I'd measured. That would leave me with about four inches of hair on my head.

I exhaled slowly and looked up at the hairdresser. One step in front of the other.

"Seriously, though," Jenna asked before I could speak. "Why?"

Because Lou loves it and I just don't want it anymore. That answer, even inside myself, surprised me. I didn't say it out loud. "Please don't ask me that."

"God, you're weird. Like really, really weird."

I didn't bother to respond to that.

"You don't have to do this," she said. "Whatever is going on, you don't have to do this."

"Yes, I do."

The hairdresser lifted her eyebrows. "Can I help you?"

The salon was on the opposite side of the mall from the wig shop. I was going to have to traipse through the whole place carrying my own ponytail.

I bit at my bottom lip. Getting the words out was a physical effort. "I'm selling my hair."

The stylist didn't bat an eye. For some reason that helped. "Want a shampoo, or just a cut?"

"No shampoo," I said. "I need my hair dry."

"You have great hair. You're sure you want to cut it off?"

I pointed to the back of my head, where my hair was already pulled back into a braided ponytail. I'd gone with thirty-two inches, just to be safe. If I was doing this, I might as well go for it. "Right above the rubber band."

The woman lifted her eyebrows, but then just took me to her chair. She used the foot pump at its base to lower the seat.

I closed my eyes when she lifted her scissors and focused on breathing as I heard and felt the first cuts. It was too late to back out, unless I wanted a pixie on one side of my head and waist-length hair on the other, but I still gripped the chair's armrests.

The weight of a hand over mine startled me. I opened my eyes and saw Jenna standing close to me, watching the hairdresser. Her fingers closed around mine.

A few more snips. And then it was done. I started to stand up, and both Jenna and the hairdresser kept me in my seat.

"Hang on," the woman said. "I at least need to clean up the edges."

"Do you trust me?" Jenna asked.

I couldn't look in the mirror. Not yet. So I looked at my sister. "Yes."

She poked around on her phone for a minute, then showed the hairdresser something on the screen.

My head felt ten pounds lighter with my braid in my lap instead of attached to my scalp. I fingered the pale strands and thought about how the ends had been with me since I was eight or nine years old.

"This what you want, honey?" The woman with the scissors looked at me in the mirror.

I shrugged and then nodded. I didn't care. Didn't even look at Jenna's phone. "Sure."

Jenna stood back with a self-satisfied smile, and the hairdresser picked up a spray bottle to spritz my head. She spent a lot of time at the back of my head, then spun me to face her. I closed my eyes as my hair rained down in my lap.

When she was done, she turned me back to the mirror. I closed my eyes.

I'd had long hair all my life. Never had more than a trim to keep my ends healthy. I wrapped my hands around the thick braid sitting in my lap and practiced Betsy's breathing. In for four, hold for five, out for six. The second time I exhaled, I opened my eyes and I saw myself without it attached to my head for the first time.

I turned my head a little, looking at my new chin-length bob. The hairdresser had given me short bangs that gave the whole cut an edginess that my waist-length hair never had.

Without all the weight, my hair had some wave that I didn't even know was there.

"Huh," I finally said, running my hand through the ends.

"Told you," Jenna said. "But Mom's still going to kill you."

I made eye contact with her in the mirror as the hairdresser pulled the plastic cape off me and shook the hair to the floor. I was holding the bulk of what she'd cut off in my lap, but there was still a shocking pile of blond all around the chair. There was no going back now.

CHAPTER 29

"You know how to ride a Vespa?" the man said to me.

I shook my head. The lack of hair was seriously making me feel off balance. "Not really."

"It's not a lot different from a bicycle," he said. "Only you don't have to pedal, of course. But steering and stopping are the same. Why don't you give it a try?"

My heart was in my throat. I'd found a Vespa for sale near the university. After I took Jenna home, I took the bus to pick it up. I wasn't sure how I was going to get this thing to Sun Valley. Right now, though, I only needed to get it to the Hive.

One thing at a time. I'd worry about getting it home when the time came.

I sat on the baby blue scooter and had such an Audrey Hepburn moment that I decided that her name was Audrey. And me and Audrey were going to figure this out.

I pushed the helmet he threw in with the sale onto my head and rode around the guy's street a little bit, getting a feel for acceleration and breaking.

I didn't fall off or crash into a parked car.

That was good.

"I think you're good to go," he finally said.

I handed him most of the roll of hundred-dollar bills the wig woman had given me earlier. And just like that, Audrey was mine.

My mother hadn't seen my head yet. And she didn't have a clue what I was doing with the money I'd made selling my hair. Jenna hadn't been kidding when she'd said Mom was going to kill me.

She was seriously going to kill me.

In the meantime, I just kept doing the next thing.

I rode Audrey toward the Hive, going slower than I probably should have, staying in the bike lane so cars could get around me.

Slow because I didn't really know what I was doing. And slow because my stomach was a knot of anxiety. What if Jason wouldn't talk to me?

Despite how slowly I drove, though, I eventually made it to the Hive's parking lot. Hard-driving music poured out of the gym's open doors. I stopped in the back and watched for a while.

Nana came out and walked to a little gray car that I was pretty sure was a Prius. Did she know that I wasn't on the competition team anymore?

I thought about riding Audrey over to her. If she was friendly to me, then everything would be OK. If she wasn't, then the Hive wouldn't ever be the same for me. I cut Audrey's engine and put down her kickstand.

This had to work. It had to.

I carried the helmet pressed against my aching stomach and walked toward the Hive.

I don't know what I expected. Mooing? Anger? Disaster?

I used to feel so comfortable there. This time I might as well have had a neon *traitor* sign around my neck.

When I walked through the doors, there was pretty much no reaction. Midge noticed me and just lifted her chin and went back to her workout.

I didn't know what Suzy or Jason had told them about why I wasn't going to be on the competition team. Maybe everyone knew I'd slept with Lou and abandoned Jason when he needed me.

Maybe they just thought I'd flaked.

But no one confronted me. Or shunned me, either.

I looked around, hoping to spot Jason. It hadn't even occurred to me that he might not be here. He was always here on Saturdays. But I didn't see him anywhere. Or Suzy either.

My heart sank.

"Oh, my goodness, Queenie. Your hair!"

I turned and saw Nana standing beside me. I put a hand to the back of my head. My cheeks burned. Not because of my hair, though. She'd called me Queenie. "Yeah."

She nodded slowly, inspecting my new cut. "Bold. I like it."

I put a hand to the bare, vulnerable back of my neck. "Really?"

"Looking for Jason?" she asked.

"Yeah." I chewed at my bottom lip a little. "I messed up, Nana."

She put a hand on my arm. "I know, sweetheart."

"You do?"

"Don't worry. I don't think everyone does. But I've been around long enough to recognize a brokenhearted boy when I see one."

I winced.

"Brokenhearted girl, too," she said, then tipped her head and looked at something behind me, before walking away.

I turned to face Jason, standing there, looking at me.

His eyes widened as he took in my hair, then he blinked a couple of times.

"Jason."

"What are you doing here?"

"I came—" I took a breath and twisted the helmet's strap between my fingers. "I'm sorry. I'm so sorry."

"Me, too." His voice was so monotone. This had to work. It had to.

"What happened at the audition?"

He huffed a hard, sharp breath of laughter. "You know what happened. I choked."

My mouth was dry, but I made myself say what I'd come here to say. "There's another one. Tonight."

"Another date with Lou?"

"What? Jesus, no."

"Then what, Celly? Why are you here?"

"They're auditioning tonight," I said. "In Sacramento."

His woodland-creature face was so shut off from me. I hated that. Hated it. "So what?"

"So. Let's go."

"To Sacramento?"

I nodded. "We can be there before dark."

"How are we going to do that?"

I held up the helmet. "Francine and Audrey."

"Audrey?"

I ran my free hand over my new bangs. "Will you come outside with me for a minute? I want to show you something."

He looked from my hair to my helmet. "All right."

We walked back out the rolling door and I took him to where I'd parked Audrey. He covered his mouth with one hand and walked slowly around her.

He ran a hand over her seat. "There's a story here."

"Yes."

For a long moment, he kept his eyes on my new scooter. Then he looked up at me. "What is it?"

"I sold my hair."

"For enough to buy a scooter?"

I ran a hand through my strangely short bob. "Apparently blond is a commodity."

"Why did you do this, Celly?" He looked at me again, and I clamped my mouth shut to keep from begging him to forgive me. He had to forgive me.

"Because—" I exhaled. Why did I do this? "I had to do something."

His tongue darted over his bottom lip and he looked at me. "We can get to Sacramento before dark?"

"I checked."

"It's not legal."

I shook my head. "It is, as long as we stick to state highways. We can take the eighty-eight."

"We'll never be allowed to go."

I shrugged one shoulder. "Some things are worth being grounded until graduation for."

He laughed again. A real laugh this time. "Yeah."

"Even college graduation.You won't choke this time, Jason."

"I'm pretty sure I will."

I shook my head. "You're supposed to be a rock star. All you need to do is let Soiled Dove hear what you can do."

"That easy, huh?"

"That easy."

He ran a hand over Audrey's seat. "What happened with Lou?"

I squinted against the sun. I didn't want to do this part. "I don't know."

"Bullshit."

Damnit. I rubbed the heel of my hand against my breastbone. And then I took a deep breath and said, "He told me he loved me and, for a minute, I believed him."

"And now?"

"Now I know better."

"You know he doesn't love you?"

"I know I don't love him." I looked back at the Hive, listened to the music coming from it. "I thought I wanted to be Vivi Hughes for so long. I'm really sorry figuring out that I don't ended up hurting you."

Jason rubbed a hand over the back of his neck. "I can't believe you cut off your hair."

I snorted and looked back at him. "Me, either. It still feels weird."

"Looks good, though."

I tilted my head. "So, are we doing this thing?"

CHAPTER 30

Riding Audrey to Sun Valley was the only practice I got before going on my first scooter-based road trip. This was insane.

The guy hadn't been wrong. Riding a scooter was an awful lot like riding a bike. On the street. With cars that were a lot bigger and louder and faster than me.

I gripped the handlebars so hard my hands hurt. But at least fear kept me from fixating on Jason and Lou and Vivi and what was going to happen when I got home the next day and had to face the music with my parents.

Jason rode just ahead of me, and I watched the back of his head to keep myself from panicking every time a car passed on my left. He looked so relaxed and easy on Francine.

His long legs were pulled up a little too high, his knees higher than his waist and jutting out to the sides. But he wasn't afraid the way I was.

He'd forgiven me. Had to have, right? Otherwise we wouldn't be doing this.

○ ○ ○

My parents were both at the gym and Jenna was at dance practice when I got home. Good thing. I pulled Audrey into the driveway, figured out her kickstand again, and then went inside.

I couldn't take more than what would fit in my backpack. I dumped my school shit onto my bed and turned to my closet. Was it too meta to wear my Soiled Dove T-shirt to Jason's audition?

Maybe. But I didn't care. I pushed it down into the bottom of my bag, added a tank top, a pair of jeans. A hoodie. Then went to the bathroom for my toothbrush.

While I was there, I took a look at my hair for the first time in private. It took my breath away. Not like cutting off a limb, though. More like shedding something I didn't need anymore.

I ran my fingers through it, pulling it back from my face.

"You're still a beast, Celly Boucher," I whispered to my reflection.

In a little while, someone was going to be walking around in the world wearing my hair. God, that was weird.

I shoved my deodorant, my toothbrush, and a tube of Colgate into my backpack. It was weird not to need heavy-duty ponytail holders to keep my hair off my face.

I stuck my hairbrush in with everything else.

And then I knelt beside my bed and pulled out my envelope of babysitting and birthday money. I pushed it into the bottom of my backpack and zipped it up.

Since I was already in so much trouble that I couldn't even comprehend what the fallout would be, I opened the hall closet and pulled my dad's leather jacket off a hanger.

Audrey couldn't go all that fast, but I was still pretty sure I'd be glad for some protection from the pavement in case the fact that I was about to drive her for hours on the open highway the day I bought her caught up with me.

And then I wrote my parents a note.

Don't worry. I'm with Jason. I'll make good choices. And I'll call tonight. Love, Celly.

Deep breath. And then I headed out.

o o o

Jason was in his driveway with Francine when I pulled up. I had to put my feet down while I was still rolling to get to a complete stop. Christ.

"You'll get the hang of it," he said.

"I sure hope so."

He looked at me a minute, then reached over and ran his long fingers over the dome of my helmet. His was still hooked on Francine's handlebar. "Let me see?"

I bit my bottom lip, my stomach doing a funny kind of flip-flop that I couldn't quite interpret. Relief that he was talking to me. That he was interested in what I'd done to myself today.

Something else. Maybe.

Something I wasn't quite ready to think about.

I pulled my helmet off and ran my free hand through my short hair. So short. "It'll grow back."

He nodded slowly, his dark eyes taking me in. "If you want it to."

I started to argue. That's not how hair works. It'll grow back, like it or not. But I knew what he meant and shoved the over-logical part of my brain aside. "I'm not sure I do."

He took his own helmet and pushed it onto his head, covering his own wild curls. "Ready?"

I nodded. Before I put my helmet back on, though, I said, "Jason."

He kept his eyes on his hands, tight around the handle bar. "I know you're sorry."

"I am. I really am."

He finally looked at me. "It's hard for me to see you hurting yourself."

I didn't know what to say to that. So I just worked on getting Audrey started again. It took two tries.

○ ○ ○

We took side roads to get from Sun Valley to where we picked up the eighty-eight in Carson City.

The farther we got from home, the easier it got to breathe. Even if I was fairly certain that we were going to be pulled over by a highway patrolman wondering why two kids were riding mopeds to California.

Even that worry faded, the more time passed without it happening. It was like we were leaving behind everything that made it difficult to fill my lungs.

Lou.

Vivi.

Moocella.

That feeling of not giving a damn.

I kept my eyes on Jason, just ahead of me, to keep from looking to my left every time a car flew past. The first time an eighteen-wheel truck passed us, I swerved so hard away from it, Audrey's wheels hit the rumble strip.

I overcorrected the first time, and for the space of a breath, I was sure I was going to die. Either crash and get run over or go into the lane beside me.

But I didn't.

I didn't want to die. I took the first deep breath I'd inhaled since leaving Lou's house. I didn't know what would happen with Jason. Or the Hive. Or school. Or anything, really. But I wanted to find out.

I was excited to find out.

Hell. I was even excited to call and make an appointment

with Ursula.

I watched Jason's shoulders shift under his denim jacket. When another massive truck barreled up behind me, I stiffened, but didn't swerve this time.

It sent a rumble up from Audrey's wheels, through my spine.

It was a little bit like being underwater, cocooned in the wind whipping around me and the road noises that were muffled by the helmet pressing against my ears.

I didn't have much to do other than hold on and think.

○ ○ ○

We couldn't go much faster than half the speed of the traffic moving beside us. That meant that the three-hour drive between Sun Valley and Sacramento would take us at least six.

Which meant we needed to stop for food.

I closed my eyes and drained half a glass of ice water in one long swallow. When I opened them again, Jason was watching me.

"What?"

He chewed on the inside of his lip. "What if I can't do this?"

"You can."

"But what if I can't?"

I shrugged one shoulder. "Then we'll go home."

"Just like that?"

"Yep. And hope we survive my mother's wrath. Graduate. Go to Las Vegas in the fall."

"You're supposed to tell me I can do this."

I took a bite of my hamburger and chewed slowly. After I swallowed, I said, "I did tell you that you can."

"Make me believe it."

I shook my head. "You don't need me to."

He leaned back in his seat, his long legs stretching alongside mine, and bumped the back of his head against the padded seat. Once. Twice. "What if I can do this?"

I lifted my eyebrows.

"What if they pick me?"

I inhaled through my nose and watched his face. "Then we go home. Hope we survive my mother's wrath. Graduate."

"And?"

I nodded. "And."

Jason beat a little rhythm on his thigh with one hand. I focused on that, breathing in hard when a minivan thundered past.

It took me a minute, but the beat fell into place.

Love knocks you over, baby. Every time. Every time.

It wasn't Victor Solo I heard in my head. It was Jason.

He was going to nail this audition. I knew it in my bones. For the first time—maybe in my whole life—I didn't know what was going to happen next in my life. And I was OK with that.

Because Soiled Dove was going on tour next year. And if Jason joined them, and he wanted me to go with him, I would.

Not because I had some sick fascination with him, like I'd had with Lou for so long.

I'd go because it would be an adventure that I didn't want to miss. And being part of that felt like the healthiest thing I'd contemplated for a long time.

A gap year with my best friend, helping him through his first year as a rock star? Yeah.

○ ○ ○

I texted my mom before we left the restaurant, to tell her that I wasn't dead in a ditch somewhere between Reno and Sacramento.

Maybe we should have just taken her car. I could have kept my hair. I might have actually been in less trouble if we had, considering that the whole I-rode-a-Vespa-across-state-lines-on-the-open-highway thing wouldn't be involved.

But this had to happen. This way. I felt that, down to my bones. And Jason needed to go through it, too, so on the other side he'd know what he could do.

It didn't matter if none of that made sense.

The little bubbles that let me know she was responding popped up immediately. I turned my phone off. I'd call her later that night. She could kill me then.

It was nearly dark before we finally pulled into a Motel Six near the Sacramento airport. I used sixty-three dollars of my leftover hair money to pay for a single room.

The man behind the counter looked up at me for a minute, then asked, "Queen or two doubles?"

My skin burned and I didn't have to see myself to know I was bright red. My face always told on me. I opened my mouth to say doubles, but Jason put an arm around my waist and cut me off.

"We're on our honeymoon."

The man narrowed his eyes. "That right?"

He kept a completely straight face. "Eloped."

The clerk turned back to me. "Got an ID?"

I shot Jason a glare as I dug my driver's license out of my backpack. I handed it over and the man looked at it, then back at me. "You're too young."

"He was joking," I said. "We're not married."

Confusion creased his forehead, then he shook his head and handed me back my ID. "I can't rent you a room."

"I'll pay cash," I said.

"I'm sorry. It doesn't work like that." When I made a frustrated noise, he added, "Where's your mother?"

Probably waiting for me to call her. So she can come get me if I need her to. "Thanks."

I turned to leave, grabbing Jason's hand as I did and dragging him with me back out the door. The bell attached to the handle chimed as I let it slam shut behind me.

"Well, damn," Jason said.

"What now?" He looked down at me long enough that it made me squirm. "I'm calling my mom."

When I reached for my phone, he wrapped his fingers around my wrist. "Do you trust me?"

The answer came smooth and easy. "Yes."

"Come on."

He shoved his helmet back on his head and trusted me to follow when he went back to the scooters.

○ ○ ○

Like riding a bike. It's just like riding a bike. At night. In traffic. I kept Jason in front of me and just concentrated on trusting that Audrey's little headlight would illuminate enough for me to keep moving forward.

We didn't go far. Ten minutes after we left the motel, Jason pulled into the parking lot of a Salvation Army.

"This will only take a minute."

I looked around. Sacramento was a lot bigger than Sun Valley. Bigger than Reno. It was unusual for me to feel small, but suddenly I did. "What are we doing here?"

"You'll see."

I did see. Quickly. Jason walked toward the back of the store like he'd been in it a thousand times. Straight to a rack filled with bed linens.

He flipped through with the kind of quick consideration that spoke of experience and picked two thick quilts.

"Seriously," I said. "What is this?"

"It's camping." He held up the blue-and-white quilt in his right hand. "Or it will be."

"Camping."

"Sort of."

I blinked at him and he nodded, then just stood there looking at me.

Right. This was going to be up to me. So if we ran into a serial killer or a bear or anything in between overnight, that would be on me, too. "Maybe I should call my dad."

Jason put his arm down. "What will he say?"

I heard his voice so clearly in my head, he might as well be there in that thrift store with us. *Don't you move a muscle, Marcella. I'm on my way.* "Shit."

"Do you even know where to camp around here?"

He shrugged. "Sort of."

"What exactly does sort of mean?"

Before he could answer, though, I knew. His parents left him when he was four. He was raised by his teenage sister, who'd given up her own baby.

By camping, he meant sleeping outdoors. Homeless. I saw the truth of that in his face. His woodland-creature face that didn't hide a single thing. Not from me.

"OK," I said.

○ ○ ○

It was full dark by the time we finally parked Francine and Audrey in a lot near a freeway underpass. The traffic that had been giving me a heart attack for the last eight or ten hours rumbled by overhead now.

Jason led me to a patch of evergreen trees a few yards away.

He knew just where to go. Just which tree to spread one blanket under. Just how far from the road we needed to be. And somehow, he knew that there wouldn't already be someone else back here.

Not even the evidence of anyone else. No beer bottles or cigarette butts or old food wrappers.

He lay down and scooted over to make room for me. We lay side-by-side, on our backs, holding hands under the other blanket. Looking up through the trees at the clear sky.

Too much light, in the city, to see many stars. But they were up there.

"Will Suzy let me come back to the Hive?" The question was barely a whisper.

Jason turned his head my way. "Yes."

"Do you—" I swallowed. "I mean, is that OK with you?"

"Yes."

I let out a breath and felt tension ease from my chest. "I really am sorry, Jason."

He tightened his fingers around mine. "I know."

"I—" I didn't know what to say. I won't hurt you again? No. Not that. "I'm not sure I want to go to Las Vegas."

His eyes widened. "Really?"

I nodded slowly. "They're going to pick you, Jason."

"You can't—"

"If you go on tour with them next year, I—"

He lifted his eyebrows. "You, what?"

"I'll go with you."

"What about school?"

"I'll go to UNR next semester. That way I can stay at the Hive, too." I turned on my side.

He nodded slowly and then rolled onto his back again.

o o o

I sat with Jason at a table near the stage. My hair was a helmet-headed, windblown mess. My cheeks were sunburned. Somehow I'd managed to sleep pretty well on an unwashed Salvation Army blanket near the freeway underpass.

"I don't think I can do this," Jason whispered.

"You can."

"I'm serious, Celly."

"Dude," I said. "Yesterday we rode scooters for six hours on an interstate highway. Crossed state lines without parental permission. And you did it with a guitar on your back."

"But—"

"It doesn't get more badass than that. Getting up there and doing the one thing you do better than anything else? That's cake."

He inhaled, then exhaled slowly. "I'm going to be sick."

"You've done this before," I said. "You sang for me."

"That's different. You're—"

"I'm what?"

"You're Celly."

I didn't know what to do with that and I wasn't ready to think about it. "You can do this. You only need to do it once."

"Unless they pick me."

I shook my head. "Until they pick you."

A guy with a clipboard said, "Jason Daley?"

Jason's eyes closed. *Get up, Jason.* Maybe he heard my thoughts, because he slowly unfolded his long body.

He made his way up to the stage. He spent a minute fiddling with his guitar, adjusting things. He was in his socks, his Doc Martens tucked under our table.

The Soiled Dove guitar player said something to him that I couldn't hear, and he answered, pointing to something on the floor. The same kind of panel he had at his house, the one he manipulated with his feet while he's playing.

The guitarist gave him an interested look, then nodded.

It took another minute for Jason to set up. He had to pull the microphone up by six inches. Do something with his toes to turn the device on.

Then, he played his first chord.

I felt it in the center of my chest. Just like the first time he played for me. I wanted to close my eyes and just listen, but I kept them open so that when he looked at me, I could beam confidence at him.

The bar where Soiled Dove was holding their audition was mostly empty this early in the day. Just them and the people auditioning for them.

There were maybe a dozen hopefuls. All of them older than Jason. Some older than Suzy and my parents. One guy must have been seventy.

We'd heard three of them audition already and none of them touched what I knew Jason could do.

He played a second chord and did something with his foot to put the first one on a playback loop. Then put that one on playback as well and started to pick out the melody to a Soiled Dove song I knew by heart.

The drummer nodded once, then joined in. Then the bass player.

Jason opened his mouth to sing. Nothing came out.

The bass player looked surprised, but he went with it when Jason started the melody over again.

He moved closer to Jason, his fingers picking out the deep undertone of a song he'd performed a thousand times. He turned his head and whispered something that the mic didn't pick up.

Jason looked out into the audience.

And he found me.

And then he sang.

45LB
45LB
25LB
25LB

For Help and Information

In an emergency, dial 911 for the fastest response

National Suicide Prevention Lifeline

Free and confidential support for people in distress, prevention, and crisis resources
A national network of local crisis centers to support people in suicidal crisis or emotional distress, twenty-four hours a day, seven days a week
Phone: 1-800-273-TALK (8255), or dial 988
Text: text 'HOME' to 741741

National Depression Hotline

Free depression help, treatment, options, and support groups, available 24/7
Phone: 1-866-629-4564

Department of Health Mental Health Resources and Support Helpline

Phone: 1-800-854-7771

National Hopeline Network Suicide & Crisis Hotline

Phone: 1-800-442-HOPE (4673)

National Institute of Mental Health Information Resource Center

Phone: 1-800-826-9438

The Trevor Lifeline

24/7 phone hotline, webchat, and text for LGBTQ+ and questioning youth
Phone: 1-866-488-7386
Chat: https://www.thetrevorproject.org/get-help/
Text: text 'START' to 678678

The Youthline

Free teen-to-teen crisis support and helpline
Phone (24/7 adult crisis responders): 1-877-968-8491
Chat: (4-10 pm PST peer support) https://www.theyouthline.org
Text: (4-10pm PST peer support): 'teen2teen' to 839863